THE RED CASTLE WOMEN

BOOKS BY MARGARET WIDDEMER

THE RED CASTLE WOMEN

GOLDEN FRIENDS I HAD:
Unrevised Memories
of Margaret Widdemer

BUCKSKIN BARONET

THE GOLDEN WILDCAT

LADY OF THE MOHAWKS

RED CLOAK FLYING

LANI

CHARIS SEES IT THROUGH

BOARDWALK

GRAVEN IMAGE

GALLANT LADY

ROSE GARDEN HUSBAND

WHY NOT

I'VE MARRIED MARJORIE

RHINESTONES

LOYAL LOVER

GOLDEN RAIN

BACK TO VIRTUE, BETTY

Poetry

THE DARK CAVALIER:
Collected Poems

FACTORIES

THE OLD ROAD TO PARADISE

CROSS-CURRENTS

BALLADS AND LYRICS

THE ROAD TO DOWNDERRY

HILL GARDEN

TREE WITH A BIRD IN IT
(Parodies)

THE
RED CASTLE
WOMEN

Margaret Widdemer

DOUBLEDAY & COMPANY, INC.
GARDEN CITY, NEW YORK
1968

All of the characters in this book are fictitious,
and any resemblance to actual persons, living or dead,
is purely coincidental.

Library of Congress Catalog Card Number 68–17811
Copyright © 1968 by Doubleday & Company, Inc.
All Rights Reserved
Printed in the United States of America
First Edition

To Louise Bogan
whose suggestion made this book

THE RED CASTLE WOMEN

CHAPTER ONE

There were two maidens sat in a bower,
And a knight came by to be their wooer:
He courted the eldest with glove and ring,
But he loved the youngest above a' thing . . .
OLD BALLAD

It did not seem like a meeting that could bring down on us all strange terrors, strange events: wakening things from the past, changing things in the future. I was so little a girl: so unafraid. The people in the old ferryhouse on the Hudson River loved me, and spoke to me with love: my Uncle Jacob, old Eliza the housekeeper, Andrew and Lorena Blackwater who lived in the cottage beside us and were my uncle's helpers, and Eliza's when she needed it.

The ferryhouse had been there always, I thought, and the road along the woods behind it and the river before it, and across to the west the Red Castle.

There had been my mother too, I knew, but she had died when I was six; I could remember long curls, and a soft fichu my head rested against, a softly gay voice, and the love I thought was everywhere for me. I had never heard of anything cruel or angry or terrible till that time the next year,

1

when I was seven. Isobel was only seven, too. I am sure she did not know what the doom was that she carried with her invisibly in her small kid-gloved hands.

My Uncle Jacob was the ferryman at Grandison-on-the-Hudson, as his forebears had been since before the American Revolution. That was a long, long time, nearly a hundred years ago: this was a safe world called eighteen-forty.

This particular afternoon was all sunny, and thrilling, with that rich scent of burning leaves which is more heady than the smells of June. I ran down to the wharf, because out the window I had seen my uncle rowing Miss Abigail Somerwell, whom I liked, in the small rowboat. Beside her on the same seat sat a little girl about my own age beautifully dressed. The other shore was behind them; the changing leaves and the yellow road; and high beyond the place they had come from, the great dull-red castle of the Somerwells. When people spoke of it they dropped their voices.

"People that lives in the Red Castle ain't never the same," old Eliza said. I didn't know why Miss Abigail wasn't the same. Or what her same had been. She had a pleasant kind middle-aged face deep in a gray silk bonnet, and a deep blue shawl with a wide border of strange flowers, smooth and warm to touch. "Cashmere," they said it was. Somebody used to sing me to sleep with a song about "Songs of Araby, and tales of fair Cashmere." That was the shawl, I thought, the fair cashmere. When I looked at her I always wished I could have a doll dressed like her.

When she had crossed before she always had with her another little girl; a little girl who had black curls. She was Miss Eugenia. This little girl had yellow ringlets below her bonnet; I could not see her face at all. I did not know her name then, but she was Isobel. Her Negro nurse sat behind in the stern, with a fluted wide apron and a long streamered cap.

2

Isobel's clothes were richer and handsomer even than little Miss Eugenia's. Her gloves were white kid and her shoes blue morocco; the beautiful bonnet, all puffed and ruffled, was pink silk. Her dress of blue silk, little as she was, had a real small hoop holding it out. She was like the one little girl who always held a fashionable lady's hand in Peterson's wonderful long fashion plate that you mustn't cut out for paper dolls. I laughed, and waved the hand to her that didn't hold my kitty.

Uncle Jacob moored, then lifted her out, with a "Here we go, little lady! And here's my niece Perdita, wanting to say how do you do."

I held my kitten up. I said, "See, she's gray like Miss Abigail's gown! Do you have a kitty?"

Miss Abigail and the Negro nurse stepped to the wharf. There was a sort of scared silence, and the grown people looked at each other. Miss Abigail caught the little kid-gloved hand.

Isobel looked up at me and smiled. "I don't have a kitty," she said. "I would like to go with you and play with yours. I like you." She held out her hand. The nurse said, "Lawk-a-mercy!"

There was still that queer feeling around us. Isobel took my free hand. "We'll go to your nursery," she said.

I said, "I haven't any nursery. But I have a bedroom with my toys and a basket for my kitty."

Miss Abigail said in a queer breathless voice, "The first time—" and then they followed us into the ferryhouse. Uncle Jacob set a chair for Miss Abigail and sat down across the hearth from her. "I mustn't let her—" she was saying, "I must take her to Lucy's school—"

Uncle Jacob said, "My dear Miss Somerwell, you are too fearful. Your niece is happy with my little Perdita. Why decide now?"

3

Miss Abigail said, "The first time she has trusted a child—but—"

I followed Isobel into my bedroom and shut the door, as I had been trained to do. Isobel sat slowly down in my little red rocker and untied her bonnet strings. I said, "Who is Lucy?"

Isobel said in an angry voice, "She keeps school. Aunt Abigail says I would be happier there than with Eugenia. But my nurse heard her saying Miss Lucy had difficult children. I wouldn't like difficult children."

"Why does she send you away, and not Eugenia?" I asked.

"It's going to be sort of Eugenia's castle, on account of a will," Isobel said sulkily. "And Aunt Abigail is all we have to take care of us. She's really an old cousin. All our parents are dead. I hate Eugenia."

I didn't know what to say, so I said, "I like your pink bonnet."

"I guess you don't know why I have to wear it," she said. "It's why I hate Eugenia. She did it." She lifted her hands and took it off very slowly, as if she didn't want to.

She had big blue eyes and lots of golden curls, and one cheek was pink and pretty. But all across the other one was a deep burned scar.

Somehow I knew I mustn't show I was sorry for her. I picked up my kitten and said, "She likes you. She was playing with the lace on your pantalette."

Isobel stared at me a minute longer. "I like her," she said. "And I like you. You haven't pointed or giggled at me. Is that because you are beneath me, as Nurse said?"

I didn't quite know what that meant, so I only said, "I just thought you were nice. I think Miss Eugenia was naughty."

"She was naughty. She pushed me against the grate fire. I

4

hate her. I hate all the other children. They point and laugh or else they whisper."

I was very sorry for her. I threw my arms around her, and said, "I won't ever point or laugh or whisper. I don't know what beneath you is, but maybe it's like your scar. Miss Eugenia always looks at me and points, or else whispers and giggles."

"Maybe it is!" Isobel said. "Then we will be friends. Do you know any games two friends could play?"

I thought. "I know tit-tat-toe," I said. "Do you?"

She didn't. So I got a pencil and slate and showed her.

The door pushed slowly open after a while. My uncle had pushed it. Miss Abigail stood by him with her hands tight together. Isobel's back was to them and she was laughing.

"Oh, I won, I won!" she said. "Let's do it again, so you will maybe win next time!"

"You see?" my uncle said. "Dear madam, you've lived with the Red Castle's legends too long. These are just two little children making friends. Shall we leave them a little longer?"

She let him lead her back to her chair by the fire. We went on playing. By and by Eliza came in and gave us milk and gingersnaps. Then Uncle Jacob called us. We came hand-in-hand. When Isobel looked at her aunt her face went angry again. "Are you going to take me away to Miss Lucy now?" she said.

But my uncle picked her up onto his knee and laughed. "Your aunt is going to get a nice pretty young lady to teach you along with my Perdita," he said. "Every morning but Saturdays and Sundays somebody will row you over here, and you will have lessons together in Perdita's room."

"I would like that," Isobel said slowly. "I like people who are beneath me." Miss Abigail looked shocked, but Uncle Jacob only laughed. "And we like you," he said.

And so it was settled. Miss Letty Moffit, who was a

5

daughter it seemed of Dominie Van Alstyne's dead friend, and had to be a visiting governess because she was poor but genteel, was rowed over and back with Isobel. She was young and pretty except for white eyelashes, and timid. We liked her.

But I never went to the Red Castle. I used to stand on the wharf and look toward it with a half-terrified, half-excited feeling. It stood on a great and very rich estate. The land ran, Isobel said, miles either way, south and north. It stood, frowning over the river road, closer and more dominant than the other great Hudson River houses. It had been built earlier, when there was need to look out for hostile Indians. ("Or any Indians," Isobel whispered. "It would be terrible if any Indians came to the Red Castle.")

When I said once to Eliza that I would like to go there instead of always having Isobel come here, she shivered and said, "You dunno what you're talkin' about, child . . . It wouldn't be lucky for you to go there. Nor me either, ugly old woman as I be." But she would not say why.

I was silent. Perhaps if I went there Eugenia would come and push me too against the grate . . .

Eugenia was not always there. She had a guardian who lived in New York City. Once I saw him and his wife. Their name was Oliver. They were stiff formal people, he with his satin stock and elegant black cape and narrow trousers, she with her striped challis with the new leg-of-mutton sleeves and leghorn hat.

Eugenia was a year younger than we were, but she was taller and seemed older. Isobel lived as much with us after that as with Miss Abigail at the Castle. At Miss Abigail's request, a room was built that opened off my bedroom. It had silk and lace curtains and draperies, and beautiful ivory colored furniture. But before Isobel would occupy it she demanded a bolt on the door.

6

As she grew older her passion for hiding from everyone but me did not change. She was duly rowed across with Miss Letty by grave black Petronius, who had belonged to Eugenia's father till the New York slaves were freed. He was called Miss Eugenia's footman, but he stayed at the Castle whether she was there or not.

I was taught along with Isobel, which was why I could embroider and do other things unfitting for my station, such as music and French. We weren't sure for years what a station was. Eugenia, who came and went, still ignoring me and seeming to dislike Isobel, we thought must have one. But it was not very important. Isobel wished that she had one too, so that she did not need to go to dancing school where other children were.

Eugenia came to the Red Castle part of the time, as Isobel had said, because the grandfather that belonged to her and Isobel and their cousin Mark, who was older, had made a will about it. Isobel was a little cross about this, and would not say what the will was about. It was Eliza, later, who told me. By that time Mark's mother, old Mr. Somerwell's oldest child, Eleanor, was dead; the other two children, his sons who were Eugenius, Eugenia's father, and Nicholas, Isobel's father, had died in a yachting accident with their young wives, when both girls were very little. And the old gentleman, who was Eugenius too, had made the will, Eliza said it was whispered, so that Mark and Eugenia had the Red Castle together when they married: if one of them didn't want to the other had the Castle and its riches. It seemed to me a very domineering will. But Eliza said that it wasn't as bad as it seemed, because they were both handsome and both would have enough money even if they didn't want each other. And the Red Castle was worth marrying even a dreadful person for, from what she said. It all seemed like a fairytale.

And the time went on until we were older. There were

more lines in old Eliza's brown face, and gray in Uncle Jacob's and Miss Abigail's; and Isobel and I were young ladies—or Isobel was—and we were nineteen. And it seemed that old Eliza's stories were partly true at least, because Eugenia and her cousin Mark Harradine were to be married, now he was back with all sorts of honors from the Mexican War.

Isobel was rowed over to tell me of it. We were in our room together.

"All the young ladies," she was saying, "preening themselves as they strutted about in their finery—Eugenia peacocking about as if nobody had ever been married before! And Mark isn't there yet, and the day so close! She says it's for important military reasons, but she looks like a thunderstorm."

Major Harradine was a dim figure as far as I was concerned. I knew vaguely that he had been fighting the Apaches in the far West before the Mexican War, almost since he left West Point. He had visited the Red Castle now and again. He must have crossed the ferry sometimes, I thought, and had a shadowy memory from years ago of a slim lad in gray like so many others—for ours was the ferry nearest West Point—but with darker eyes, and black hair wind-tossed.

There had been a long silence. She was rising to go. She passed my glass, and stopped suddenly, setting both small gloved hands on each side of it. She stared and stared in it—that lovely, that hopelessly marred face. I was frightened. I took her by the shoulders and pulled her around and kissed her. She buried her head against me and sobbed wildly. I tried to soothe her. Presently she dried her eyes.

"If I could only live here forever, hidden! Perhaps they'll let me, once that accursed Eugenia is married. We can go to Aunt's house in Peekskill."

8

It was a more violent crying spell than usual.

"Stay overnight, dear," I said. She usually did when one of her spells of anger and tears was over. This time she shook her head. She poured water from the ewer on the marble washstand, and, as steadily as she had stared at herself, stared again, while she washed tears and cosmetics from her face. She overlaid the scarred side with rouge and powder, then made the unhurt side match. She turned to me and laughed.

"It would be shockingly fast at her age and social position, if it were not for the reason, poor thing," she said in a mincing voice. "That's what I heard Eugenia say to her bosom friend."

"Oh, Isobel darling, can't you stop taking it so hard?"

"If I couldn't let go before you I don't know what I'd do. The little ferry girl is a quite wonderful mercy" she was quoting again. "Sufficiently educated beyond her station to be a companion. And in spite of her good looks, of course, she could never be a rival, because of her unknown past."

"My—past?" I couldn't think what she meant. "But I've lived here always."

She laughed again—that hard laugh.

"Oh, listeners never hear any good of themselves, or anybody else, for that matter. I could be jealous of your looks: you're lovely, they say. They say you're like her: 'That lovely little ferry girl, so like Madame Honor—'"

"You mean my mother?"

"Yes. Nobody ever knew her last name. So nobody knows who you are." Before I could answer she had kissed me. "But I don't hate you. It's Eugenia I hate. Proud and arrogant and selfish—" She stopped and smiled and tied on her bonnet. Then she unlocked the door, and passed through my room into the keeping room. As she turned to the door she spoke over her shoulder.

"But I can wait . . . They brought Eugenia from some-

9

where else to the Red Castle, as they did me, as they did Aunt Abigail. She'll be shamed as I was shamed, as Aunt Abigail was shamed for all her piety. The Iroquois girl will see to that . . . I can wait."

She was out on the wharf, blowing the horn for the ferry, before I could ask her what she meant. Or cared to ask, indeed; I had enough to do to try to think out what she had shown me about myself . . . about my past. I stood, as Isobel had stood, staring in the glass. What Eugenia had said meant that nobody knew who I was, who my mother was . . . I had no past . . . I was a waif—perhaps a foundling —I did not know my half forgotten mother's name, my own name . . . and I remembered that Perdita meant "Lost . . ." I had been called that on purpose, perhaps. I made up my mind that I would know.

CHAPTER TWO

♖

There oft a restless Indian queen
(Pale Shebah with her braided hair)
And many a barbarous form is seen
To chide the man who lingers there.
                              PHILIP FRENEAU

All my life things have come to me not singly, but in twos. I made up my mind next morning that I would go to my uncle and demand to be told all he knew. But because of the approaching wedding he and Andy and young Joseph were busied taking people to and fro in everything from the little boats to the big flatboat for the horses and carriages. I went out to work in the gardens. The purple asters were beginning.

I was in the landward garden when I saw Alonzo Beggs. He was an awkward great lout from the nearest village who had been coming and going forever of late.

"I haven't time to talk to you, Alonzo," I said. "I have to go in and set these bouquets round the keeping room."

"You been sayin' that the last three times," Alonzo burst out. He stood there doggedly, big and slouching. His tow-colored hair was greased down flat. His neckcloth was wrapped up to his ears, trying to look like a stock.

"Look here, Miss Perdita," he said, rocking from one foot to the other, and moving round so that he was between me and the house. "You know I'm crazy fer you. Let's get wedded. Onct we was tied up my mammy couldn't say nothin', no matter what you be."

My uncle was there, nearer than I had known. He jumped down the steps and gripped Alonzo's homespun shoulder, whirling him round. "Get away and never come back!" he said. He flung the boy, for all his gangling height, from the porch into my bed of late petunias.

Alonzo pulled himself out.

"You hain't no right to do that!" he shouted. "I'll have the law on you."

"That's enough," Uncle Jacob said sharply. "If you don't want to be thrown into the river instead of the flowerbed, make tracks this minute." I hadn't known my gentle-spoken uncle could be so angry.

Alonzo shambled slowly across the lawn onto the path toward his village. "Some wouldn't want her," he called back as he moved. My uncle threw an arm round me and drew me into the house.

"What—what did he mean?" I asked.

"He meant to be a fool," he said more harshly than I had ever heard him speak. His mild blue eyes were angry. He pushed back his whitening hair. I faced him.

"You have to tell me! Why would a boy like that feel he was doing me a favor—to marry me? And why do I have . . . an unknown past?"

"Who else has been talking to you?"

"Isobel said something too," I faltered. "Please—"

He said, "I've been wrong, putting off making things clear to you. I hadn't realized you were old enough to be treated like a woman. It's nothing to fear, darling. I have to see Lawyer Granger tonight: tomorrow night we'll talk."

12

He was gone to his work before I could entreat any more. There were horses and carriages, I could tell, waiting to be poled across. Eugenia's marriage to this Major Harradine was a great event.

I could not wait. Old Eliza might know something. I went straight into the raftered kitchen. She had been leaning near the window. She was still grinning, I supposed at the sight of Alonzo's dismissal. Nothing much escaped her.

"Eliza," I said, "can you tell me about myself?"

She did not show surprise. "I s'pose it had to come sooner or later," she said. "That lowdown Alonzo with his nasty gossipy mother. I ain't the one to tell you, child, your uncle is. It ain't bad, don't look so. Your mother was as pretty as a picter an' good as gold, an' people liked her, an' she was a lady if there ever was one. Only thing was, she'd been hurt when they found her, and she couldn't remember things—"

"When they found her?" It seemed strange to me, suddenly, that all these years I had never asked questions or had anything said to me until now . . . I had never gone to any school. Uncle Jacob had taught me till Miss Letty Moffit did. I had never had a playmate till Isobel came. And nobody had acted as if there was anything strange about my mother. I had taken it for granted that she was Uncle Jacob's sister; a much loved sister. I had, I thought, perhaps been kept in my pleasant ignorance deliberately: I do not yet know.

"Who found her?" I asked. "Where was she?"

Eliza looked at me as if she had said more than she meant to.

"Well, it was one awful stormy Fall night. She was ridin' somewhere with you on her sort of cushion before. Andy Blackwater found her: I think they heard you cryin'. She was thrown off her horse. They found you wrapped up on the wood-edge, safe by a miracle. Her head was hurt. Her portmanteau was broke and the things in it scattered. Andy carried her in and Lorena and I tended her. There was a letter loose with the clothes and such that began 'Dearest Honor.' That was how we knew her first name. She couldn't remember who she was. She wore a wedding ring all right."

"Then—I'm no relation to Uncle Jacob—"

"He couldn't love you more if he was your own father. He'd liked to been. That's all I know. Ask him." Eliza shut her lips like a trap.

As the day wore on, one of the sudden changes we were liable to struck the river. A storm swept down from the north, with heavy rain, jagged lightnings and ever louder thunder. It turned chill. I watched the increasingly turbid, increasingly rough water off and on all day from our windows that opened west on the river and Eliza's hand came on my shoulder. She spoke sharply behind me. "Tain't no use staring out, child. Mr. Jacob won't git back *this* night."

I saw she was right. He had not left us until late afternoon. It was a long ride, even in clear weather, to Lawyer Granger's. My uncle was to have stayed to supper. But I could not leave the window. I was waiting—waiting for something I did not know. Our two old bloodhounds, restless too, began to bay in their kennel, and I put on my waterproof and went out and unchained them and brought them into the keeping room with me. Eliza scolded a little, but I think she too was glad of their company.

"Red Castle's all lighted up for company," Eliza said, behind me at the window again. "Guess won't nobody come by tonight."

It was: against the darkening sky, deeply blackened, it towered, now startlingly sharp—outlined as the lightning wakened everything to eerie clearness, now, in the increasing twilight, a great mass of stoned darkness. In the storm its heights and towers seemed as sinister as the Ogre's castle in the storybooks; inescapable, terrifying. One faint light in the

14

highest turret was not yellow and comforting but frighteningly small and wavering.

I tried to remember that somewhere inside were living, commonplace people moving about their affairs: the Somerwell ladies, their guests, their servants, their little animals; and that the preparations for the great wedding were going on humanly. Perhaps if any of them looked through the wild, crying storm at our low house it might seem terrifying to them. But I could not make it true. The only truth was that implacable shape, lowering against the zigzag lightnings and one with the thunder and shrieking wind.

"Miss Abigail and her nieces are over there getting ready for the wonderful wedding," I said. "I wonder what it would feel like to have a life like theirs: a French dresser putting your clothes on: a groom following when you rode out; and a bridegroom chosen for you by someone else marching in, with glittering epaulets and medals."

"Be glad you haven't naught of the sort," Eliza said grimly, "with the Iroquois woman's haunt waitin' for you on a night like this."

She had at last made me turn from the window. "The Iroquois woman?" I said. "Was she a guest?"

"She's been more of a guest than the Red Castle women wanted," Eliza said, still grimly, "for pretty well a century now."

My uncle had always been stern with Eliza about telling the old legends and stories of the countryside. But tonight I welcomed anything that would make me forget the sense of dread the storm-ringed Red Castle had brought, and the more dreaded story I awaited my uncle's telling—the story that made a lout like Alonzo feel he condescended in asking me in marriage, and Isobel speak of my unknown past.

I said, "Sit down here by the fire and tell me about the Iroquois woman, Eliza." I think she too was glad to talk of

15

something else. We dropped down on each side the hearth-fire. Young Joseph came in, as always at this time, and built the fire up. I heard him go back to the little room in our house he always occupied when Eliza and I were without Uncle Jacob. He would go to sleep; he read himself to sleep with *Lives of Great Americans* usually. His routine made things less strange somehow.

"Now tell me about the Iroquois woman," I said, getting my uncle's shirt I was making from my sewing stand by me. Eliza took her knitting.

"Well, I suppose you know who the Iroquois were," she said.

"Oh yes," I said. "The Six Nations. The Hodenasaunee. They were a powerful league of Indian tribes upstate before the Revolution." One of the books Uncle Jacob and I read to each other in the winter was Morgan's book about them.

"Well," Eliza said, "one of the six tribes was the Oneida. They was almost the only ones stuck to us patriots in the fightin'. Well, my grandsir and granny was butler and house-keeper for the first old Somerwell, the one that built the Red Castle. Master Edward Eugenius Somerwell. Folks said he'd been the blacksheep son of high-up people in England. They said too he'd had to leave England in a hurry because of wicked things he'd done there. He wasn't young when he settled and married here. It was pretty much an open secret that he'd made his fortune by being a slaver, stealing poor blacks over from Afriky and selling them here. It was looked down on by gentry rather. Maybe that was why he built the biggest, handsomest mansion on the river. Plain stone from round here an' good ballast brick wasn't good enough for him. He sent down South for red sandstone . . ." Her voice dropped. "But 'twas said 'twas right to call it the Red Castle because it was built by the blood of all the poor blacks that died in the holds of his slavin' ships;

16

that he'd built on the flesh an' blood of human bein's with souls to save, like the wicked people down South."

A little before I was born our state had freed its slaves. I heard the gentlemen that talked to Uncle Jacob say that it had ruined a great many upstate landowners. They talked too about the South keeping slaves now. It hadn't interested me much. "Go on about the Iroquois woman," I said. "Did Master Somerwell make her a slave too?"

Eliza shook her head. "No. It all came more of old Master Somerwell's devilment. You see, he wanted all three of his sons to marry up high and rich. Well, his third son, Eugenius, was wild. They had these fancy names, Sallust and Hercules and Eugenius. Eugenius got into some sort of trouble and went upstate with a parcel of traders in a hurry. His father didn't bother much till the two older sons took smallpox the winter it was bad an' died. So he searched till he found Eugenius. Seems he was living with the Oneida Indians. He'd been taken into the tribe, and married legal by Iroquois rites, like all the Six Nations had been gettin' married for centuries. They had a baby. He didn't want to come back, but his father kept on at him, an' he did, along with his wife an' son. He settled in to be a grand gentleman again easy enough. But the girl was restless. Presently they had a beautiful young white lady to visit. They felt Eugenius wasn't really married to the Indian girl: Onnorate her name was. It meant Leaf in English, seems."

"Like naming a white baby Ivy or Rose," I said when she stopped talking to get breath.

"I suppose. Well, presently Eugenius got to like the young white lady."

"Oh, he was cruel!" I said.

Eliza shrugged. "You can hear plenty stories about white men treatin' Indian girls that way in the old days. They mostly end with the girl jumpin' off a cliff or into a lake,

17

and that's why it's called Lover's Leap. But this one didn't. When the old father told her they was sendin' her home with some money, she said, "I will not go. I am a chief's daughter. I should be shamed before my tribe."

"What was Eugenius doing about it?"

"Oh, they'd sent him to New York City. Well, when Onnorate wouldn't go, the old gentleman had two of his strong blacks tie her to a horse, with a black girl to carry the baby, and the overseer to see she went home."

"How do you know all that?"

"You s'pose the slaves didn't tell? Niggers has a grapevine post like nothin' on earth, even now. And my great-granny was housekeeper. What she didn't know wasn't worth knowin'. Well, the overseer and the three blacks came back sayin' she'd taken it quiet finally."

"Then why do the Red Castle ladies worry about her?"

"Because," Eliza said slowly. "She came back!"

"Oh, her ghost? But that was long ago—if it really happened . . ."

"No, her livin' self. The weddin' invitations was out, inscribed on white satin. The slaves went up- an' downriver carryin' them to the gentry. My ma showed me one my great-granny saved: my eldest brother's wife has it: it says 'Eugenius Somerwell and Isobel Van Vooren' yes, our Isobel was named fer her. She's a picter in the Red Castle gallery. Well, the bride and groom was standin' together under the great chandelier in the high stone hall, with fifty candles in it, Ma said. The fiddles an' all was playin'. An' the Indian girl walked up to them an' faced them. An' everything sort of stopped dead. They could hear her all through the room. She said, 'I have talked to the Honundeounts: the wise old men and women of my tribe. And they have told me to say this to you, and to all the clan of this house. As I have been shamed, Onnorate, the Leaf, a chief's daughter,

18

so shall every woman brought to this house to live be shamed. When wind blows from the north and you see a leaf blowing across the windows, and no wind elsewhere, you will remember it is true. And it shall not end until Onnorate the Leaf returns, an honored wife, to this castle.' And before anybody had courage enough to say or do anything she was gone. They heard the horse-hoofs goin' away."

"Didn't anybody ever know any more about her and the baby?" I asked.

Eliza shook her head. "Nobody ever did. Seems when the old man died Eugenius tried to get back the baby. I guess wives was patienter those days. Eugenius' bridesman, Mr. Philip Freneau that some said he'd been in love with Onnorate himself, went with the overseer to see, up where the Oneida was still. They'd stayed here when the other Iroquois mostly went to Canada. They come back with no news. I guess Mr. Freneau'd maybe married her himself if he found her. He wrote poetry some said was about her and the Indians' hauntin'; 'Pale Shebah with her braided hair,' he called her. But nobody never knew. And the poor little white wife, Madam Isobel—well, there was other women. She pined an' died with her second child. She said to her mother, who came to be with her, 'I cannot bear the shame.'"

"But that was long ago."

"Things has happened since," Eliza said darkly. "Miss Abigail was brought to the Castle when she was a young thing. She was betrothed. And while she was there her beau went abroad on business. And he come back with a bride."

"But—but that could happen without—"

"Then why—" Eliza said triumphantly, "the day she heard did a great brown leaf keep blowin' against the pane of the front window? Miss Isobel's old nurse Keziah told me that herself. For the matter of that, what about poor Miss Isobel herself, when the Nicholas Somerwells brought her visitin',

19

and all four of them, Mr. Nicholas and his wife Sibylla, and Mr. Eugenius and his wife Juliana that was Miss Eugenia's pa and ma, went sailin' in Mr. Nicholas' yacht on the Sound and was drowned and the boat sunk and no bodies ever found? Mr. Eugenius and Mr. Nicholas married sisters, an' when the two little orphans was brought up together here by Miss Abigail, everybody said how good they could grow up together. And look what came of it—the poor child's scarred face. If that's not bein' shamed, what is?"

I had heard the story all my life of the tragedy that left old Mr. Somerwell, the girls' and Mark Harradine's grandfather, childless except for Major Harradine's mother, who lived with her husband in New York City. I only said, "But nothing has happened to Miss Eugenia."

"We're all born but we're not buried," she said. "All I say is, if I was the Somerwells I'd never stop till I found that Oneida village and hired one of their medicine men to fix that curse no matter how expensive it come. Well, time we went to bed."

I shook my head. "I'm going to sit up a little longer. If Uncle Jacob should come back, he'd be glad of a hot toddy and a bright fire."

Eliza said, "What you s'pose he did before you grew up?" She went off to bed.

I heaped up the fire. I was strong, slim as I was, from a lifetime of rowing and swimming and riding. I pulled off my white apron and tied on my company black silk one. I sat there sewing and singing to myself for maybe three hours. The clock in the corner said below its moving moon and stars that it was nearly one. The storm quieted. I folded up the shirt I had not quite finished and stowed it in the little drawer of my workstand and turned to go to bed. Then I heard the horn from the other landing.

I went mechanically to the window and stared through

20

the rain, but of course I could see nothing. Then I heard a man's voice, deep and decisive even in calling across the water. Before I knew what I was doing I had fastened my waterproof on and pulled its hood over my hair. I opened the door on the wharf: the waves were not as quieted as I had hoped. I saw that I would have to call young Joseph. I hoped he was reading late.

Fortunately he was. He was lying on the bed of his little room, and he'd kept the fire in. He was deep in his *Lives of Great Americans*. When I told him what I wanted, in an instant he had on his coat, its hood over his head. He was nearly as strong as a man; like me, he had rowed the river since early childhood.

We went out with our lanterns. We untied one of the rowboats, after I had lifted the horn that hung inside the boathouse. I called, "Coming!"

Though rain and wind had died down, it was hard pulling. But we could make it. The voice had sounded in desperate need. Indeed, who would demand to be set across the river in storm otherwise? It did not occur to me to fear the man I was rowing toward; everyone knew Van Dorn's Perdita, and most had a pleasant word for me.

There were two figures outlined against the next flash as we reached the other shore. A tall erect man wrapped in a long blue cloak, a wide hat worn low over great black eyes that, unafraid, were smiling at my surprise. His arm was thrust through the bridle of a horse whose handsome head showed behind his shoulder. The woman behind him was small and slight, in a drenched riding habit, her arm too through a horse's bridle. They must have ridden up from New York City, I thought, but what a time and hour to cross the ferry, and why?

The gentleman spoke quickly, in a deep beautiful voice.

21

"Get us over quickly—" he began, and stopped short. "Why it's a woman! And a boy!"

"The ferryman and his assistant are both stormstayed on your side," I said. "But we can take you across. You will have to swim the horses behind you."

He had evidently done it before, as he did not stop to ask how.

"If you will take my horse's rein," he said, "I will take your oars, if you please. Sit in the stern with my companion."

The rain mercifully quieted again: it was abating, I thought. The young lady had not spoken. She sat very still beside me as they put off. She was about my height and slender. The next flash showed me that the veil strapped across her face and falling behind her stiff hat was thick. The gentleman was speaking again.

"It is important that we continue our journey, or I would not have summoned you so late, and in this weather. Indeed, I would not have summoned a young lady in any case, had I known."

"There's nobody else, as I told you," I said. "We are used to this. I'm the ferryman's niece, Perdita Van Dorn, and Joseph here is his helper's son."

"In spite of that the boat is safer with me than you this weather," he said. "I too know the Hudson well. And you, somehow . . ." He stopped himself short. Suddenly we were both silent. It was as if we had forgotten the other two. We reached the other side still in silence, lighted the last little way by the lantern hanging from its pole on our side. He helped us both ashore, and I showed him where to find the gate leading to the stable.

"I must rub them down," he said, as Joseph steered the boat a little aside to the stable landing. "If you will take Miss Drusilla into the ferryhouse, I will join you shortly."

I led her in and over to the fire. She had a cloak over her

habit, but it and the habit were wet. I took the cloak off and unpinned her hat and veil. She had a sweet and soft voice, but with an accent a little strange to me.

"Wait here a minute," I said, "and then if you will come into my room I will try to dry your clothes: I have a wrapper you can wear."

She sank down as if she was too tired to answer. Her drooping head was brunette and beautiful: small delicate features, very large soft dark eyes, and a skin with a curious olive transparency. Her hair, heavy and waving, was wet too. By the way she let me unpin it, she was used to being tended.

Her escort entered as I finished. I could see him clearly now. He had a soldier's carriage: a magnificent figure, tall and wide-shouldered. His eyes were like eyes I had known somewhere in their flashing heavylashed blackness. It was a strong face: a slightly aquiline profile, firmset lips under a long military mustache, and a clear darkly tanned skin. But now in the light of the mantelpiece lights I could see that he too was very tired. I led Miss Drusilla into my bedroom, took her wet habit and underclothing, put my quilted wrapper on her and heaped the patchwork quilts over her. She was asleep before I closed the door.

I came timidly back to where the gentleman waited. "Can you not both stay the night?" I said. "There is an extra bedroom behind my own where I could accommodate Miss Drusilla. And the cottage where Joseph's people live is next us—he will show you." For Joseph had slipped back to his little room.

The gentleman smiled down at me. "We have come a long way, and we are tired, it is true," he said. "But if you will let us rest here perhaps an hour, it is all we may. Our haste is imperative."

"Ride on at this hour—in this weather?"

"Yes," he said quietly. I sat, so that he might sit also. He threw off the long blue cloak and did so.

I went to the kitchen, and came back with a glass of milk and bread and butter and cold meat, and set the tray beside the sleeping girl in my room. Then I went and came again with food for him on a tray that I set on our cherry table. Looking up to ask him to come there I saw he had fallen into sudden sleep, his black thick-curled head fallen against the chairback.

"I am sorry to waken you," I said, a shy hand on his shoulder, "but you should eat and drink: you said you could not stay long."

His eyes went wide. "You are as beautiful as I thought you by the flash," he said drowsily. Then waking fully, he rose, and said, "I beg your pardon. I was too near sleep still to know what I said."

I could feel my cheeks burn. I wished I could say to him, awake though I was, how handsome he seemed to me, how strong and sure, how much at once my friend. I said, "Shall I put the tray by you on the stand?"

"No: leave it on the table, if you please. And will you not sit with me?"

I dropped down across from him: I poured coffee for him, and for myself, so that he would not feel he was eating alone. I wondered what it would be like to sit across from him always, serving him, as now.

I forget what we said: we talked, strangely, as if we had known each other always; small friendly things. Presently he looked up at me and smiled again, he broke the roll by his plate, and leaning across gave half to me. I hoped he did not see how high I colored again. For I had seen men do this before, half-unconsciously. An old, old gesture from a man to a woman who was his to share all with. He straightened himself at, I suppose, some motion or look of mine, and smiled. "I beg your pardon," he said. "I scarcely knew I did that—"

"You are still not quite awake," I said softly. Neither of us spoke much after that: we were content not to. Presently he stood up.

"May I ask you to call Miss Drusilla?" he said. "I fear we have rested as long as we may."

I went to her. She sprang awake, finally, in terror. "It's only Perdita, who rowed you over," I said. "Your escort tells me you must journey on. You will have to wear my habit. Yours is damp still. I have put it in the little valise you threw in the boat."

She only stared: she seemed unable to think or act. So I found my habit and put it on her as if she was a child. I gave her my riding hood, for her beaver was still damp. Her shoes, set by the hearthfire, would be dried, I thought. The gentleman was cloaked and ready when we came back into the keeping room, striding restlessly up and down. I set her down and put her shoes on. "Get her a glass of wine," I said. He had it poured and at her lips before I could gesture to the sideboard. I was kneeling still, fastening her shoes, and as he gave her the drink I felt his livingness pressed against me, and saw that he too flushed a little.

"Bring her, if you will, to the mounting-block opposite your landward door," he said. "I will meet you there with the horses."

I obeyed as quietly as I had throughout. As we women stood a moment awaiting him I saw that the storm was quieting. One or two stars, even, were dimly visible among the blowing wrack of the sky. He came then, leading the horses through the other stable door. He tossed Miss Drusilla up, and put the bridle of his own horse in her hand as well as her own, saying "Wait." He turned to me. "I did not know that any girl could be as brave—and as wonderful," he said.

25

"Thanks are so little to give; and yet I must demand more of you than you have given."

"Ask," I said.

"I ask your promise that you will tell nobody of anything that has happened this night, and exact the same promise from your young servant. Tell your uncle only. It was he whom I had hoped to find. Whatever you hear, whatever you imagine, say nothing."

"I promise," I said. "And my word of honor is good. I have been taught to keep faith as well as if I were an officer and a gentleman."

The smile that broke through his intensity answered mine. As before, something in us each knew the other well. "You did not need to tell me that," he said. "One more thing." He held out two letters. The ink on the envelopes was not yet dry. He must have written them while I dressed Drusilla. "Will you, or will Mr. Van Dorn, see that the one not addressed to him reaches its destination as soon as possible? It is imperative."

I nodded, holding out my hand. He raised it to his lips. After that long moment he straightened up and, holding it, laid his letters in it. Then he mounted; hoofs faded out on their path. It might have been a dream. . . .

I waited on the back stoop till the hoofs were only echoes. The rain suddenly dashed down again and stirred me into returning into the house. I stood still in the keeping room. He was no longer there, but the feel of his presence was still: the smiling tall sureness, the deep beautiful voice speaking to me as if I was a lady. And that strong horseman's hand which had unthinkingly shared bread with me as men share with their own.

"You are as beautiful as I thought you by the flash."

I crossed to the gilt-framed mirror that hung between the windows. It was an odd thing to belong to an old ferryhouse.

My uncle had picked it up long ago from some old mansion's auction sale. I faced the girl who stood staring out at me from between the gold roses and cupids. She had never looked like that before. She stood straight and intent, her wide blue cambric skirts crumpled from the heavy waterproof. The black silk apron I'd forgotten to untie clipped a waist too small to need tight-lacing. Isobel would never believe that my corsets were loose-fitting. I could see that my eyes were dilated and far-looking still, my cheeks burning. I'd seen myself standing here, and dressed like this, often enough. The crocheted collar; the white undersleeves still immaculate below the long blue sleeves; the clearcut childish face with its blacklashed gray eyes, the long brown curls that parted above my brow and were caught high behind my ears. But never like this. I was all alive, my cheeks a deeper rose color, my lips burning red, my eyes wide and waiting and shining. Perhaps I would not be beautiful tomorrow, but I was tonight.

I made myself walk over to the mantel to put the two notes he had given me there. The address on the uppermost stood out clear and black: *Miss Eugenia Somerwell, Grandison-on-the-Hudson.* I turned it over. The name I sought ran across the back above the seal. *Mark Harradine.*

I set both notes carefully beside the clock.

"Of course," I heard myself say. "He is Eugenia Somerwell's betrothed. They are to be married two days from now."

I don't know how long I sat there not moving. I know that after a time I took out my uncle's cambric shirt from the drawer in the stand and began to sew once more. Presently my mind began to move again. Why had he crossed the ferry with such haste, with a girl I had never seen? But their attitude to each other was not intimacy. They were escort and escorted in all courtesy and in the usual fashion; for a young lady must be in charge of a gentleman while traveling, of course, if no elder lady was available. But . . . her terror . . . their haste . . . And why had he left the letter for Miss Eugenia instead of seeing her? Why, two days before the wedding, was he riding north along the river in the worst storm in years? "Perhaps it was something to do with his military duties," I thought, and realized how foolish that was. . . .

I felt cold and very, very tired. I rose; there was a damp spot by the table where I had wrung out and folded and put in her little valise the habit too damp to wear. There did not seem to be anything else to do . . . I went to my room. Strangely, I slept.

I did not toss or waken. But all through my dreams Major Harradine moved again: the raindrops glittering on his hair and making it curl out of its smooth waves; his dark eyes watching me. He was always going to tell me all the things I wanted to know. But just as he was going to I would see him crossing the room and opening the door and vanishing. I dreamed it over and over. When I waked I was very tired.

Uncle Jacob had come back, and had breakfast, by the time I came out of my bedroom.

"You shouldn't have sat up so late, my dear one," he said as I sat down at the table by him. "You look very tired and pale."

He looked tired himself: though, it seemed, he had stayed the night harmlessly enough with Lawyer Granger. He had been exhausted too easily, I remembered, of late.

I spoke brightly: "Oh, but I had such an adventure. I must tell you. He said I could—he said you knew—"

"He? Who?"

I flushed up, I could feel. "Who but Major Harradine, Miss Eugenia's betrothed."

Uncle Jacob looked at me gravely. "What was it he said I knew, child? And what was he doing two days before his wedding riding north?"

"He was escorting a young lady," I said. "A Miss Drusilla Huntington."

Uncle Jacob looked blank.

"It seemed—something he had to do. It seemed—a duty," I said hurriedly. "There is a note for you on the mantel shelf, so it was not something he was ashamed of—"

I brought the two notes to him where he sat. He tore the one open, and read it—once quickly; once slowly. Then, very carefully, he tore it into small pieces, and dropped them on the coals.

"You are right, my little girl," he said finally. "It is not a thing to be ashamed of—"

He broke off and, picking up the other note, walked through the house to the western shore. I heard him blow the small horn that hung by the door, the horn for Andy: the blast that said "Haste." And in a moment I heard him speak to Andy, hurrying to him: Andy's low reply. A moment after that my uncle came back into the keeping room: there was the splash of oars. I had seen the address on the other envelope, of course.

My uncle frowned and sat down again. "The boy should have taken time to stop off a moment at least at the Red Castle," he said. "Miss Eugenia—" he stopped himself. "Well-well, the great folks' affairs aren't our affairs."

I said, "I suppose not. But he asked me to promise to say nothing about any of it except to you. I gave him my word."

"That is right, dear little one," my uncle said. "It is far from a thing to be ashamed of."

I did not want to talk about him any longer. I was to keep it all a secret; they both said that. I knew another thing; that

29

I must forget. Forget everything; his voice and what he said, half-awake; his look, the quick grace of his leap to his saddle . . . Everything but that when Miss Eugenia and her bridegroom next crossed the ferry they were the same as the other gentry who lived in the great manors along the Hudson, no more, no less. I spoke hurriedly to Uncle Jacob.

"He said nothing—he was very tired; they both slept a little—" I stammered. "Uncle Jacob—you were going to tell me about my mother."

"It's a busy time, what with all the weddingeers coming and going," he said. "But wait till Eliza has cleared, now. Come over by the hearth and sit down, child. There isn't much to tell, actually." But before he had come over and settled into his chair across from me, the horn blew again, and a girl's voice called "Boat!"

I could see the figure on the other side. Running to the window I saw that it was Isobel.

"I'm afraid we'll have to wait till this evening, my dear," Uncle Jacob said, crossing to the door.

I knew that I would. When Isobel came, she always stayed the morning, sometimes all day.

She entered as always, quietly.

"So soon again!" she said, "but I can't stand it there with all the people coming and going. And Eugenia has disappeared with a megrim of some sort, her bedroom door locked and her fine French demoiselle on guard. She wouldn't be able to come down for dinner, she said—and all the bridesmaids, her friends, not mine, to entertain! I left it to Aunt Abigail." She laughed a little, not gayly, I thought, as she tossed her cloak, and her hat with its thick veil, to Keziah. The old woman—she was the same woman who had nursed my friend, and was with her now as her maid—took them quietly, hung them away and as always moved to the kitchen and Eliza. We went as always to the pretty room behind my own

30

that had been built for us of long ago as children; she bolted the door.

"But dear Isobel, you aren't going to stay away from the Red Castle till the wedding day, are you? What will they think?"

She did not move. She was sitting as she always did, on the windowseat, her scarred cheek pressed against the cool stone framing the window. Only the unhurt side of her face showed; she was always happier, I suppose, so. She was so lovely like that that it always made my heart ache to remember the other side. She had a young, classic profile. Her fair curls fell loose down along the smooth cheek with its delicate rose color. She spoke dully.

"I hate the Red Castle. If I hadn't been brought there, Keziah says, my accident wouldn't have happened—she calls it an accident," she ended bitterly.

"But I don't know why she says that. You and Miss Eugenia would have been reared together in any case," I said. "There was only Miss Abigail suitable to care for you."

"It wasn't Aunt Abigail that mattered; it was the Red Castle itself. I'm not supposed to tell anyone. But Keziah is like you, Dita dearest, she'd do anything to comfort me. You know her people have always been servants and tenants of ours: her grandmother and grandfather were in the house when it happened, before the Revolutionary War. They knew."

"If it is a family secret should you tell me?"

"It is a nonsensical superstition, the Somerwells always insist. Why be so secretive about a mere folly? And—if I could not talk everything out to you I should go wild sometimes."

I knew it was true. How many times had I seen her through her unhappy moods, the flooding tears she let no other human being see? If I checked her now she might be

31

in no fit state to return. I went on quietly with my knitting, a comforter for Uncle Jacob against winter. "What was it Keziah's people remembered, then?" I said. "And remember how such people exaggerate, dear."

"Oh, what would I give to have as untouched a heart as yours!" she said. I turned my face away.

"Never mind me," I said. "Go on."

"You want to know what Keziah's people knew? About the Iroquois woman. She told me. Girls born and reared in the Red Castle are safe enough. Mark Harradine's mother, my father Nicholas' sister, was. She married a rich New York aristocrat and was happy till she died. But girls *brought* here—they are shamed." She stood erect, her hands clenched at her sides. "*I* am shamed," she said. "What man will ever want or love me? Unless some fortunehunter who knows what my dowry is lies to me that he forgets my marred looks—and keeps a pretty young mistress on my money!"

"Oh, my dear—it isn't true that you aren't loved. Miss Abigail loves you, and I, and your servants adore you—and if we why not a man?"

"You don't know what you say, and why should you? You with a lovely face!" I tried to turn her mind. I said at random, "But Miss Eugenia was brought here after they all died, like you, and nothing has happened to her." As I said it I remembered saying it to Eliza, and her quoting the old saying, "We're all born, but we're not buried."

Isobel's look darkened again. Her head lifted. "Something will—it will! That is what I am waiting for, living for! To have her shamed as my face shames me! Shamed before Mark Harradine!"

She began to cry wildly. I held her close. "Dearest, he isn't the only man in the world," I said. As I spoke I felt my own heart hurry. . . . I spoke almost as much to myself as to her. "He belongs to another woman; he must praise her and

32

only her. But presently there will be a gentleman who will love you as he does Eugenia and you will love him. You've lived too long with only the Red Castle people and the ferry girl." I made myself laugh a little. "Isobel—remember that we're young, with many, many things to come."

"Then why do *you* cry?" she said, raising herself from my embrace.

"I—I don't know. Because you were, I suppose."

"I have a right to. What have I?"

"Well, what have I, compared to you?" I said. "Old Eliza says my mother died before she could tell them anything about either of us."

"Yes, I would rather be like you. Your long gray eyes, your flushed ivory skin—would you give them to me?" As she spoke she stared at me almost as if I were the Eugenia she hated.

There was a sharp knock on our door: Eliza's knock.

"Miss Isobel, Miss Abigail's sent for you," she said sharply —I suppose because she saw we had both been crying. "She says Miss Eugenia's sick and won't come out of her room, and you'll have to play hostess in her stead again to her young friends."

Isobel laughed, the hard little laugh I had heard before. "Perhaps she grieves because there is no news of Major Harradine," she said. "The wedding is set for day after tomorrow, remember. No love note—no trooper riding up with tidings?"

"It wouldn't be my place to ask, miss," Eliza said primly. Isobel strapped her thick lace veil across the face still wet with tears, and said, "Well, I should be happy. I have a rich new blue velvet for the affair day after tomorrow, to set off my pretty curls and sweet blue eyes, with a lace bertha worth ten summer dimities, Perdita. And as Aunt Abigail says, when my curls are combed loose by my scar and it is creamed and powdered it is not bad at all!" The sharp laugh came again.

I watched the boat setting out . . . Mark Harradine would have to cross, I knew, from the side whence he had ridden with Drusilla Huntingdon and he had not come. . . . Well there were two days still—and like Eliza, it was not my place to ask or know.

Eliza was back with a hand on my shoulder. "There's a Quaker boy from upriver left a parcel for you," she said. "I dunno who'd be sending you any such." She did not ask me to open it and show her, but I knew she was dying of curiosity.

"Is it anyone you know?" I asked to gain time.

She shook her head. "A decent lad enough," she said. "Them Quakers bring their children up right." She laid it in my hand; a neatly wrapped bundle in brown paper, directed to Miss Van Dorn in a hand I did not know, covered something soft and oblong . . . My own riding habit, of course, returned by the young lady Drusilla. I opened it and shook out the well-known folds. I heard myself say quickly, "I forgot to tell you that I loaned my habit to a lady who came through in the rain awhile back, whose own was saturated. I wrapped hers up and gave it to her."

"When was it?" she asked inevitably.

"I can't quite remember." I hurried into my bedroom with it over my shoulder.

CHAPTER THREE

♜

My true-love hath my heart, and I have his,
   By just exchange one for the other given:
I hold his dear, and mine he cannot miss;
   There never was a better bargain driven . . .
                                   PHILIP SIDNEY

I sat still at the front window, watching Andy helping Isobel and old Keziah into the boat. I wondered how much of the legend was true. There were tales enough, if you asked the village people. But they were more usually Dutch legends. Hendrick Hudson and his crew playing at bowls when the thunder sounded. The poor man who had said he would cross the Hudson in a storm on Sunday "spuyten duyvil"—despite the devil—and rowed there still. And the American one of "Mad Anthony" Wayne galloping to his rendezvous with some long-dead lady, on his demon horse. . . . But stories of deserted Indian maidens, oddly, I had not heard here before. As Isobel had said, they were more apt to be told of inland hills and waterfalls.

Andy came back, and entered to tell me that Eliza had said it was time to change to my blue silk and black apron for supper. I said, "Stay a minute, Andy, please. Did you ever hear the story of an Indian girl whom one of the Somerwells married by Indian rites before the Revolution, and brought home with their baby?"

As always he took a moment to frame his slow reply.

"You can hear most anything, Miss Dita," he said. "A lot of proud whites took Indian girls in the early days, before the white ladies came out here. Streak of Indian in a lot of folks up and down the river."

He moved to the open window and shut it. Then I heard my uncle's voice, quiet and cheerful as always, and ran to my room to be ready to sup with him. Eliza was having partridges and jelly and trout from the stream, and one of the apple pies with cream that he liked. I heard her marching in and out. Nothing was too good for Uncle Jacob, we both felt.

He came in, and I ran to kiss him before I went to change my gown and smooth my curls.

"Oh, I am glad to live here with you and Eliza and the Blackwaters, Uncle," I said, when I had come back from washing in cool water from my pretty china ewer, and was dressed in my Sunday silk. "I think I am better off than if I was one of the young ladies we've been ferrying across to the wedding tomorrow, or even the Somerwell girls."

He smiled at me across the table. "I'm glad you feel so, my little love, for I don't know what the old ferryhouse would do without my little Perdita."

I said boldly, "Uncle, I heard one story today from Isobel; a wild legend about an Indian girl and—a family curse of all things!"

"Oh, the one about the Oneida girl they called the Leaf," he said. "You can make things like that plausible if you try: tie everything unfortunate that happens to it. The first Somerwell and his wife were hard folk by all accounts. If anyone was punished it should have been those two. Perhaps it was

36

enough for them that they were left childless except for the grandsons by the Eugenius who had the Indian girl and Isobel Van Vooren. Well, you never know, little dear one. I've known of too many strange things happening to deny too stoutly that nothing strange may." He was quiet and sighed a little. I said what I'd been leading up to:

"Uncle dear, I heard one strange story today. I want to hear another now: what you promised, all you know about my mother."

"I hoped you'd forgotten," he said, "and there's not much to tell. But I will tell you everything I know," he went on quietly.

We talked then, as we finished our meal, of small things that did not matter, how the ferry had taken in so much money, because of all the people crossing to and fro for all the parties and festivities, that I could have a new winter dress. Miss Abigail would buy the dress-pattern for me, as she always did, when she went on her fall trip to New York City, to buy materials for herself and Isobel. And how Andy had shot enough of the wicked minks who were after our chickens so that there was plenty of fur for a tippet and muff for me, that the old tailor in Grandison Village would make.

"It isn't elegant fur," my uncle said smiling, "but my pretty Perdita will be as warm as if it was sealskin or chinchilla."

"It will be lovely and warm," I said, "and mink lasts well, too. And maybe some day a prince will come and marry me, and give me a sealskin cloak and cap, and even a muff like Miss Eugenia's!"

I was only talking bravely to make my uncle feel that I was happy. "It's a nuisance to get the minkskins ready for the tailor," I said. "It's good of Andy to take the trouble."

"Andy is almost as fond of you as he is of his own

children," Uncle Jacob said. "He has known you even a little longer than I have."

I thought my uncle was trying to put off telling me what I wanted to know. But I was wrong. He leaned back in his chair across from mine and spoke on, staring into the flames.

"It was Andy who brought you in," he said. "I had been across, taking a party to the other bank. It was a very cold night, and snow was beginning to fall. When I came back into the keeping room I saw that Andy had built up a blazing fire. A lady lay on the old settle, white and unconscious. She was covered with comforters, and Andy's Lorena was putting hot bricks at her feet. She finished as I came near, and turned and took you from the big chair where you had been put. She took you on her lap and began to undress you, and put dry clothes of her little girl's on you instead. You were quite unhurt. You might have been between one and two.

"'The baby's all right, but she's hungry,' Lorena said: you know an earthquake wouldn't shake Lorena. 'Hold her while I go get some warm bread and milk.'

"I was a young man and an only child: I'd never held a baby before. You were the prettiest baby I'd ever seen. Your hair was yellow, then, and your cheeks still deep rose from the cold. You smiled when I picked you up: you looked at me in that way some babies have, as if you knew all about me and were thinking it over. You put your arms tight around my neck.

"I was in a sort of daze when Andy spoke. 'I brought them in here because they are gentry,' he said, 'and our house won't hold no more than us.'

"Then I turned as I saw the lady on the settle. She wasn't much more than twenty. She opened her eyes as I looked: great long dark gray eyes with thick lashes, eyes like yours. She looked at me, and her lashes fell. Her hair had come loose. It was almost the color yours is now: it fell over the side of the settle almost to the floor. Ill and white as she was, she was lovely. I learned she was as good and gentle as she was beautiful.

" 'Where did you find them?' " I asked Andy.

"Lorena came back and took you from me, and sat down and began to feed you from the porringer. 'I think she was on her way to cross the ferry,' he said. 'She was lying a little way above the road to the ferryhouse. The snow was beginning to fall on them both. She was in a riding habit.'

"We found the horse next day, sheltering under a clump of trees, with his bridle caught on a low bough.

" 'Has she said anything?' " I asked.

"Andy shook his head. 'She was stunned. A mercy the baby didn't wander off.'

"Eliza came in then: and the women agreed that the best thing to do was to put the mother and child to bed, for it was too late to go all the miles to the doctor, and she seemed to be in natural sleep. So they took the baby upstairs, and I followed with Honor."

"What was her other name?" I asked.

He shook his head. "We never knew."

I stared at my uncle. "Why? Wouldn't she tell you?"

He said gravely. "She did not know. When we managed to get Dr. De Witt next day—the snow was so heavy that traffic was almost impossible—he said that she must have fallen or been thrown from the horse, with you in her arms: and by a miracle protected you from hurt. The back of her head must have struck a stone, he said, under the snow. It was the next day that Andy found the horse. He was a valuable beast, a lady's hack. There were saddlebags, packed with your possessions and hers. Everything was of expensive make and material. There were—there are—jewels. But we found nothing to tell us what her last name was, anywhere."

"No letters—no papers of any sort?" I asked. "But surely when she came to—"

"There was one letter," he said. "It began 'My dearest Honor.' It begged her to have a little more patience, he loved her and would return to her and their child shortly. The months away from her had been long. It enclosed money. But the signature was only 'Your own always' and there was no address on the blank side of the letter, only a seal with no crest or inscription."

"But when she came to?"

"She recovered consciousness," he said gravely. "In body she was well after a few weeks. Bodily she was a beautiful young woman, perhaps twenty or twenty-one—graceful and gay. Mentally—mentally my poor Honor remembered nothing that had gone before her accident. You can recall her: the most gentle, gay, charming child. She loved you. She remembered her mother-love, we thought. But she did not remember that she was your mother. She was puzzled about you: she asked me where you came from. 'Is she my little sister?' she asked finally. 'She must be some relative of mine, because I love her.'"

"But when my mother said, 'Try to remember, my dear. She is your little daughter,' Honor only shook her head. It troubled her so to try to remember anything that we stopped trying to make her. The doctor said that was best. That our best hope was to build up her physical health and make her as happy as possible: perhaps memory would return of itself. He spoke of the possibility of an operation. I was saving money for that. But she died; there was an epidemic of fever. She had been happy with us."

"But did you make no inquiries?" I asked. "You say her belongings were expensive. She had—Eliza said she had—a wedding ring, the ways and manners of a cherished young lady—"

"Yes." He suddenly rose and walked to and fro. "Heavens, yes! We sought all up and down the river. A beautiful gently bred young woman—a pretty baby girl—they should have been missed. And she must, we thought, have either been a wife—a loved wife—or thought herself so. Heavens knows it didn't matter which so far as I was concerned."

I remembered something I had been told.

"But surely there was an inscription inside her betrothal ring—or had she none?"

"There was a betrothal ring. It had an inscription, but as was coming to be the mode, with only Christian names: Honor from Edward. We advertised in the New York and village papers. We searched from Grandison as far south as New York City, and north to Albany. There was no result."

"But the name—Edward—didn't she remember it?"

He shook his head. "Nothing behind her fall."

"But, Uncle Jacob—the man who gave her the rings. You could not find him? He must have died."

My uncle spoke very quietly again. "I went to my clergyman, my old friend Dr. Van Alstyne. I said, 'Honor cannot remember anything. But if she had a husband, or a man who feigned to be her husband, by now he would have combed heaven and earth for her . . . and if he does not love her and is not her husband, she is free. You know that I would make a good and faithful husband to her. I have told people that she is my widowed cousin from New York City. Our ways and manners are different, and the way she was found might be known any time Andy and Lorena broke their word to keep it still. Andy's safe—how can you tell about a woman? And there were the advertisements.'

"'Does she love you?' my friend asked.

"I said, 'Yes, she clings to me. She says and acts it. She does love me.' And I was right, Perdita!

"'In seven years of desertion remarriage is legal,' he said.

41

'She has been with you a year. Can you wait, if you love her as faithfully as you say?'

" 'Six long years?' I said. 'No. And remember the letter. I do not think it the letter of an honest gentleman. It is more like the letter of a man who tries to keep a girl who loves him quieted.'

" 'Or a weak man, who for selfish reasons, or financial, or someone's domination, temporizes,' he said. 'These might be, along with honest love—'

" 'Honest!' I said. 'A coward's affection, that holds other things more important than the girl who has given him all—'

" 'I agree with you—almost—' Dr. Van Alstyne said. 'Let us, too, temporize. Wait a little longer, son. Another year may bring back her memory, or the facts may come to light.'

"I said, 'We love each other.'

" 'Well, what of the other man's child?'

" 'I love her also, as if she was my own,' I told him. And I always have, my little Perdita."

I leaned toward him and touched his hand. "I wish you had married her," I said. "I wish she had not died."

He smiled at me. "My own dear little girl," he said. He was silent a few moments more. Then he spoke on.

"Then the fever came," he said. "By my old friend and rector's persuasions, I waited two years longer, after all. They were not unhappy years: sometimes we were very happy. And we could look forward. She was content, a loving child. I had her love, and her presence—sometimes a joy—sometimes a torment, but always better than not to have known her. The great folk were not interested. The villagers were used to long betrothals. There was less talk than I had feared; at least she heard nothing. The cub Alonzo who was insulting—more because he was a fool, I think now, than willingly—was I imagine of a family which was evil-minded. I suppose there are some. The last evening before Honor died, she came to her senses. It was, I expect, what the old women call the lightening before death. She turned on her pillow to me, with her wonderful hair flowing down as it had when she was first brought in and laid on the settle. She looked at me and smiled. Dr. De Witt stood at the other side of the bed. He too, of course, heard.

"She put her small burning hand in mine, as she had so many times. 'I remember everything now,' she said, 'and I remember our love. It is all right, dearest.' She spoke like a woman, not a child. 'As soon as I am well we can be married.'

"I supposed she was raving. I held water to her lips and she drank and spoke again, in answer to my question.

" 'What is your name, darling, besides Honor?' I said. 'Why did you come—'

"She smiled. 'Because of my child. And she has nothing to be ashamed of. I was a wife—my name—' Her head fell back on the pillow. She could only whisper. 'It has to be heaven, dear love,' she said. She was gone."

My eyes filled. "Oh! And you never knew any more."

"No. But whatever her errand, why she had ridden far in that cruel weather, her word was enough for me. She could never have been other than truthful. So I know that neither she nor you had anything to be ashamed of. 'I was a wife,' she said. She must have been widowed, young as she was. And in spite of all, those three years she was in my house were the happiest of all my years."

He leaned back, looking suddenly very tired. He had seemed more wan lately, I remembered. "Tomorrow, if you like, I will show you her possessions. You are old enough to have her jewels."

Before I could answer there was a violent knock on the front door. It was flung wide before I reached it. It was Miss Eugenia.

"Tie my boat, Jacob," she said shortly, and was inside before he could hurry to fasten the little skiff. He knelt just in time to secure it as it was floating off. She made two swift steps to where I stood, careless of the wet edges of the deep blue satin skirts that flew wide around her. One heavy black plait was half-down across her white shoulder. Her eyes were angry. She stood over me.

"Tell me about my letter!" she said sharply.

I was slow to answer and her nails sank into my wrist. "Your letter—"

"Jacob Van Dorn was not here that night! Andy Black-water rowed him. They couldn't get back, they didn't. It was you—it must have been you!"

I knew what she meant now. And I could not help thinking, as one's mind flies to irrelevant things in terror, of the sort of rage which had flung the little Isobel against the fireplace. Before I could speak again my uncle was back and beside me.

"If you will release my niece's wrist she will find it easier to answer you," he said, and I had not known that he could speak so sternly.

"Make her tell, then!" she said sullenly. Old Regina, always most quick to protect me, lying on the hearth as ever, lifted her head and growled softly, and Rex sat up. Uncle Jacob quieted them, and said, "Please accept a seat, Miss Eugenia. You must not find us lacking in courtesy." His tone was ironic; she flushed and dropped into the chair. "And now, what is it you wish my niece to tell you?"

Her hands gripped the chair arms and her eyes flashed, as she spoke. "Your man Blackwater brought me a note from my betrothed, Major Harradine, the morning after the storm. The major had passed through your ferryhouse. Only Perdita here, and the old woman Eliza, could have been there. He"— her hand flew to her lifted throat—"he crossed the river without pausing to see me. Our wedding day was set for the day after tomorrow. He told me to trust him—trust him! It was a sacred obligation to a gentleman who had saved his life, and had since died. He hoped—hoped, mind you!—to return in time. He would make every possible effort. He asked that I feign illness, in the possible case he could not. A vow to a dead man coming before his marriage vow!" She stopped, choked by her anger.

"Have you told your aunt and cousin this? If not, why do you describe it to us, who are no relation—not even your friends on an equality?" he asked coolly.

"Why? Because Perdita was alone with him here. She had his letter in her hands!"

"Stop. My niece is honorable. She has never opened a letter not meant for her in her life. You cannot say the seal was tampered with. If you are honorable also, tell us the truth."

"It did not look so—how do I know? I tore the letter open too soon to be sure . . . if there is any possibility, I *must* know. She must tell me! Did she open it? Did she take anything out? What did he tell her?"

"Miss Somerwell," he said, "we Van Dorns are neither your slaves nor your tenants. This ferry has been freehold longer than the Red Castle has been standing. If you cannot accept her word I must ask you to leave us. I cannot wish to use force to a young lady: I hope you will not make this necessary."

"She has not given me her word," she said angrily.

"I give it," I said. "Your betrothed sealed your letter. I put it on the mantel and only touched it again to give it to Andy."

Eugenia sank back in her chair. To my surprise she spoke more gently; her voice, directed to him, was winning and suddenly melodious. "Dear Mr. Van Dorn, I did not mean to insult either of you," she said, smiling at him. "But oh, surely

45

you see that Perdita is the only human being who can help me, the only one who saw my betrothed, who had converse with him. She can at least tell me all that occurred that dreadful night. There might be a reason—a clue."

I had given Mark Harradine my word of honor. Even if that had not been final, my uncle had told me that the night's doings must be kept secret. I looked for him now for help; but he only shook his head. He said gently, "Tell her what you can, my dear."

I knew what he meant. I drew a long breath and spoke.

"Major Harradine called the boat in a lull of the storm," I said. "I managed to row over with Joseph. He took the oars back to the ferryhouse. As you say, I was alone. Old Eliza was in bed. He was wet and weary. He put his horse in the ferryhouse stable with ours, and rested here a short while." I stopped for a moment. I sat straighter, and spoke on in a voice as clear as her own. Had the time been short or long? I could not remember. "He did not say who he was. I did not know him. I gave him food while he rested and dried his cloak. He slept a little: I waked him as he had asked. He wrote the letter. Then he rode away."

"Did he say nothing of why he was going and where?"

I kept faith with him. "Passengers do not tell ferry people their affairs," I said. "He did not."

"You were together long enough for him to dry his cloak," she said satirically, "and to minister to him. Had you never heard said of Mark Harradine that no woman could meet and know him with an untouched fancy—or an untouched heart?"

I made myself continue to answer quietly. I could hear my own words dropping one by one as if indifferently.

"We said little. I was in my room most of the time, and he in the keeping room. He came late and went at dawning. He rode north, to what destination or on what errand I do

46

not know. Indeed, if you will consider, Miss Eugenia, it would be strange if I did know."

I was done; and I had not lied; I had not betrayed him.

"Then why are you so white?"

I came to my feet. "Because I am afraid of you and your anger!" I said, angry myself at last. I reached back to grasp my uncle's hand.

"My girl has told you all she can," he said. "Unless you wish to cross-question our old servant, which you may do, we will consider this interview terminated, Miss Somerwell."

"I think not," she said. "I know your old woman; she is besotted with your—niece, as you wish to call her. Take me to the other side."

My uncle went to the door and held it for her. She stood still while he knelt to tie my little *Foam* to the skiff's stern for his return journey. In the minutes he took, Eugenia whirled on me, hand on the door.

"You know more than you've told, with your hypocritical angel-face they talk about! I tell you this! If you've deceived me—your punishment won't be long coming, and one you won't forget. You shall be shamed as no woman has been shamed since they whipped the Indian harlot from the Red Castle long back!"

"You will not push me into the fire, I suppose?" I said. I had stood enough. I moved a little toward her, and my great dogs moved at either side of me. They knew what our voices meant. I laid a hand on either collar, or they would have advanced on her.

She laughed. "Not with your friends ready to attack, naturally," she said. "There are things which burn deeper."

The long silence was broken by my uncle's voice. "I am ready, Miss Eugenia." She laughed a little again, and went.

47

CHAPTER FOUR

♜

Sleep on, my love, in thy cold bed,
Never to be disquieted.
My last goodnight! Thou wilt not wake
Till I thy fate shall overtake:
Stay for me there: I will not fail
To meet thee in that hollow vale . . .

HENRY KING

I sat, my guardian dogs pressing close at my knees, till I heard the click of my uncle's oars and the bump of his boat against the wharf. He looked drawn and white, as he entered, his hand pressed against his side.

"Is anything the matter?" I asked.

"No, my dear. I strained myself a little pulling Miss Eugenia's skiff up on shore—a night's rest will cure it. Go to bed now, little dear one: we are both tired."

I lay awake a long time thinking: not of stormy Miss Eugenia—my own story mattered more. If, as Uncle Jacob said, my mother had recovered her memory before death, his inference was right: she was a lawful widow . . . But then what did she need or whom seek, to take her baby and ride through wild roads in wild weather?

And yet—the outside world would feel that the one *if* was

a strong one: only my uncle and the doctor could testify that the girl who called herself Honor returned to sanity when she spoke her last word to her lover . . . I began to think of the only proof, the letter which told so little . . . Tomorrow my uncle would show me that and the other things. Perhaps they might hold something my young eyes could find that others had overlooked . . . Or something still lay leafcovered in woods near where the horse had been caught—a token of some sort. I finally made myself sleep. The echo of an old tune Uncle Jacob loved was in my ears as I sank down into dreams . . .

> *Shall I e'er forget her? Never,*
> *No, loved one, no—*
> *She's the star I lost from heaven*
> *Long time ago . . .*

I slept ill that night: Eugenia's wild anger had disturbed me more than I knew. I kept awakening and wondering if I had said too much or too little: what had detained Major Harradine: if it was love for the exquisite frightened girl he called Drusilla, which had made him ride with her and take a promise of secrecy from me.

I was finally waked by Eliza at my bedside. I saw her face.

"What is it?" I said, sitting up and making ready to spring out of bed. "Is anything wrong?"

Her hands, down at her sides, clenched and unclenched. She tried to speak twice. Finally she managed. "Child," she said, "I never did know how to break things easy. . . . He was a good man . . ."

He *was* a good man—I stared terrified. "My uncle—is he sick?"

"He—he won't never be sick no more, child. He's in heaven. In heaven with poor Madame Honor that he never did forget, that he said he told you about last night—"

I did not feel anything at all. It was not true. It couldn't be true. Then when old Eliza herself burst into a wild weeping I began to know it was true.

I rose and put on my wrapper and crossed to his room. He lay there very quietly, as if he might waken at any moment. The only thing new to me was the faint half smile on his thin kind face, the death-smile new to me then. I bent and kissed his forehead. It was cold. Suddenly everything was unreal. I began to remember all the things to be done. It was well I did, for Eliza at my heels was still sobbing aloud.

"We must send first for Dr. De Witt, Eliza," I heard myself say steadily. "Where is Andy?"

She sobbed that she did not know, she supposed in his own house out back. I told her to go and call him. Still sobbing, she went. I passed into the chilly living room and sat at the escritoire to write the necessary notes. I remembered that Dr. Van Alstyne, my uncle's old friend, was my co-guardian with Dr. De Witt, and wrote to him as well. Andy, tense and holding on to himself, came back with Eliza. "I git coffee, child, you must eat," she said. "You got to write any more letters?"

"No. I've written the doctor and the clergyman."

"Your uncle made a will," she said. "You better write Lawyer Granger, too."

I went on writing, like an automaton. Andy, when I looked up, was silent, and I saw stricken, still. I sat quite still, with the pen in my hand. Presently I felt arms round me; Andy's Lorena, still crying a little as she spoke.

"Dearie, you better come lie down, I've made your bed up. You don't need to worry, Eliza and I will look after everything. Would you want I sat by you?"

I shook my head. I went docilely after Lorena. She loosened the buttons on my wrapper and made me lie down and pulled the comforter over me. Presently she came back with hot bricks for my feet. I heard myself saying, like somebody far off, "You are very kind."

She took my hand, sitting by me, and I saw she was crying a little. She went on talking. Presently Eliza came in with some camomile tea, and I drank it to please them.

Dr. De Witt was sitting beside me when I woke. I heard him say crossly to the women, "What did you give her?"

"It was just a little mite of laudanum like everybody keeps in the house," Eliza said. "We was scared; she was like a sleepwalker."

"So you made her sleep deeper," he said crossly. I said, opening my eyes, "It didn't hurt me, Doctor."

"And see, she's been cryin' in her sleep!" Eliza said eagerly. I felt my face. It was wet with tears.

"Why do they all want me to cry?" I asked the doctor. But he only patted my hand.

"But why?" I said.

"It was heart disease. I think you should have been told. But he did not want you to worry. Don't think about anything," he said.

Dr. Van Alstyne, my uncle's old friend the clergyman, came soon. He stood silent for a moment; then I heard him say under his breath, "All, all are gone, the old familiar faces." I opened my eyes, and he spoke kindly. "You are young, my dear child: life is ahead of you. And your uncle has seen to it that you will be well taken care of." Then he held my hand and prayed by my bedside, kneeling stiffly with his gold-headed cane.

My uncle had been loved. The long train of carriages that followed him to the grave proved that. The three old men—Dr. Van Alstyne, Dr. De Witt and Lawyer Granger—stood round me at the grave, Andy Blackwater and his wife and children a little behind us with old Eliza. It seemed like a long

long play, that would never be over. I said that to the clergy-man, whom I knew best, as the carriage took us back.

"Pompa mortis—" he began and changed to "Yes, yes, poor child, the pomp of death is harder to bear than death itself. Only one more thing, and you shall be left in peace. Lawyer Granger must tell you about your uncle's will."

I had forgotten about that. Andy and Lorena had gone back in their little boat before ours took us over. There was a bright fire in the keeping room, and we sat around the table.

Lawyer Granger read the will. The ferry and all its build-ings and what the will called tenements, ready money and some bank stock, were his, and everything was left to me, "My beloved adoptive daughter Perdita."

Mr. Granger explained that tenements meant houses—houses in New York City, whose rentals came to me.

"You are not wealthy, my dear," he said, "but you can be called well-to-do. You can afford to hire a duenna and re-move from here."

Andy and Eliza had not been forgotten: there was even a legacy to Andy's son young Joseph. They were, if they so desired, to carry on the ferry.

When the other gentlemen had gone, Mr. Granger lingered a little.

"There is something else before I go, unless you are too weary to receive it; and a message from friends who were unable to come in person immediately."

I said, "No." I thought I knew of what he spoke.

I was not mistaken. He rose and crossed to the nearer of the oval gilt frames which held the India-ink colored portraits of my uncle's parents, lifted and laid it on the mantel. Behind it, unknown to me till now, was a sunken wall safe. He un-locked it and lifted down a metal box which he laid on the table and opened with a smaller key. I came near: a yellowed letter lay on the top of a number of velvet-covered boxes. Mr. Granger put it carefully down and lifted the boxes out.

"This is the jewelry which was your mother's," he said. "It does not, of course, represent a fortune. But I believe it could be disposed of for a couple of thousand dollars, which would if you wish further education cover a couple of years in a ladies' seminary."

We laid the pieces out on the table; a string of pearls, pearl-and-jet bracelets, a bracelet with sunken diamonds, diamond earrings, some handsome cameos and gold chains, a small gold ladies' watch, and two lockets. In a box by themselves, two diamond rings, a diamond brooch, and a pearl and amethyst. I snatched up the nearest locket and opened it . . . but there was only one picture in it: a sweet faced elderly lady whose hair and what showed of her gown were of a period perhaps twenty years ago. I looked closely, and cried out.

"Look, Mr. Granger! There has been a picture in the empty side. See, here are the marks of the glue that held it. It has been wrenched out."

He set on his silver spectacles.

He said, "A woman's eyes are sharper than a man's. We had not noticed it before." He spoke on slowly. "Your uncle, or so I suppose, for he spoke of being about to do so, told you what little we know of your mother," he said.

"Yes, yes," I said eagerly. "He spoke of the letter there. It had no signature . . . May I?"

He nodded as I eagerly, yet carefully, opened the folds. The signature my uncle had spoken of was there, "*Your own always.*" I looked closely.

"Something has been destroyed here also," I said. "Look, sir. I think my father's signature has been cut away."

He looked closely and nodded again. "Cleverly; only the lack of a margin proves it," he said. "I had not seen the letter. Yes, there are a couple of black marks which would be tops of capital letters, too small for any but your young eyes. Someone has wished to erase all clues to his personality."

I pushed down my wonder. The fact was all that mattered now.

"You said," I answered feverishly, "that my mother's jewels would educate me. Would they not pay for further search?"

"Yes," he said, "but my dear child, why pour out your possessions on a will-o'-the-wisp? Jacob Van Dorn, as he told me, searched deeply. Hired seekers could do no more."

I did not answer but my mind was unchanged.

He laid the jewelry back in the boxes. "Put them in the tin box where they were," he said. "They are all right for the time being; we will engage a safe deposit box. Do you wish me to keep the keys as before?"

"All but the jewelry," I said. "I would like to look at it. There might be some trace there of my mother's identity."

"My dear young lady, these belong to you," he said. "I would only like to remind you that they are valuable, and that jewels are easy to steal."

"I will take great care of them," I said. "Nobody knows of their existence beyond ourselves, I suppose, and I will keep them locked in my dressing case."

He looked serious, but he said no more: he replaced the tin box, locked the safe, and pulled the portrait over the place.

"Now for the last matter I have to discuss with you," he said. "The message of which I spoke."

I waited, a little tired.

"Perhaps you have wondered why Miss Abigail Somerwell, your patroness, and your young friend, Miss Isobel, did not attend Mr. Van Dorn's funeral. The reason was that Miss Abigail could not leave home; her other niece, Miss Eugenia, was and is dangerously ill."

Eugenia dangerously ill! But—and with a leap of the heart

I realized that in the grief of my uncle's death, I had not remembered that Major Harradine had never recrossed the ferry . . . and that today was to have been their wedding day . . . Eugenia, then, had done as his letter requested: she had feigned illness.

"But—the marriage—" I faltered.

"It was of course postponed; a letter sent to Major Harradine I understand the night before your uncle's passing: they feared cholera." It was only I who could contradict the story of the letter. And she could be sure I would not.

"And is it cholera?"

"No. It is a false alarm. But it seems her nerves prevent her from seeing anyone for some days. Her aunt is about to call on you—"

"And when—" Before I could bring myself to ask about the marriage there were the well-known steps without. Old Eliza had heard the knocker that echoed first in the kitchen, and was throwing the door wide to Miss Abigail and Isobel.

Mr. Granger was greeting both ladies in his slow formal way. I ran to seat Miss Abigail by the fire as always, and turned to Isobel, my hands in hers. Miss Abigail threw back her lace veil, and rose, beckoning me near. She put an arm around me. "My poor child! We came as soon as possible," she said, and kissed me. Isobel was close, too, a hand still holding mine.

When their words of affection and sympathy were done, and I had got control of myself, Miss Abigail said, "Our good friend Mr. Granger has perhaps given you an idea that our visit is not only one of condolence, dear child."

I caught my breath. What new thing was to befall me or had? But Mr. Granger only said, "I had only time to explain the reason of your non-appearance at the late sad event and that Miss Perdita might expect you here." He sat down across from us. He said, "Shall I speak for Miss Somerwell and Miss Isobel, or does Miss Somerwell prefer to?"

Clinging to Isobel's hand, I felt a certain relief. Whatever it was could not be too bad if my friend was a part of it. Miss Abigail smiled.

"I am sufficiently intimate with this young lady to speak for myself and my niece," she said. She faced me again. "My dear Perdita, I have discussed the plan I am about to offer with your old friend and legal adviser and yours here. We feel that you are too young and too alone in the world to remain here at the ferryhouse with only old servants. I have known you almost since your infancy, as has my niece Isobel. My other niece Eugenia's approaching marriage will leave Isobel without a female companion of her own—" I caught my breath—then I remembered—naturally they would not know any details of Eugenia's and Mark Harradine's future plans. . . .

Isobel interrupted her aunt. She was pulling me close. "Oh, Aunt Abigail, don't take so long about it!" she cried. Her arm round me, she said, "We want you to come live with us at the Red Castle." She even laughed a little. "Aunt Abigail thinks you are good for me!"

Miss Abigail took up the story majestically. "I have noticed," she said, "that Perdita's naturally cheerful nature has a cheering effect on that of my niece Isobel. Perdita's education, also, thanks to my late worthy friend Mr. Van Dorn, is, excepting in the lighter accomplishments, nearly equal to Isobel's. I would propose that she share Isobel's studies in this respect. In fact, as you know, Mr. Granger, I offer her a position of equality in our home as Isobel's sisterly friend."

I stood silent for a moment. "But—to leave my own house—" I stammered. I looked round the old room I loved . . . Mr. Granger frowned slightly. I knew he was thinking that the offer was more than a girl in my position could expect: and that my words were ungrateful. I said, "But, dear Miss Abigail—I am only a ferry girl!"

She smiled slightly. "If we do not regard that, you need not," she said. "Your manner and breeding, thanks, I think I may say, partly because of your friendship with my Isobel, are unexceptionable. You will have an opportunity to meet the young ladies and gentlemen of our acquaintance. In short, you will share my niece's social life as well as her studies."

Isobel pulled me still closer. She spoke low. "Dita, you will, you must! I want you—I need you. Oh—to live with you, instead of that arrogant Eugenia—" Her feverish small hands clutched mine tight. I saw that in a moment, if I did not accede to Miss Abigail's invitation, one of her spells of hysterical weeping would come on. I turned to face Miss Abigail and curtsied.

"I thank you, dear Miss Abigail," I said. "I am grateful. I will come."

Miss Abigail rose and kissed my cheek. "It is settled, then," she said. "You should be able—do you not think so, Mr. Granger, to be packed and ready in another week."

I felt a moment of dismay; her words made it so final . . . A week . . . But by then, surely, Major Harradine would have returned: I would not have to be there until they were married and gone.

"But Eliza?" I asked.

Mr. Granger said, "I have apprised the Blackwaters and Eliza of the probability that Miss Perdita would remove to the Red Castle. They expressed regret, but agreed with us that it was best."

I saw that I had no choice. It was, indeed, an offer for which any young person in my position, I knew, should be grateful.

"I will do my best to deserve your kindness, Miss Abigail," I said, and for the first time was able to burst into tears.

Isobel's arm came round me again: she was hurrying me into our little room.

"My aunt has promised," she said, "that we may still come here to be private. And your little boat will be at our boat-house, so we can cross when we wish."

"Oh, I am glad," I said, "I will not lose my old home altogether."

"I thought of that," she said. "But I was selfish, also. Oh Perdita, I never had secrets from you. I want to be able to return here, to escape from the pomp and fuss of Eugenia's wedding."

I looked at her in surprise. "But I will not be coming to you for a week," I said. "Surely she will be—" I stopped myself. "Surely she will be well before then."

Isobel's voice dropped.

"Perdita, she was not sick! I saw her through the keyhole of her room. She was pacing up and down, angry—I know her angers. I don't know how much our aunt knows. But I do know that your Andy Blackwater brought a letter for her. It is my belief that Cousin Mark wrote her to postpone the wedding. All I know is that letters canceling the date of the wedding flew out everywhere like a flock of birds. And we don't know when it will be; Eugenia has sent word downstairs that she cannot decide until she knows when she will be well."

I did not answer. I knew why she could not decide. "It will be ended one way or another before too long," I said. I wondered—but how could I speak? What had kept the bridegroom from return? He had not said how far he must escort his beautiful, frightened Drusilla. I only knew that he was honorable, and so must keep his word to his betrothed. And that I must keep my promise of silence no matter what the cost.

58

CHAPTER FIVE

I would not have thy married heart
    Think momently of me,
Nor would I tear the cords apart
    That bind me so to thee;
No! While my thoughts seem pure and mild
Like dew upon the roses wild,
    I would not have thee know
The stream that seems to thee so still
    Has such a tide below.

RUFUS DAWES

The change from the only home I had known is, strangely, vague to me still. I remember Eliza crying while she helped pack my things.

The two rooms that belonged to me and Isobel were to remain untouched. Standing in the doorway before we crossed together, Isobel smiled.

"So we leave our refuge!" she said. "Thank Heaven it is here to return to! Who knows how much we may need it!"

I did not answer. I realized that in spite of my bereavement I had not so sorrowful or bitter a view of life and living as poor Isobel. . . . I had something to give, as well as all I was receiving. And then I heard the horn on this side blowing.

Andy had finished putting my possessions in the boat, and we must cross. The Red Castle awaited.

It towered on the height of the slope of the western shore. I looked at it in a new way. Till now it had only been the great, eerie mansion, castle-shaped, of red sandstone, that the first Eugenius Somerwell had erected from his wealth as a slave trader. Today it was more than that—a place whose great doors would open for me and close on me, for—who knew how long? For the first time I was a little afraid.

And then, irretrievably, I was in the boat; in the carriage; borne the short way to the carriage drive of the Castle itself. The great doors beyond the paved court opened. I shrank back a little. The lamps shone bright in the long hall; the tall black butler stood aside: but it was only kind Miss Abigail, just as she always was, holding both hands out to welcome me, while Isobel's arm round me drew me in. I smiled not only at my friends, but at my own transitory fears.

Isobel led me up the steep stone stairs: presently I stood alone in the high tapestried room they had given me. The great fireplace burned bright. Behind me a heavy curtained carved bed stood; carved chairs, a carved desk, stood between the deep-cut narrow windows. My homely valises and I seemed strange in this place.

And then there was a knock at the door, but only Isobel's old Keziah stood smiling and curtsying there.

"I come to put away your gown," she said, "Miss Abigail say you maybe choose your own out of the maids to be your dresser. Miss Isobel say I come to you first, you don't feel so strange."

I thanked Keziah, and watched her open the doors of a great dark wardrobe that I could have hidden in and deftly unpack my valises. The gowns in the wardrobe; the underwear in a carved walnut highboy. And then Isobel, running in, smiling, to show me that her bedroom was next mine.

I had feared dining with Miss Eugenia at the table. But she was not there. Miss Abigail began talking to me pleasantly about the materials she was writing for to the New York drygoods stores; the sewing woman engaged for Eugenia was here still, she said. I was a little aghast at the cost ahead; and then recalled that I could afford it, and said so gratefully: at which Miss Abigail smiled and said there would be time enough to think of that. As I knew that my gowns were not suitable or sufficient, even if I had not needed a suit of mourning, I said no more. But I determined I would pay for my own clothes.

The fact of Eugenia's absence looked as if she was still obeying her betrothed and feigning illness. They began to talk of her without my asking.

"I must make my niece Eugenia's excuses," Miss Abigail told me. "She is better but still not able to descend from her apartment."

I took courage. "What does the doctor say?"

"Since his first visit," she answered, "she has gone into such a state of hysteria when his further attentions were mentioned that we have not dared to suggest it again. But she seems slowly recovering."

I wondered how she had managed to slip from the Red Castle and visit me at the ferryhouse. I had not then learned what a cowing effect a person with violent rages has on the household. Apparently few questions had been asked, especially on emotional subjects, for fear of reawakening the storms.

Isobel answered one of my questions without my needing to ask, after the meal was over.

"As long as my lady Eugenia has Petronius she can send messages to all the world," she said. She had led me to her little sitting room, whose stone walls were masked by azure silk coverings that matched the furnishings. "He's left over

61

from the time they freed the York State slaves: he is as much her possession as if she could lash or sell him. He was her father's body servant."

I knew the man she meant. The middle-aged, well dressed, well mounted Negro who had—it came to me now—crossed the ferry those days back with plump saddlebags full of—it must have been—the notes postponing the marriage.

"He may be with Major Harradine now," Isobel added. "He went on another of Eugenia's mysterious errands some days back and hasn't returned."

I reminded myself again that it was not my affair. I must have control and patience. Major Harradine would emerge from his mission of escorting Drusilla Huntington, Eugenia would emerge from her feigned illness . . . Oh, if I had only asked my uncle, if he had willed to tell me, what it was about! For he had had the clue to it all; he had said it was right . . . If he had said so, it *was* right.

I was more fortunate than Eugenia, at least. I had faith in both men, the living and the dead. . . .

The ways of the great household went smoothly on. And the new ways that I must learn. To be waited on by the pleasant young Scottish girl Janet, whose father was head gardener here. To receive pianoforte lessons, and dancing lessons with Isobel from the old French dancing master who came twice weekly. To drive with the ladies in the afternoons; to be introduced to the ladies and gentlemen who called on them and were called on. Miss Abigail seemed to wish to see more than it was usual of society. I guessed that she wished the explanation of the postponement given to as many people as possible.

For the rest, Miss Abigail decreed that I must be gowned as well as Isobel. I could, of course, wear only black and white. So there were hours in the sewing room with the seamstress who made for Isobel and Eugenia, and a pile of my garments in review on one of the tables there. She chose from the jewels that had been my mother's a single string of pearls with matching earrings, brooch and bracelet as suitable for me. She had been told, she said, my mother's story by my uncle.

"Indeed," she said, "I did not need to hear the story and see your mother's relics, to know that you must have been a lady by birth. I would not have let you and my Isobel grow up so sisterly otherwise."

So the days went on, placidly enough: till, perhaps ten of them passed, and Eugenia, beautiful and elegant as always, swept down to dinner. But she spoke to me pleasantly if a little distantly. The rage at the ferryhouse might never have been.

"Blackwater from the ferry brought me news today of my cousin Mark," she said, as if it was the merest chitchat. "I had summoned him, feeling recovered. He should arrive to-morrow afternoon."

"Where is he, and where did he wait your pleasure?" Isobel asked. If there was mockery in her voice Eugenia ignored it.

"He had been waiting my pleasure," she said smoothly, "at the house of an old friend, some twenty miles away on the other bank of the river."

"There will be a good deal to do," her aunt said. "You will want at least a fortnight; the invitations to repeat, the bridesmaids—"

"No. I feel that my newly recovered health would not permit a repetition of all this formality. I shall need nobody present but the family, and of course the clergyman—I suppose necessarily our lawyer. We will use the great parlor. The announcements you may attend to at leisure when it is over." She rose and was gone.

Miss Abigail said, looking troubled, "She is not herself yet. If something has brought on one of her storms . . . but Mark could always handle her. I will be glad when he is here. I think, Isobel, we will venture on asking Dr. De Witt to be our house guest. He is an old friend; it will seem natural . . ."

"Could it be that she dislikes having me here?" I ventured. "If so—"

"No," Miss Abigail said firmly.

When I was alone with Isobel again she said, "My aunt is right. If it is you Eugenia is annoyed with, if you don't mind being a lightning rod for a few days, she's the less likely to say or do something to the rest of us that can't be covered up. And she won't dare make an actual scene about you before the old gentlemen. It would put her in the wrong, for you've done nothing."

"But"—I spoke before I thought—"if the scene should be with her betrothed?"

Isobel laughed. "Is that our affair?" she said lightly.

I did not see Miss Eugenia again until later that afternoon. We were all three gathered in the sewing room with the seamstress. At Miss Abigail's wish Janet and I had brought all my gowns there, so that it might be decided what more I needed. To my dismay they were firm that several garments I had supposed would last for some time to come must be discarded. Isobel was laughing at my efforts to keep a white poplin with black velvet trimmings which I was sure had another season of life left to it, when suddenly Miss Eugenia was among us. She moved, with a swish of her sweeping silk skirt, over to the table where my clothes were piled.

"And what is this you are doing for your little protégée, Aunt?" she inquired in the soft voice I knew too well. As she spoke she was deliberately lifting and inspecting the pile of my dresses on the cutting table.

"Put those down—they're not yours!" Isobel said more sharply than I would have dared. Eugenia gave her strange little laugh.

64

"I am sure Miss Van Dorn, who I hear has the disposition of an angel—and the crystalline truth of one, of course— cannot mind," she said. She continued to lift garment after garment from the pile. Presently she lifted and shook out my riding habit. "This," she said, "if I may be so bold as to suggest, should surely be replaced. I understand our generous aunt is seeing to it that Perdita is being properly outfitted. She did the same lately for the undergroom's little orphan, I remember."

Before Isobel, who had flushed as high as I, could snatch the habit from Eugenia's high-held hands, she had eyed it keenly from shoulders to hem, and laid it down.

"Eugenia—" Isobel began to say; her cousin's voice drowned hers.

"It has been cleaned and pressed, I see. But it has, if a practised horsewoman may offer her opinion, had its day. There will always be marks of red mud here on the hem. And there is an old mended rent on the shoulder. Hard service, my good girl."

Miss Abigail interrupted, her voice for once stern. "Miss Van Dorn appreciates your interest, I know. But all decisions as to her personal affairs are in my hands. She has, as I recall, been already measured for a new habit. Had you not, my dear?"

I said yes as quietly as my anger permitted.

Drusilla Huntington, or someone for her, had put the habit in as good shape as was possible. But the heavy rains had beaten down on it as thoroughly as on the one of her own, and there were stains which nothing would remove. The tear Eugenia spoke of had been mended six months ago; it might as well have been a brand.

"That is well—I knew she could trust your generosity," Miss Eugenia said, and smiling still, swept from the room.

I had carried my little desk to my bedroom, and was writing in my diary. The high narrow window by which I sat overlooked a great sweep of lawn. The wind blew wildly, and the great pines were bowing. Fascinated, I did not hear the rap at my door: it flung wide and Eugenia came in.

"I could not make you hear," she said in her sweetened voice. "My aunt requests that you come to the great parlor. In fifteen minutes it will be time for afternoon tea."

"I am dressed and ready now," I said, rising. She waved me back. "Not yet."

There was a fine fire in the great fireplace. She dropped down in the highbacked chair across from me. I was a little frightened. But I was near the tapestried bell-pull, and I knew Isobel's room was next mine and her maid still with her. And that Eugenia did not wish her secret known, I knew too.

"It is as well that we should come to some understanding," she said. She seemed calm; not on the verge of one of the rages that I heard so much of. "Things stand thus: you know that I feigned illness to protect some errand of Major Harradine's. You recall that I crossed the river to demand what you and your uncle could tell me. Now that he is dead, you are the only person who knows the truth. You could have betrayed all this to my aunt, and my cousin Isobel. As you have not done so, it is obvious that you have promised Harradine to keep his secret. He can always do what he will with women—how easily with one like you!" Till now she had held herself to calm; she rose and stood over me, her voice risen. "*Have* you given such a word?"

I thought quickly. Insulting as she was, it was best to tell what truth I might. "Your betrothed did ask that we keep his journey secret. My uncle regarded it as a necessary journey. I did give my promise, and it is good."

"So you will tell me no more?" Her hands clenched; her eyes burned down on me. I wondered why.

"He did not inform me of the reason for his journey. My uncle seemed to know more than I: but he did not, either."

Her eyes still glared down to mine. Suddenly she laughed. "Your word seems good—pity your behavior does not follow it!" she said. I did not understand her. She went on, "Give it again then, not to speak of my visit to you."

"I give it," I said, "and it may occur to you that if I had spoken you would have known it from your aunt already. But—Miss Eugenia—"

"Well!" she said eagerly.

"Would it not be better to confide in your aunt? Surely if you believe in your betrothed's honor, Miss Abigail will do so also; and know how to deal with any difficulties that may arise?"

She stared at me in what seemed honest astonishment. "Of what brazen stuff are you made?" she said. "You have forgotten, I think, that my aunt's sole experience with betrothal was falsehood and desertion. And that behind her—behind women in all generations of our family—have been other such experiences. Whether it is true or false that a savage mistress caused it by her spells or not, it has happened. Neither she nor Isobel could be trusted to judge fairly—to believe I was not shamed—" Her control broke again. "How do I know that you too do not delight in my shaming?"

"But you are not shamed," I said. "You must know better than I how honorable a gentleman is Mark Harradine."

She laughed again. "Aye, we both know well!" she said.

I was beginning to fear again. I crossed to the door, and spoke turning back to her. "Miss Abigail will wonder where we are," I said. Isobel was coming from her room: "Just in time," she said taking my hand. I pulled my broché shawl close against the chill hall, and we went to the great parlor.

It was so large that despite the hangings, two fireplaces were needed. Miss Abigail's calm presence behind the teatable

67

comforted me. Eugenia followed us in, and sat quiet and smiling. The scene we had passed through seemed unreal.

But as I took the delicate Dresden cup from the footman's hand, it was nearly with anguish that I wished Mark Harradine would return swiftly. That the marriage would be over swiftly, that they would go, or I: and I learn to hold myself quiet, forget him, forget her, forget the wild emotions that beat in the Red Castle, inescapable.

I forgot to lift the cup to my lips, trying to force my mind to belief in quiet coming; quiet years with Isobel and her aunt: quiet routine of lessons and visitings and pleasant trivial talk, with my grief for my uncle, and my memory of Mark Harradine's strong thrilling presence, muted like an old dream. Oh, soon—soon!

. . . I had lost myself, gone far in myself. Then I heard a step outside; the sound of a man's spurred foot. The footman flung the door wide and Major Harradine came in. He came forward, then paused for a moment, frozen, his eyes on mine. It was only a moment: Miss Abigail was rising in delight from her place; Eugenia was moving forward with an out-stretched hand. He kissed Miss Abigail's hand: he took Eugenia's, and the two tall stately figures crossed the room together.

After the first flurry of welcome was over, Miss Abigail beckoned me to join the group, seated now.

"I do not know if you remember Jacob Van Dorn's little niece, Mark. She has always been Isobel's close friend; and now that our good Jacob is gone she is a part of our household: she will go with us when we retire to my house in Peekskill."

He had risen: our hands touched for a moment. "I was told of Mr. Van Dorn's death at the ferryhouse," he said, "to my deep regret. And I remember Miss Perdita."

Rising from my curtsy, I looked quickly at him and away.

He was unchanged: after all it was a short time. The same flashing heavy-lashed eyes, like, I knew now, Eugenia's; the soldierly tall carriage, the unhurried grace. I heard Isobel's light voice from far off.

"And where have you been awaiting your lady's pleasure, Cousin Mark?"

His answer came calmly. "With an old friend of my early school days, Cousin Isobel, Andrew Peterson, who has a mansion near Albany. We were glad to meet again."

I wondered, then knew. The answer was doubtless true as far as it went. But how long had it taken him before that to escort Miss Drusilla to her unknown destination, of course, I did not know. I doubted if even his betrothed would.

"And now," Miss Abigail's voice was saying—I had known it would come sooner or later—"What are your plans, my dears?"

When had they time to plan? I wondered. By letter, I supposed: by the messenger Petronius. For Eugenia answered.

"As most preparations were made before my unfortunate illness overtook me, we think day after tomorrow. I fear my health is still not sufficiently stable to endure a flood of guests and parties. There will only be ourselves, my old guardian, Mr. Granger, and of course the clergyman."

Miss Abigail said, "As you still feel a convalescent, Eugenia, we had best have also as a guest our old friend Dr. De Witt."

She smiled, "Why, if you will. Though I assure you all my nerves have to stand they are ready for."

The talk went on. Presently it was time to dine.

"You will wish to be alone," their aunt said when the meal was over. "And shall you stay here tonight, Mark?"

He smiled slightly and shook his head.

"You forget the etiquette of marriage. But there is no need for me to return as far as Andrew's house. I am sleeping for

69

the next two nights with our old friend Mr. Granger, whose house is nearest here. For the nearest inn is a long road away."

"And we wish no accidents to occur," Eugenia said, smiling.

And then Miss Abigail motioned with her brows to Isobel and me, and we left them together.

The whole conversation had been carried on quietly; it was like a scene far off under water. And yet there had been a curious undercurrent, a tension. Leaving, I found myself taking a long breath, as if we had all been talking and acting under penalty of something that would shatter, would scream, if the lightest extra touch was laid on it . . . Looking secretly at my companions as we moved up the stone stairway, I saw, in my almost clairvoyant condition of suspense, that they, too, were tense and pale, and, as I was, controlled by an effort. And yet there was no overt reason for it all.

Isobel spoke with the same hushed quietness I felt, as her aunt turned aside to her own room and we went on together.

"Eugenia's man Petronius has been absent some days. He returned yesterday and she gave him audience for two hours. I believe she had sent him to spy on Major Harradine."

I said without surprise, "She could not do that. She loves him."

"There is love and love. And where there is excessive pride there is jealousy. Eugenia is not of those who desires to please a lover. She would win, or dazzle, or subjugate. The lover must hasten to please *her*. He must give all, she take all, or she does not call it love."

"But what man is like that?" I said before I thought.

"With Eugenia's armament—beauty, power, charm—there have been many men. But though he is my cousin, I know little of Mark Harradine. Only that he has honor and loyalty, and great self-control. And these, alone, of course would hold him to a long given word. What I do not know is—"

She stopped and smiled. "I have been thinking aloud. We give too much thought, you and I, to a love affair that is none of our business. Good night, Perdita: you at least I can trust."

She kissed me at my door; her candle held high, she entered her own.

I did not know what she had been going to say. Whatever it was there was another thing still she had no way of knowing. That Eugenia, jealous and proud and high-tempered as she was, brooded angrily and bitterly over the true reason for the delay; the thing that must needs wake public gossip if any word of it slipped out; Mark Harradine's postponement, his unexplained journey.

My fire still burned deep and bright. I settled on the rug before it; I knew I could not sleep yet. I thought of Drusilla Huntington; beautiful, grateful, terrified, clinging. And I thought of the thing he had done for her, the thing that might gamble his life's pattern away, his life's happiness. Done, I had supposed, while still giving faith and love to his bride . . . Could any man, no matter how deeply held by gratitude, risk all he had risked, untouched by all that Drusilla was and had? Suddenly Eugenia's jealousy and fury and unfaith seemed reasonable. How did I know? How could I believe? I sprang up and walked the long room to its chill corners, wildly. Presently I checked myself; I faced the girl in the mirror, the girl I had seen that first night in the ferry-house: flushed and wildeyed now, with clenched hands. She had trusted. She was right.

"I will trust!" I said aloud. "I *know*. She is innocent; he has done what he did for honor and pity alone. He cannot be otherwise than true."

I made myself kneel and say my prayers. I made ready for bed. I quenched the candles; my prayers went on: I held myself to them: I prayed for him: At last before I slept I

71

could pray for Eugenia Somerwell. As I fell asleep, the wind rose high; the moonlight through the window showed a brown leaf beating against my pane. My eyes, opened by the wind's crying, focused on it. Somehow I was not afraid.

"God, if poor Onnorate's soul still beats about the Red Castle, give her peace," I whispered. "She loved unloved, and her heart broke." I did not fear her. I reached to her in love and pity. Finally I slept.

CHAPTER SIX

No shade has come between thee and the sun,
Like some long childish dream thy life hath run:
But now the stream has reached a dark, deep sea,
And sorrow, dim and crowned, is waiting thee.

ADELAIDE ANNE PROCTER

Isobel stood in my door next morning. "Let us go over to the ferryhouse," she said. She looked pale and tired. "We shall be in the way of the preparations for the wedding; for I suppose there must be something in the air: the servants are all aquiver, at least. I have spoken to Aunt Abigail."

Our own wedding preparations were of course done, such as they were; our white muslin frocks, and the white kid slippers, freshly set out. I was glad to go; as she said, the suspense in the air was wearing.

At the ferryhouse our rooms were unchanged, for Eliza was to stay on and kept them as they always had been. I found myself picking up my old role of looking after Isobel. I took her white work from its old drawer, the collar and cuffs to be embroidered, and laid it in her hand. Beside it was my knitting, the scarf for Uncle Jacob not quite done. After the first pang it comforted me to finish it. He would have wanted it given to some poor man against the coming winter cold.

"By this time two days it will be all over," Isobel said.

"Oh, yes," I said. I tried to speak brightly. "And we can settle into our old peaceful life. The Peekskill house where we are going sounds pleasant."

"A peaceful life!" she said. "Is that all you want? We had enough of dull peace till Eugenia came back to the Red Castle."

"But doesn't it belong to her?"

Isobel shook her head. "No. It is in the hands of the trustees, and Aunt Abigail is in charge of it and may share it hospitably with any of our family she desires—actually Eugenia and Mark and I are all that are left except for a distant cousin, an old lady who is queer—an old recluse really, who lives upstairs and never sees anybody. Miss Anna somebody. The Castle is so big she might as well be in the next country. Aunt Abigail drops in on her every so often, and she has a servant. I suppose we ought to be kind and go see her, but she's away upstairs, in the top floor— The Castle is held for Eugenia and Mark. They get it when they marry each other. If they don't, it goes to the one who is refused . . . Our grandfather, old Eugenius, was an old tyrant. But Aunt Abigail says it was all arranged so long back that Eugenia and Mark were children . . ."

"Oh, but do they have to marry or have nothing?" I asked.

She laughed. "Mercy no, Mark's father was rich. He is. Our grandfather left Eugenia and me both well off. So is Aunt Abigail. There were just the three of old Grandfather Eugenius' children; Aunt Eleanor, who married a New York City gentleman named Harradine: Eugenia's father, another Eugenius, and my father, Nicholas." I nodded I knew the story. Mark Harradine's parents had lived until recently. But I knew well the story of the two sons and their wives who

74

had gone on a pleasure sail on Long Island Sound, long ago when their daughters were little. And a storm had risen; and the yacht had been wrecked with everyone on board drowned. It was still a favorite Village tale. Miss Abigail had been summoned and given charge of the two children.

"I suppose if I'd been named for all the Eugeniuses, instead of the second Eugenius' poor little wife, Mark would have been given his choice," Isobel said in a voice bitter under its lightness. "Grandfather was bent to keep the Castle in the family. He made them promise when they were children, before Mark went to West Point."

"But—"

"Oh, Eugenia is in love with Mark, and he with her—if you can be devoted from the other end of the United States. What I don't understand is why she's cooking up for one of her rages. I know them, I've cause. Have you angered her in any way? My conscience is clear."

I was so tired of evading! But I said, "Perhaps she is annoyed at my being brought here to live with you all."

"Good heavens, after the wedding she need never see you again."

I said, "If people lose their temper easily I suppose any pretext will do . . . Shall I read aloud to you? I am tired of knitting." I picked up the book that lay on the little table without waiting for her answer, and began Gray's *Elegy:*

> *The curfew tolls the knell of parting day,*
> *The lowing herd winds slowly o'er the lea. . . .*

The slow soothing lines went on and on. Presently Isobel sat more quietly. But glancing up I saw that tears were streaming down her face.

I heard the horn on our side of the river, calling Andy; presently the knocking of the big flatboat that meant a carriage and horses. There was a window which gave on the

75

water. I went to see; it was a vehicle I did not know, with a crested panel; and aside from the coachman and footman, apparently empty.

"I think it is the equipage they will leave in," Isobel said from behind my shoulder. "Aunt was saying that Cousin Mark had ordered it, writing from the West, some time ago."

"But one can't use a coach among the wild Indians in the West!" I said.

"Oh, she will make him resign. There's a big estate and a lot of city property to take care of. And the Mexican War is over, and he did brilliantly in it. He can resign his commission with honor."

Then Eliza knocked, and came in to ask how long we planned to stay in the ferryhouse. Isobel said sharply, "Till the last possible moment." Eliza said that then she had better send Andy's boy for more chickens. And why didn't we take the little rowboat and go out up the river a piece? It was a bright day and with quiet water. So we did. Rowing hard, at least for me, calmed me, as I suppose Eliza knew it would. When we came back, she remembered that there was nobody but ourselves to go on a forgotten errand to the nearest little village. And somehow the time passed, and it was time to return, on the morning of the wedding.

"Better hurry," Eliza told Andy. "Windstorm coming."

The wind was suddenly high, indeed. The little whitecaps were cresting all the length of the river. The known Red Castle carriage awaited us, blown for, on the other side.

Suddenly as we drove up the road to the Red Castle grounds Isobel clutched me. "The leaves! The leaves!" she said. "Look."

I looked, but I did not understand. "It's November," I said, "of course the leaves are falling." The high wind was stripping the trees. A gust carried them across our road, like a flight of brown birds.

76

"Not like this," she said. "They blew thick and wild like this, old Keziah said, the time this"—she touched her scarred cheek—"happened."

I said, more sternly than I was given to speaking to her, "Isobel, that old woman should be stopped from telling you those things. And you should stop thinking of them. What good does it do?"

"If you were going to live any longer in the Red Castle it would make you think of them," she said. "We know that the Indian woman Onnorate, whose name means the Leaf, cursed the women who should be brought to the Red Castle. And the curses did fall."

"Oh, my dearest," I said, "surely you have read the Bible! And surely you remember the place where it says, 'The curse causeless shall not come.' You never did anything to that poor Indian girl, nor did I, even supposing the story is true. So even if she did curse the Somerwells, her curse is causeless where you and I are concerned."

"Yet it fell," she murmured. As she spoke the horses, blinded by a still wilder gust of leaves, jerked aside. The coachman was having trouble with them. "There," she said.

"And there!" I answered smiling as he curbed them and brought us to the steps. "We are safe despite November weather."

"Safe? Not yet!" she said, pointing.

I looked up. The high narrow windows, glazed and red-curtained, were already lighted. And across the nearest one a single brown leaf was beating, beating, as if propelled by something invisible. She screamed.

"Junius!" I said, to the footman who had moved round to hand us out. "Take the coachman's whip and reach up to where that brown leaf is swinging. It is caught in a cobweb, I think."

I had not remembered that the Negroes, freed in New

77

York twenty-odd years, were still superstitious in spite of their Christian upbringing. Junius turned the ashen color which with Negroes means pallor.

"Nonsense!" I said. "Give me your whip, Apollo!" For the coachman, too, was staring and gray-faced. His hold on the whip was so loose I could take it. I came close under the window and, reaching up the full length of my arm, struck against the window just above the leaf. The leaf went on beating, beating. I clambered up to the high seat beside him, and said, "Drive under the window!" I used the whip's tip this time, reaching over. It fell, loosened from whatever invisibly held it, and blew against my cheek, slipping gently down. It felt like a caress.

"Miss Perdita—Miss Perdita—" the coachman moaned, "you done take de curse!"

I was suddenly gay. "It was a beautiful leaf!" I said. "It stroked me—it loved me!" I scarcely knew what I said, I was so intent on calming my friend. "Come into the house, Isobel," I said. "If you are all right it hasn't hurt you—and if I love it how can it hurt me?"

"You are a woman brought to the Red Castle," she insisted in a monotone. I threw an arm around her and drew her up the steps, against the strong wind and its flood of leaves still blowing. I ordered the shaking footman to open the door, and we entered. Isobel pulled herself from me, and fled through the hall and up the stone steps as if pursued. I followed slowly.

Miss Abigail came to us from her bedroom door, elegant in her plum-colored satin. "You have just time to dress, young ladies," she began, and broke off to say, "What is the matter?" for Isobel had caught her in a desperate hold.

"The leaf—the leaf!" Isobel sobbed. "It came on the window—it beat against the window outside the room where they will marry—and Perdita has taken it on herself—"

I looked to see the elder lady laugh Isobel out of her folly.

I was appalled to see that, instead, her arms dropped from around her niece. She backed against the wall, white.

"It was caught in a cobweb," I explained, smiling. "I brushed it down. And if it will cheer my Isobel, I take it gladly!"

But Miss Abigail still stared. And I remembered that she too had had a part in the legend. But in a moment she controlled herself.

"It is November after all," she said, making herself smile. "Go dress, my dears."

I was tying the last of my black sleeve-knots when she came in. "Nearly ready? That is well," she said. "But, my child, one does not wear black ribbons at a wedding. Have you no white?"

I had not. She sent Janet for some of Isobel's. "There," she said when they were at my throat and wrists and in my hair. "I should have told you before. You look very well, my dear." We went down the narrow stone stair to meet the gentlemen. My spirits had evaporated. I was suddenly weary.

The three elderly gentlemen were waiting for us. The clergyman, of course; the doctor, as Miss Abigail had insisted; and Mr. Granger, Eugenia's co-guardian. It made me feel safer and better to see them there . . . And then I wondered—why did I fear, why feel I needed safety? I was safe in my very unimportance.

Miss Abigail greeted her old friends. Isobel and I curtsied behind her. We moved to the great brocaded sofa along the wall which faced the front windows. A small table, draped as an altar, stood between the windows: a tall Gothic chair behind it for the clergyman till he should stand to marry them. He moved over now to Miss Abigail; they spoke low for a moment; he went out and returned in his vestments. He sat down on the tall chair to wait: the other two gentle-

79

men moved to a sofa like our own, at the side, and waited also. The wait seemed forever.

I had gone so far within myself that when the door opened to admit Major Harradine I nearly cried out. I do not know what I had thought: I only know that suddenly it was real and irrevocable: I was to sit quietly where I was and have it happen. He stood there presently, the clergyman waited ready. The door would open in a moment on Eugenia— Eugenia, beautiful, arrogant, conquering . . .

It opened. What else had I expected? Lawyer Granger, who had moved there, escorted her to the altar where, straight, grave, splendid in his uniform, his dark vivid eyes steadfastly on her, the tall bridegroom stood. They were well-matched; alike in coloring, and in stature; alike in pride and strong will. Her eyes, so like his, shone undimmed even through the Brussels lace veil that covered her sweep-ing, wide-flowing white satin gown from head to foot. She had no attendant. The quiet, dark-clad Negro Petronius stood, effacing himself against the door.

The service began. I knew it well; what girl did not? It went on in the old clergyman's slow reverent voice till it reached, "I require and charge ye both, as ye will answer at the dreadful day of Judgment, when the secrets of all hearts shall be revealed, if either of you know any impediment—"

Eugenia's voice cut through the slow words like a sword.

"Stop, Dr. Van Alstyne. There may be an impediment—" Mr. Granger tried to stop her, but she went clearly and coldly on. "Before I give myself and my possessions to this gentleman, there is something I need to know. With what young lady, Mark Harradine, were you riding, and on what errand, the night you wrote me to delay our marriage by lies?"

Isobel's hand gripped mine. In the pause before he an-

80

swered, she whispered, "The leaf's curse was for her this time! It is she who has been shamed!"

Major Harradine was answering now, as coldly as she had spoken.

"You should have interrogated me at a less melodramatic time than this, Eugenia. Also I am risking a good deal by informing you. But with one exception, and that a trustworthy one, as I have learned, I am among honorable old friends. I can trust to their secrecy. The young lady I was escorting was the only child of a gentleman who had saved my life and who died from wounds then received. He laid it on me to rescue her from so grave a peril, even had I owed him nothing, that I or any other man of honor would have obeyed at any cost. For even now, if the secret be spread, she may be lost."

"An excellent story. But the facts I have learned are against it," Eugenia said. She gestured to Petronius, quiet and unspeaking. He moved forward till he stood a little behind her, his devoted eyes on his mistress.

I felt Major Harradine's eyes on mine. I had not known he saw me.

"Miss Van Dorn here can witness for me. I release her from her promise of secrecy as far as these present are concerned. She was at the ferryhouse the night I escorted the lady toward safety."

I stood up. "This is true," I said. "You will remember, Mr. Granger, the stormy night my uncle stayed with you, because the weather was too wild for him to return by the time you had finished your business. My servant Eliza was abed and asleep, the Blackwaters abed and beyond call. Major Harradine and the lady summoned the boat. I crossed to them in a lull of the storm. He rowed us back, the horses swimming behind us. Major Harradine left letters of explanation for my uncle and Miss Somerwell. And when my uncle returned—oh, gentlemen, you knew him for an honorable man —he told me that Major Harradine had done right and well."

There was a moment's silence, then Eugenia spoke again. "I believed your letter then, Mark. So I lied as you asked. I postponed the wedding, I pretended illness. If I still believed, this ceremony should go on."

His control broke. He said, "You do not believe my word of honor? What sort of woman are you?"

She turned on me, her eyes flashing, her gloved hands clenched beneath the veil.

"I believe what my servant here, who has been with me since babyhood, was sent to discover. He found two witnesses, unlike Miss Van Dorn, with no personal reason for lying. Two men and a woman, riding on the far bank, who can swear that it was this waif, this nameless creature, riding beside him, unmistakable, through that night's—that early morning's—rain!"

Miss Abigail said, shocked, "Eugenia, this is close to madness!"

And Mr. Granger, after her quickly, "You have been ill, my dear. Try to control yourself. Perhaps it even might be well to postpone today's occasion to a later date. There would be time to send out the cards again . . ."

It seemed to me that they were both more alarmed than was necessary; though I was grateful, of course, for what was also a defense of me.

"I am not ill. I have not been ill at all. Like a fool, I pretended illness at my—*faithful*—betrothed's demand, fool that I was!"

It was the wild and dreaded anger I had heard so much of. The elders looked at each other, with fear. Not only Mr. Granger, but her servant Petronius, moved closer to her.

Major Harradine spoke, his deep, controlled voice a contrast to her wildness. "Why you make this statement about

Miss Van Dorn I cannot understand. Except that as we know, when you lose your temper you speak wildly. She never left the ferryhouse."

Eugenia laughed, facing him close. "When you rode that night from the ferryhouse Perdita was seen riding beside you unmistakably by a farmer traveling at dawn, by two women returning from a friend's deathbed. You and she entered a bridle path leading to one of three small lonely farms. You were not seen again till recently; Perdita was seen in two days. They signed written papers. They described you to my servant Petronius, whom I sent to find out. The blue habit with a tear on the shoulder. The slim erect figure of middle height; the dark hair under the blue veil. I have had the habit in my hands since, with red clay that cleaning could not erase, on its hem. I had known the mended tear on her shoulder for months."

"I loaned the habit to the lady," I said desperately. "Hers was wet through. It was brought back to me by a messenger days ago."

"And where is her own, then?"

"I gave it to her that night, partly dried," I said. I could hear how false it must sound.

"That is enough."

"I agree with you," Major Harradine said sharply. "And I also agree with your good guardian that you are in no state to talk further. I suggest that you retire; and when you are yourself again apologize to Miss Van Dorn and myself."

She seemed daunted, for the first time. She said in a lower voice, "For the sake of the old tie between us, Mark, I will even give you a chance to be forgiven. Gentlemen have their little weaknesses. Better it should be with a low-class girl than an equal. So admit the truth, and I forgive, and our nuptials shall go on."

"I am to purchase married bliss, then, at the cost of my

83

truth and honor? And what of this lady's fair name?" I was to learn later what the silken voice meant.

"This *lady*—with her false angelhood and false gentility! Ask Alonzo Beggs' mother—ask the clown himself, if she has not been as lost as her name since her fourteenth year! It is any decent lady's duty to expose her to the gentlefolk she has been forced upon!"

The silken voice cut across hers like a rapier. "To whom, in your own phrase, have you exposed Miss Van Dorn?"

Her voice triumphed. "The whole list of our wedding guests! And her own village folk. The circle of ladies and gentlemen who have had the girl forced on them by my besotted aunt and cousin! Dupes who have been fooled into accepting her, and even praising her—to me! The soldier who accompanied her in this last escapade I leave anonymous, in my letters."

Miss Abigail cried out, "Eugenia, are you mad?"

"I merely deal justice—and a little mercy, Mark. My messenger is ordered to ride out in twenty minutes unless I send word. That word will be given if you admit the truth before these witnesses; that the Van Dorn woman was the partner of your illicit honeymoon."

He did not answer her at once: he said something low to Lawyer Granger, who slipped from the room: There was a chance, then, of stopping the messenger—if they could find him and he was obedient . . . My hands clutched and I prayed silently as I never had.

Mark Harradine's voice was clear and unmoved. "Cousin Eugenia, I do not need your mercy—unless the freedom you give me can be so considered. You have twice broken our engagement in your jealous rages. I accept your decision now once and for all. And as what you have said and threatened may be said again in your next break from sanity, there had best be a barrier you must accept—a barrier of law as well as

84

love . . . Miss Van Dorn, will you accept me for your husband?"

There was a stunned silence in the room. The vibration of his closeness so dazed and thrilled me that I could only remember that what he asked was what I wanted most in the world. What did it matter that he spoke in chivalrous protection of my name . . . We had met only twice. I remembered the words spoken half-asleep—*You are as beautiful as I thought you by the flash*—the old gesture, the sharing of bread with me, unthinking—the speech between us while we waited, as if we had been each others' forever . . . that strange knowledge of each other . . . Could it be that he had loved me as suddenly and deeply as I knew now I had loved him? My brain, my reason, told me as swiftly that I so wanted it that I could be lying to myself.

The thoughts, the passions that swept me had taken scarcely a moment: I felt Mark catching me half round, and heard a cry from Miss Abigail. Eugenia had flung her heavy silver prayerbook, and the blow had fallen beyond me, striking Miss Abigail's shoulder. Dr. De Witt held Eugenia fast. "This is enough," he said. "Mark, your chivalry and Eugenia's jealousy have carried you both too far. You have considered your betrothed of years past, when not herself, forgivable twice before. Mark . . . these inherited rages . . ."

"Does it need chivalry"—Mark's voice was calm—"to sue for such beauty and goodness and charm? I take my freedom. I may make use of it as I wish."

I knew what I must say: what I would rather die than say.

"Major Harradine," I said, as steadily as he had spoken, "you do a rash thing. Remember that I am as far as I know nameless. My upbringing was of a class below yours—you scarcely know me. You would regret—"

I heard him laugh. I felt his arm tighten. "I shall not regret! Answer me, Perdita!"

I wanted it more than anything in the world. Suddenly there was no more resistance in me. I felt Eugenia's clawed hand clutching my shoulder; Mark's tearing it away and pulling me closer to him again.

The old lawyer was speaking. "Mark, have you forgotten that you rob Eugenia not only of her bridegroom, but of the Red Castle? Your grandfather willed it to you together, on condition that you marry. The one of you who refuses lose it to the other. She has refused, but cannot you forget her wild words?"

"I had forgotten: but she may keep the Castle. I have enough. I await your answer, Perdita."

I loved him. I was young and quick to learn. I wanted what he offered more than anything in the world. I heard my own voice saying clearly, "I thank you for the honor you do me, Major Harradine. I will be your wife." I heard Eugenia' gasp, and her heavy fall. Mark's hold did not loosen, but could see Eugenia, prone on the floor, her white skirts wide her eyes rolled up in her head. The Negro Petronius knelt beside her and lifted her.

"You know they always end like this, the rages, Miss Abigail," he said, without surprise. "If the gentlemen will open the door, I take her up."

As the silence fell again, I heard the horses' hoofs. They were not going out; the riders were taking them slowly around the driveway back to their stables. The door opened and closed; Petronius' heavy tread went up the stair outside But I heard both dimly, for Mark was bending, gravely quietly, to kiss me. And as I lifted my face to take that kiss I forgot Isobel, crying out, Eugenia borne away by the dimming footsteps, the perilous future—

Everything.

CHAPTER SEVEN

♖

On my finger is a ring
Which I still see glittering
When the night hides everything.
ELIZABETH BARRETT BROWNING

I can only remember of my wedding that it seemed unreal;
I have been told since that this is fairly usual. I went through
the ceremony almost absently—without actual feeling. I
heard my mind saying, "It was a good thing Miss Abigail
made me take the black ribbons off my dress, for a bride
does not wear black" . . . and wondering why this was so.
Even Major Harradine's deep clear voice repeating something
after the clergyman seemed far off and unconnected with us,
until one phrase sprang out, piercing my mind—"Until death
do us part." So this was what I had done—what he had
done . . . Presently I was being told to repeat the words after
the clergyman also. I had, as it happened, never been present
at a wedding, I heard my own voice, also, like someone else's.
Everything went farther and farther away, even my bridegroom's light kiss and lighter embrace at the end. Presently
the old men's voices were wishing us well, then Miss Abigail's, broken a little; Isobel's, strangely metallic. I so far

forgot where I was as to nearly turn and ask her to come away with me to talk and cry it out, as always when she was moved and on the edge of breaking down. I just remembered in time that I was no longer to be responsible for my dear Isobel. I had no idea what my bridegroom intended doing with me. But my allegiance of course was with him from now forever.

Miss Abigail, presently, after drawing Major Harradine aside and talking a little with him, came to me, and drew me away and upstairs. She must have sent for Janet, because the girl was quickly in the bedroom also. They were packing for me, I saw. I stood still: "Am I to go somewhere?" I said finally.

Miss Abigail looked at me, a little shocked. Then she came close and shook my arm slightly. "You are married and going on your wedding journey," she said a little sharply, and then, more gently, "Oh, you poor child, don't you know what you've done?"

I said, "Oh, yes. I have married Major Harradine, because he wished it, and because I love him more than anything in the world."

Janet gasped a little, but Miss Abigail only said, "I am glad to hear you say that. For, my dear Perdita, you may need all your love and patience and courage. As for the immediate present, your husband and I have agreed that the best thing you can both do is to continue with the plans already made."

"But I do not know what they were . . . may I be told?"

She said, still half laughing, half sharply, "Of course you must. You will take the carriage that awaits you both: you will travel in it to New York City. I imagine you will stay there a day or so before going on to Niagara Falls. You will need to do some shopping, by the way; here is a note to the manager at A. T. Stewart's. You may use my account; consider it my wedding gift."

I thanked her and promised not to be extravagant, at which she smiled and said she had known that. I began to help with the packing. After a time I asked rather timidly what would happen to Eugenia. "Is she staying here?"

Miss Abigail sighed. "It usually takes her several days to recover from one of these fits of anger," she said. "Also, she forfeited the Red Castle, of course, by the terms of the will. Mark wishes her to keep it, he says, but I doubt if it is possible. I suppose she will return to the city, or travel. You are its chatelaine now."

I stared, aghast. "I?"

"You are its owner's wife, child. But he has asked that Isobel and I stay here for the present."

Janet had left the room. Her calm had been a comfort. She had only said, "Oh, Mrs. Harradine, may you always be happy! We shall miss you, even for this little while!"

She spoke as if she meant it, and I thought that if I had made the little dressing-maid like me in such a short span, perhaps I could make Major Harradine care, at least, sometime.

Then Miss Abigail was kissing me and holding me close for a moment. Afterward, she held me off and said quietly, "What a mercy that black velvet walking-suit with guipure lace was ready! But the gray poplin with the black moire trimming, the one which replaced your old white—you had better wear that as a traveling dress, my dear."

I was still in a half trance. She called Janet back, and had her help me to change quickly. She fastened the mink tippet above my cloak, and gave me my muff. "Remember to get a sealskin coat and muff as soon as you are shopping in the city," she said . . . I thought of my light words to my uncle about the prince who should give me a sealskin sacque and cap . . . and hoped I might keep instead the modest furs that had come from the village man, Uncle Jacob's last gift.

Miss Abigail followed me down the long stone stair. She kissed me again for goodbye, and led me to where Major Harradine stood awaiting me in the hall.

"Be gentle with her; she is little more than a child," she said.

He laid my hand on his arm. "I promise that," he said. I dared to look up and found he was smiling a little. The long dark eyes were looking down into my own with kindness, and something more that I did not quite understand. But it was something I was safe with.

"Tell Isobel farewell," I said. "Tell her I will always love her."

Before Miss Abigail could reply I was being led down the great hall: across the porch between the great stone columns into the crested coach I had seen. Dimly I noticed that my little trunk had been fastened behind, together with his own. The coachman bowed to us. And then we were together, shut in. The bridegroom I had only seen three times sat beside me, alive and real: his arm went around me and he bent to kiss me, very gently, once more.

The feeling of unreality was suddenly gone. I almost cried out. What had I, what had that little Perdita of the ferry, done, that she was shut here alone, kissed with a gesture of fond possession, held by the great gentleman who was Eugenia Somerwell's betrothed two short hours gone? And then, as the thrill of that nearness and caress went through me, I knew that come what might I would not alter this wild thing I had done.

"You must not be afraid," he said, very gently still. "You have been very brave till now, my little bride."

It was then that I should have said to him, "It was not bravery; it was because I loved you." But I did not dare. "I am not afraid," I said. "You must know how much I trust you. It is strange, that is all. But I will try not to be strange-feeling long."

He laughed out at that. "What a good girl! I shall see to it that you are not." And in spite of everything the old feeling of oneness with his thought came to me, and I laughed with him.

"That's better," he said. "For the moment I felt as if I was talking to a ten-year-old. How old are you, Perdita?"

"You know I am older than that, at least! I shall be twenty next birthday."

"That is a terrible age. I wonder if mine terrifies you. I am near twenty-nine."

As he spoke, lightly still, his ungloved hands were busy about me, loosing my tippet and collar, taking off the little black velvet hat with the long plume and drawing my head against his uncloaked shoulder. "It is a long drive," he said. "It will be dark before we leave the Albany Post Road. You may as well be comfortable, child."

It was a strange word for what I felt, his arm pulling me closer, his cheek leaning against my hair . . . Perhaps it was only the way of gentlemen. But it was his right, I re-membered . . . Oh, why think, why wonder? However little it meant it was happiness.

He was speaking on with the same pleasant intimacy. As to the good child he had called me, the child he must set at ease.

"Under the circumstances I suppose a wedding breakfast would have been almost too much for our grave and reverend seigniors, wouldn't it? Even Cousin Abigail's state-liness, I saw, was shaken, and little Isobel fairly fled from the room! But we should find a comfortable tavern enough around one o'clock." He looked at his watch. "Is that too long to wait?"

"Oh, no," I said out of my pleasant dream, "We breakfasted past seven."

"And I. That is settled, then. We should reach New York City and its hotels—the Astor House, I think, do you like it?—by dark. They are holding a suite for us there unless you dislike it."

"I would like it," I said shyly. "I have never been to the city before."

They had expected us at the tavern. The host came bowing to meet us, leading us to a private room with fine damask and flowers on the table. His wife, plump and smiling, led me away to refresh, hovering around me with arch smiles and praise of my looks and ways and his. All had been planned—for Eugenia. For a moment I was chilled again; the words before the wedding . . . the barrier . . . I saw myself, smoothing my curls in the mirror. No stately dark beauty. Almost the child he called me, wide eyed, a little shy; hands unused to gloves, feet unused to dancing—

But I was his; he was kind. If it was still only the friendliness one gives a dear child, it must be enough for now. I lifted my head and smiled too and thanked her, and returned to where my bridegroom waited, smiling. He had thought me beautiful, and he did still, for the dark eyes looked at me approving . . . Be thankful I was married to such a gentleman.

And I found that he was more than kind; considerate, for he said, "It has been a strain, my little lady; come drink your wine. And remember we have been friends since that wild night when you came so bravely to the rescue."

It was true. There are people who are immediately friends, easy together from the first meeting, and of such were we. And—even if it was never to be more than this it was more than many wives ever had.

And so I took heart, and ate with appetite, and found things to say, and suddenly thought that if I could go on living, as now, in the moment, I could have happiness—and that I would try. Between our words and smiles I said silently a little prayer for it, and carried on.

He said—it was one of our flashes of mental oneness—"You are wondering about something. Do not fear to ask me, no matter what it is." His eyes were still deep in mine. I was a little frightened that we were as close as that; but took him at his word. It was greatly daring; I found myself secretly twisting the fine handkerchief I held: I found later that I had torn it. "Why did the will name Eugenia for your wife, not Isobel?" I asked.

"I am afraid it was something our relative knew or feared about Isobel," he said. "What, I never knew—nor even the lawyer who made the will." It must be, poor child, the scarred cheek, I supposed: or, perhaps, her moods of grief for it. Some men felt that the wife of a gentleman who was placed and admired as Major Harradine was must be beautiful, unmarred, and able to be socially esteemed and admired; as Eugenia, of course, with her beauty and arrogance of manner, was in spite of the rages. It seemed cruel. Yet he had stepped aside from Eugenia . . .

He said presently, as if he was still thinking it over, "It may have been that he thought Eugenia the handsomer, or she may have been the granddaughter he saw most of, or her name. One never knows what whim may take an arbitrary old gentleman. As I remember our grandfather, he was something of a tyrant. Fortunately I saw less of him than my cousins did: my mother, naturally, did not live with him. I was only a visitor at the Red Castle. Uncle Eugenius, the heir, was pretty well tied down: Uncle Nicholas, the younger, had a home of his own on Long Island near the water, and a profession. They all four came and went. My uncles married sisters, you know—the elder sister, Juliana, came to visit her sister Sibylla, and eventually married

Eugenius. I was there, as I said, very little—I don't really recall what they were like. I was not there when they went on the ill-fated trip on Uncle Nicholas' yacht."

"It is still a village legend," I said. "Hard they should go so young. But there are so many tales about the Red Castle . . . Somerwells . . ."

"Too many!" he said half laughing; but I thought he meant it. "My dear, none of them is important—our life is our own, dear girl, and in the future, not in the tangle of superstition the old place has always known. Put the Red Castle and its shadows out of your mind, my love—our world is wider than that."

As he spoke, smiling at me in the sunlight, it seemed as if he might almost be glad to be free of Eugenia. Oh, if it could be true! For as he talked I learned more of what he was— Not only the brilliant soldier and gentleman women loved too easily and well, but a good and stable man, capable of principles and affections.

And then it was time to prepare for the further drive: the return to our coach, his arm round me as if it was a wonted thing now, the clip-clop of the horses' hoofs, and the scenery going by—the wide dear water of the Hudson, still awhile, and on the other side the greenery and beauty of great estate after great estate.

After a while we turned and drove through lane after turning lane; we were leaving the vista of the river. We began to cross car tracks: city railroad lines, their horse-drawn cars with the backs of bonneted and tall-hatted heads showing through the windows. It was still pretty country. The roads were bad and good by turns: presently we turned on a wider road, macadamized partly, partly cobblestoned. There were more stages now, than coaches; an occasional gentleman in a gig or rockaway with a single horse. I had never seen so many people and vehicles in one day before. It was still a lovely countryside: pretty scattered villages, rural cottages with bright autumn gardens still, now and again an elegant estate.

"It's the Bloomingdale Road," Mark said, "it will take us straight—or nearly straight—to the Astor House." They had not changed its name to Broadway then. After a while it was twilight; and the first four-in-hand we had seen dashed past us, overtaking the stage ahead of us. As it passed I had a glimpse of its only occupant. A magnificent green silk bonnet lined with quilted pink framed the brown, wrinkled face of an old woman with cascades of lighter brown curls down each cheek. I said, "I wonder who she is? Those dyed ringlets are so pitiful."

"You can find something to be kind about, love, in most people," he said. "Few can in old Madam Burr—or Jumel, as most call her. She is one whom men do not let their wives so much as greet in passing, old and pitiful as she is: everyone knows her and her grand equipages and her elegance, up in her country place at Mount Morris: an adventuress, and some even say a murderess."

I shivered a little, there close to him. The word he had used to me mattered more than what he had said of the poor aged creature: usual between man and wife, yet it made me happy. And hers was the only unhappy face I saw; I was interested next moment in the crowded stage passing us, the ladies' hoops packed uncomfortably between them, the faces that peeped from the deep bonnets mostly pretty and young; the gentlemen more absorbed in their papers or figuring, but prosperous looking too. I wondered if I would be allowed to ride in the stages . . . and then the word of murder waked an echo. I remembered old Eliza, saying of my mother's accident, "The doctor did say it might 'a been somebody wanted to murder her—it was a strange place for a blow to be; but then they'd a taken her baggage, and they didn't . . ."

Then I forgot it; Eliza liked horrors. I was fascinated to watch the tall street lamps going slowly past me, the lamplighters reaching up their lighted poles to make the oil wicks flare out. "It's like magic," I said.

"Wait till you get down to Thirtieth Street," Mark said, smiling. "They have this new gaslight all the way down from there." I had not known about gaslight. There were elegant chandeliers, and lamps, of course, at the Red Castle, as, I'd heard, with other of the great Hudson River mansions. I had never been through the greatest part of the castle, for there was story and suite on suite, reaching far and high, strange rooms, indeed, where even Miss Abigail had not ventured. The gaslight sounded frightening. But when we came to where the gas had been laid on, it seemed underground in some odd way. Its fans of light were so pretty that I could not be afraid. Which, Major Harradine said, was as well, because the Astor House was almost entirely gaslighted.

We arrived in excellent time for dinner. Indeed, it would be an hour at least before we needed to think of it.

"Which is as well," Mark said, when he had directed the coachman where to go for the night. "It will give you time to rest."

We passed through the great elegantly furnished red-and-gold foyer, up the wide winding stair. The bowing waiters flung open a door. Here, too, all was prepared. For Eugenia, again. The pretty sitting room was decked out for her. The curtsying chambermaid took my sacque and hat and flung another door open. As I hesitated, Major Harradine, his own cloak still across his arm, waited beside the parlor's door.

"I have an errand," he said. "It should not take me more than an hour. You will excuse me?"

I said only, "Surely. But—you will have no time to rest before we dine, then—" I asked no questions.

He smiled. "An old campaigner like me? I am not tired,

my dear; it is only an inquiry that I must make at the Arsenal on Fifth Avenue." I knew that military things could not wait, and smiled and said so.

"It is only military at one remove," he said, and was turning to leave when his cloak caught on the opened door, and something fell from an inner pocket. He shook the cloak, velvet side out, then picked it up—a letter—half laughing, half rueful. "Good heavens," he said, "I should have given you this as soon as we were in the carriage. Cousin Abigail said it was a farewell note from little Isobel."

"Then there was no great hurry," I said, taking it. "Now was a good time to receive it: I can read it while you are away and maybe answer it. You know we have been like sisters since we were little children."

He lifted an amused eyebrow. "It seems I have married that *rara avis*, a reasonable woman!" he said. He bent to kiss me and was gone. Flushed, my heart beating a little harder, I dropped on the nearest seat, a low rose satin-covered *pouffe*, and opened the envelope when the door closed behind him. Poor Isobel—she had been crying too hard, I supposed, still, to emerge and say her farewells. The paper was crumpled and wet—she had even cried while she wrote . . .

The beginning was wild, but that was Isobel . . .

"Oh my dear, my own poor Perdita!" it said. "What have you done? How could you? How do you know what secrets have been kept from us all . . . what are still being kept? I am afraid for you: it was more than daring; it was a step that may end terribly for you . . . were you mesmerized or as I have thought seeing your docility with your uncle, trained to obey any man, no matter how shocking his demands? But perhaps, dearest, it can be annulled—changed—something to protect my Perdita . . . Remember I have money of my own. I will help you to free yourself, if what I dread comes about. A man you did not know, whose past you do not know, only the things Eugenia who does know him, said. . . . Always, if he does not watch you, keep me *au courant* of your whereabouts; tell me everything he says and does to you, the things you find he hides from you. Promise that?"

I read no further. Isobel always looked on the dark side, but this was worse than anything I remembered.

"It doesn't make sense!" I said aloud. "Oh dear, I wish I had been able to take time to talk to her before I went: I could have quieted her, made her see—"

See what? That I had done what I most wanted to do? That was no answer, even with the long pleasant ride, the lovely surroundings, Mark's kiss on my lips, his normal, light ways and words about me. She would only think me the more mesmerized, enthralled. As I was—I was! And delighting in it. But the old habit of comforting, cheering, laughing her out of her tragic times—I could no longer. I belonged to her no longer. I belonged to him, come what might . . . And then I realized that my last words sounded as if I was shaken . . .

I would not be shaken. And his own last laughing phrase came back to comfort me. I was that *rara avis*, a reasonable woman. I had not, like my poor Isobel, been reared in a great dark castle, half of whose rooms and byways even were too many for me to know; I had not had my face and my life scarred by a half mad jealousy . . . I remembered her legends of those great lost unknown rooms, and the dark stories that despite Miss Abigail's disapproval Negro and white servants alike told us children. I remembered that one was about an enormous room so far upstairs and so hidden that few people had known about it, or seen it, whose walls had strange painted people and villages papered all over the stones: it was like a far off town or even half world. And there were times, the old women said, special days, when the people from the walls could come down, and slip half seen through the halls, and you could hear whispers in an unknown language. And there was the other room, locked fast and dark, from which sometimes there were cries that came out, screams and laughter and pleadings. The castle was so great, with so many empty rooms, so many floors and staircases and little hidden turns: And there was a room on the very top floor where Isobel had told me, terrified, that she herself, running away to be by herself, had heard a woman's voice singing in the dark emptiness: and she had fainted, and been found by Eugenia's servant Petronius huddled against the door in the cold dark.

And she had lived there, always. Not only in the bright rooms with the heavy Honduras mahogany furniture, fashionable, with fires and lamps and candles; she had gone all over it secretly, sometimes at twilight.

No wonder, I thought, that she believed in dark things. Even in the bright, cheerful ferryhouse where I was always told that God would take care of me, and knew that Uncle Jacob would, Isobel's stories frightened me a little. But if I thought or spoke of such things there would always be somebody's warm hand and warm love close; and prayers for comfort, and hymns: I remembered one now:

> *May no dark dreams disturb my rest,*
> *Nor powers of evil me molest . . .*

They could not, over there. And they would not, here. I folded the letter back into its envelope, and gazed happily around the bright luxurious parlor where I sat: the flowers, my great soft satin armchair, the silver-striped paper with French color-prints hanging against it, coquetting Watteau gentlemen and ladies. The little ormolu tables, the glittering chandelier. And Mark Harradine returning soon. I made myself reasonable. I must rest now, and tomorrow by daylight answer the letter. As I rose and crossed to the bedroom where the chambermaid had shown me in to take off my wraps, I had a good thought. Why not, when we had returned from this wedding trip to Niagara Falls that Miss Abigail had spoken about, have Isobel visit us here in the bright busy city, where as far as I knew there were no haunted rooms or gloomy stories?

The chambermaid had partly unpacked for me. She had laid across the bed the soft rosy silken negligee, at its foot the soft satin slippers. I would have time to bathe and another three quarters of an hour for resting. There was a private bathroom beyond; through its half opened door I could see a long mirror. I bathed, and slipped into my chemise and the gown and slippers. I put my corset and petticoats and gown on the chair by the bed; a half hour's rest and then time to dress . . .

I had not known how tired I was: the warm water had relaxed me. I slept immediately; I was only awakened by the click of the key to the outside door and his step across the floor and into my room. I had slept deeply till his return.

CHAPTER EIGHT

🏰

O let the solid ground
Not fail beneath my feet
Before my life has found
What some have found so sweet;
Then let come what may,
No matter if I go mad,
I shall have had my day.
ALFRED LORD TENNYSON

He stepped softly into the room. He smiled down into my opened eyes.

"You slept—that is good," he said. He stooped, and lifted me close against him. My heart beat hard. I felt his, against me, quickening too. Then his hand was pushing the laces from my shoulder, his lips were there first, then on mine. Then he pulled himself away. "You're tired, you just wakened," he said. "Forgive me—but you were so lovely— there—"

Before I knew, I sat up and clung to him again. I heard the little exultant laugh I loved. "Sweetest—dearest—" he said.

Presently he drew away. "Give me fifteen minutes, love," he said. "Don't change, nothing could be prettier than that silken thing. We'll dine up here."

He tossed his coat on a chair as he turned. Why, I thought, of course he can do that before me: I belong to him. He took up the dressing case the maid had laid open, and crossed to the little dressing room. I heard the splash as he poured water from the ewer, before he closed the door.

I made myself rise, I went to the cheval glass to shake straight and tighten the ribbons of my negligee. I am afraid I was vain of my slender waist, nearly as small without my stays. I hadn't time to lace them back on, I knew, if I brushed out my hair and arranged it again. I hoped he hadn't seen my corsets tossed there on the chair by the bed. I slipped back to the sitting room as he had told me to, the train of the soft rosy silk trailing, the lace-ruffled sleeves falling loose.

There were twin love seats, on either side of the bright little fire against an inner wall. I dropped into one to await him.

He followed me in exactly ten minutes by the marble mantel clock. He was somehow more the man I remembered at the ferryhouse than before. I realized in a moment that it was because his black thick hair was wetted from its brushing as it had been from the storm, and curling more in spite of being smoothed. I wondered vaguely why he had borrowed my dressing room, for there was another door opposite mine, opening from the parlor. As he passed the hall door he rang, and almost by magic the waiter was there with the bill of fare. In a little time more we had ordered, or rather Major Harradine, with a question or two to me, had—and we were alone again.

He came over to where I sat, and sat down by me on my love seat. His lips brushed mine again as his arm went round me. He said, "The first time I kissed you you were five years old."

I said before I thought, "Oh, is that the reason we have never been like strangers?"

"It might be one reason," he said seriously. Before I could answer I realized what he had said meant. Of course, he had crossed the ferry.

"Why—I remember you a little, too," I said shyly. "A tall boy in gray . . . oh, did you know my mother, then?"

"Naturally," he said. "Why, love, it was a nine days' wonder, the beautiful young lady who had been rescued from the snow with her child, who was being nursed by old Mrs. Van Dorn and her son, and who had been so hurt that she had forgotten everything. We called her Madame Honor . . . She did remember her name, then, I suppose."

"No," I said. "They found a letter calling her that. Oh, tell me what you remember of her! I was so little when she died."

He said, "I was fifteen, I think. I had been sent to spend the summer at the Red Castle. We knew no more, of course, than I have said. She had ridden as far as the ferryhouse on the other side: she had been thrown from her horse and hurt her head. Her baby daughter was miraculously unhurt; her last conscious act must have been to protect you . . . It was rarely anyone saw her. I was fortunate. It was a beautiful afternoon, and she had taken you walking along the edge of the woods opposite the ferryhouse. In the direction we went the night you succoured Miss Huntington and me. It was sunny and windy. She smiled when we met and asked me if I knew what lay beyond the wood and if it was too far to walk. I remember how the ribbons on her hat, and her wide white skirts were blowing, and how her hair glinted. It was like yours now. But yours was gold then, not gold-glinted. You were quite unafraid. When I introduced myself and asked what your name was, you looked up yourself and said, 'Perdita. I will kiss you if you like.' And Madame Honor said, 'She does not often take to strangers.' She had a very sweet voice—a lady's voice. So I lifted you up and kissed you. I didn't think that some day I'd be sitting with you alone and close, before our hearthfire!"

I did not answer . . . How could it all be true! I wished I had not had Isobel's letter. But oh, let it go on, let me believe it a little longer . . .

Presently he asked, "If she could remember nothing of the past, where did you get your name?"

"She called me that. Because I was lost—like her."

"You must have been christened by that time. Was there nothing in the letter—"

"Nothing about me."

"Perhaps it was Honor, like hers—you are all honor, all fidelity—" He checked himself—he had spoken swiftly, intensely: "Tell me what you do know of your story, my dear."

So I told him: the snow-blurred letter, the box of jewelry, the wedding ring, the little trunk in the attic of the ferry-house with her belongings.

"We must go over everything again," he said thoughtfully, "when we are next at the Red Castle."

"Oh, I wish—I wish for your sake I knew!"

He laughed. "It doesn't matter to me. I wish it didn't to you."

I said, remembering, "But oh—Eugenia—"

"Dear child, we are all so used to Eugenia's wild rages and their wilder accusations, that I had forgotten how they might hurt someone unused."

Used to her wild words! But—he had defended me against them. If it had not been for her insults I might not be sitting here in the firelight, alone and close with him, as he had said.

I was unprepared for the next thing he did; he was laughing a little again.

"I want to see if your beautiful hair is as long as your mother's was," he said. His hands were busy while he spoke, pulling out the pins that held the loose curls in place, and shaking free the great knot at back. He said, "You are a very lovely woman, my wife."

There was a knock at the door, and I caught it back, flushed, and wound it hastily behind my head. It was the waiter with the great tray. The table was glittering; the man was back again with something else, and I saw it was champagne. Shortly the man was dismissed. "I will wait on madame," Mark said to him. "We will ring for the dessert."

The waiters—there were two by now—bowed at his apparently extravagant *pour-boire*. The elder waiter spoke an extravagant phrase of thanks and compliments to me, in French. I found myself smiling and replying. It was all, I thought, a little like the Arabian Nights.

"You speak French?" Mark said, surprised, as they went. I nodded. "There was time to study a good deal in the winter evenings. It was only accomplishments I needed to learn with Isobel."

"My little miracle!" he said lightly, and then we went to the table. He poured me champagne. "To our future, love!" he said as we drank. Oh, if the enchantment would not break for a little while longer! If the words, the caresses, were even the knight-errantry which had rescued me from public slander, the barrier to being passion-held to a termagant, it would be enough.

"To our future!" I echoed, smiling.

I remember thinking then that if we had been bride and groom in a novel of Sir Walter Scott or Mrs. Radcliffe's, we would have had no appetite. But the fairytale food and drink were part of the delight. He rose, a hand on my shoulder in passing, and changed the plates from the bouillon to the guinea-hen under glass, and the asparagus from the chafing-dish—there were more courses than any two people could possibly eat, so I was glad the waiters had been dismissed: they had shown signs of wanting to press all too much on us.

"I like waiting on you, my Perdita," he said. "You waited on me before, remember?" He waited on himself and sat down across from me, the smile in his eyes again. He took a roll from the basket near him, and, still looking in my eyes, broke it and shared it with me.

He was not half-wakened this time. The man was giving his woman the share, the oneness, with everything that was his.

I gasped. Before I knew I had said the thing. "But—but then—Mark—you love me!" I said, and could have bitten my tongue off.

"I've loved you ever since I saw you in the lamplight at the ferryhouse," he said. "It may have been even before, when we were crossing in the dark. I went through Hades, knowing myself honorbound to Eugenia. When she gave me my freedom— Good God, my own wife, my own love, did you not see and know?"

"You were a great gentleman," I faltered. "You were betrothed to a great beauty, a lady you had known always. I could only love you and hope no one would know."

He came round to me. "Something in me did know. Because, my love, being what you are, no matter how strong the reasons were, you would not have married me, unloving."

I said, "Yes. That is true."

The wind was high again, even here in the city. A sudden gust blew leaves against the pane. One clung in the chink between the drawn curtains, and I shivered. He rose and passed behind me. I turned and saw that he had opened the door there, to take out my fleecy shawl the chambermaid had hung in a shallow closet.

"Come back to the fire, love," he said. There was a knock,

he said "*Entrez*" and the waiter came back. "I thought monsieur had forgotten to ring for the dessert," he said. We laughed, sitting by the fire. We had. The waiter brought it to us there, ices with creams and fruit, demitasses, on a low table, and went, carrying the trays from the table where we had been. I took a spoonful and laid it down, his laughing eyes on me. "You don't really want it, do you?" he said. "Nor I. Shall we call him to take it away? Drink the liqueur —it is made of violets—or would you rather have the Benedictine?"

It was only a tiny glassful; it stung my lips sweetly. He rang again and the man came and went. He drew me up, an arm around me; we stood a moment so. Then, still holding me, he put out the candles, and the gas-jet by the door. The fire had burned low now, but the one in the room beyond was bright still, as he opened that door.

CHAPTER NINE

. . . I love him far beyond all telling—
My love is he,
Give him to me—
His love is mine, my heart has he.

FLORIAN'S SONG

"I don't want to go to Niagara Falls," I said early the next afternoon. I was as spoiled as that already.

"Can you offer me a good reason against it?" Mark said, his black eyes sparkling. For the great gentleman I had married, I had already found, could be a laughing boy too, sweeping me on to gayety with him.

"Yes," I said. "That was where you were going with Eugenia."

"And you are human enough to be jealous!" he said. "Thank Heaven—I was beginning to fear I'd married an angel. By all means, my little love! I was rather dreading being part of a wilderness of brides and grooms, myself. The Falls will still be existing if our grandchildren want us to escort them there. Where would you prefer going?"

I said, rather ashamed of myself, "Anywhere you say. But

first, Miss Abigail said that I needed to make some purchases. I was to use her account."

"You shall make your purchases, and I will go with you," he said. "But you won't use Cousin Abigail's account. Had you forgotten our marriage ceremony so soon? All my worldly goods—"

He stood me up and looked me over, hands on my shoulders. "You need a fur sacque and muff to begin with, I know that much. Better make a list while I write my cousin Laura. I can add to it when you're through."

"Your cousin Laura?"

"My cousin Edgar's wife, Laura Harradine. They live not far above here on Madison Avenue. And perhaps I should be indiscreet enough to tell you that she did not wish me to marry our cousin Eugenia. So I shall send a note to say that I have married instead a young lady with all the virtues—except perhaps a slight prejudice against my late fiancée—"

We were both laughing. The sun shone in at the windows: in spite of the November day there were English sparrows twittering on the trees whose tops were at the windows.

"I'll write Miss Abigail also," I said, "and say that you are still treating me well." My little traveling desk had been set on a small table near: I found paper and pens in it, and after I had made a shopping list, began the letter. Mark was at the escritoire.

"I'm telling Laura that she may make us a bride-visit tomorrow," he said. "I think you may like her. Besides, she had been kind enough to promise to set my house in order for us. I want her report."

"A house? Here in New York City?"

"A house, certainly. It was my great-grandfather's. He brought my great-grandmother there as a bride, as I shall bring you. And"—he was teasing again—"Eugenia did not like it at all. She has a curious and unbridled affection for the

Red Castle. I don't think she's left it for more than a few weeks at a time since she was old enough to have her way. She knows every inch of it, ghost rooms and all. I hope they'll let us give it back to her!"

"You aren't writing to your cousin Laura. When can I see the house?"

"Say 'When can I see *our* house.'"

I said it obediently. "But—"

"I know. But talking to you and looking at you is so much pleasanter."

But he did go on with the note.

"The furrier, first," he said, when we were in our carriage again.

"But should you—"

His arm was around me where we sat, so it was easy for him to shake me a little. "The etiquette books say that a lady should never mention money. There's nothing said about how much she may spend of it. My darling, try to get it into your head that I have a good deal of money, and that it is difficult to spend much of it while fighting the Mexicans. Also I am in love with you and this is our honeymoon. I'd like to give you the moon and stars, and the sort of furs a lady needs are a very poor substitute. But on second thoughts, if you need time to get used to it, we will go buy something else first."

His rebuke was gay: but I would remember it.

The something else proved to be found in a store called Tiffany's. It took two grave clerks as well as Mark to decide what rings my hands, laid on a black velvet cushion, were to wear. I helped a little but not much, each ring was so beautiful and dazzling. My hand felt so proud with the jewels slipping over the wedding ring that still felt un accustomed. Finally we chose a single big diamond set high on a slender gold band, and Mark went away with the senior

110

clerk to have it engraved. There was a cluster of sapphires and diamonds; there was a carved amethyst with a rose made of seed pearls set in it; there was a circle of pearls: and I found the remaining clerk laying an emerald set in little velvet boxes; earrings, necklace, bracelets, brooch. I took out the plain gold earrings and hooked the emeralds through my ears immediately; they were so lovely.

When we were in the carriage again I turned to Mark and tried to thank him, but I found my eyes filling with tears. "It is so much," I started to say.

I was pulled close again, and this time he was not looking or talking lightly. He said, "My wife Perdita, listen. If you had accepted the fact that you must marry where you did not love: if, endeavoring to love the lady destined for you, you had found unreason, violence, an emotion that demanded subservience in yourself, and wild rages rising from insensate jealousy: and if honor, promises made too early to know their meaning, held you fettered—"

"You mean that you did not love Eugenia?"

"I never loved her. I made my profession, my life among men, my chief interest. I lived the life of any man—sport—the wilds—passing light amusements with women—and then, almost on my wedding day, I found the woman who belonged to me—a hell that could have been heaven. Perdita, do you know what it was like to write reassuring Eugenia, to spend those last days knowing what I might have won—to find you in our very house the day I waited to marry another woman—and then, my blessed gift of freedom, and your assent, my Perdita! Could anything on earth be too much to give and do for you, for the gift of yourself in that moment?"

I said through my tears, "Not in that moment! It was with me as with you—from the moment we met."

"Then always?"

"Then always."

I looked up into his eyes and saw that they too were dimmed. We were silent for a moment. Then I felt him drawing off my glove and setting the betrothal ring above the wedding ring. He was smiling. "It's a little late, but it's forever," he said, "so no more talk about a trivial piece of fur or so!"

"You sound as if you were giving me a kitten," I said, laughing with him, as we would always laugh, together.

"Wait and see."

And so I accepted, I hoped, as a matter of course the rich sealskin sacque, the muff, the little cap with its floating veil; and then the set of soft whiteness, with the flecks of black here and there, the muff and cape that went with my black velvet walking suit, all in chinchilla.

"It is delightful, buying you things," he said as we left the furrier's, the bowing, laden salesmen behind us. "Are you too tired for just one gown, or maybe two? And I think there is something Laura calls a *sortie du bal*. Balls spring up under Laura's satin brodequins, I have noticed. And you will find."

I said meekly that I was not too tired. So we went to A. T. Stewart's after all— Mark told me a wild tale of his having been a pirate, and of having founded his fortunes as a dry-goods millionaire by means of some herds of captured cows— and bought the gowns. It was evidently on the cards about the balls, which partly scared and partly excited me, because Mark found a model evening gown, a pale blue satin with trails of rosebuds to hold it on my shoulders, and in long sweeps all across the skirt, which was so billowing that there had to be a wider hoop than my own to go with it. I didn't dare ask how he managed to get it away from them because they did not want to let it go—it was an import, to be copied, and they wanted to sell me the dress pattern to be made up. But we came away with it and its slippers and its

112

white kid gloves—a dozen pairs, which seemed to be the way gloves for ball gowns were usually sold. So I then got myself a staid brown broché, because after all I was a married woman now, and a tiny lace cap to remind my husband of the fact. There was also the *sortie du bal*—a knee-long tasseled, flowing velvet cape, in a rose that matched the flowers. And when we got back to the Astor I found that I had not been told about the bracelets.

"I feel like Tarpeia," I said, lying back on the couch, while he strung them on my arms . . . Suddenly I shivered, and clung to him. . . . "Oh Mark, it is too wonderful, all this—shall I be crushed under the enemies' shields, to pay for my happiness?"

"Nonsense—" He held me fast. "Only like this! Tarpeia was betraying her country: You are giving as much happiness as you take, my well-read little girl. Indeed, from what I have understood, you have done more than that. You are something of a miracle, indeed; reared between a grave-minded old uncle and poor gloomy Isobel, you are as light-hearted, until this moment, as a child."

But who would not be, I thought—nineteen, in love and loved! And what he had not quite said was true: Isobel's grieving, Isobel's harping on the evils and old legends of the Red Castle, had moved me more than I had realized . . . But—if the legend that any woman brought to the Red Castle was shamed was true, I had been. Eugenia's wild insults, before the group assembled there, her worse threats, were shaming enough, surely—even though they brought me what I wanted most in the world. So I smiled up at him: and saw that he was leaning back in his chair beside me, serious.

"There is something I have to tell you," he said, "now that you are my wife and our interests are one. It is about Drusilla Huntington. You had faith in me without knowledge: you deserve to know."

"Naturally I've wondered," I said. "But I knew there must be a reason. Don't tell me unless you wish to—you do not owe it to me."

"I wish to, my love. It was not a story for the ears of an unmarried girl I did not know."

I liked his name for me. And I thought, more than I thought of Drusilla, how good it was no longer to be Perdita—not the lost one—now.

"Everard Huntington was my Colonel, as I have said," he told me. "He had saved my life at the Battle of Chapultepec, and did not recover from the wound received then. This you know. What you do not know was what he laid on me to do, and why it had to be done at any cost."

"I knew you were duty-bound to escort her—no more."

"Yes. When I knew my Colonel first, I also knew his wife. They were wealthy Southerners. I spent one leave at their South Carolina plantation below Charleston. Mrs. Huntington was a gentle and charming lady, blue-eyed, fairhaired, fair-skinned, with a faint, attractive French accent. Their daughter, then, was at a boardingschool in Boston, I was told, where many Charlestonians sent their girls. Last year Mrs. Huntington died, and her daughter, her education finished, came home to keep house for her father. She was a belle, I understood: and engaged to marry a young Englishman who was then traveling in Canada, visiting his relations. I met them both—Drusilla and her betrothed—a little later, near the border, when the Colonel took me with him for a few days' short leave: things were darkening. I remember envying them. All seemed so right, so happy for them. I need not have done so, poor Drusilla!"

"What was it—did her lover die?"

Mark shook his head. "No. Worse than that. The Huntingtons, like most Southerners, had flocks of dependents: poor relations, hangers-on to whom they gave their unstinted

114

hospitality. It seems there was one cousin, a young man, poverty-stricken, who had courted Drusilla and been refused. She was at this time back in her home, alone with her duenna, another cousin, an elderly lady. Colonel Huntington had been recalled to his duty in the West. On the eve of battle he received a letter from the kinsman who had aspired to Drusilla's hand. Huntington showed it to me, in hospital, after the victory.

"The man—I cannot call him a gentleman—had been interested, he wrote, in the fact that Mrs. Huntington's background was not entirely known. He had, he said, therefore spent some time investigating it. He had found the proved facts.

Mrs. Huntington, blonde and well-bred, was, nevertheless, one of the community of New Orleans quadroons who are a caste by themselves. They are educated, trained, given every advantage: made exquisite ladies, to be mistresses of the New Orleans aristocracy. Even though, as was the case with Eveline Huntington, generation after generation of white gentry had chosen her foremothers, until the drop of black blood was minimal, for she was fairer than you or I, she was legally as black as Eugenia's old Petronius. Her marriage to the Colonel, legal in the state where they had married, was null by the laws of South Carolina. So that Drusilla, also, by those laws, was not only illegitimate but her father's slave. And when he should die—and he knew he was dying—she would be the slave of the hanger-on, her cousin, the next heir."

I shivered and held his hand more tightly. "How terrible!"

"Worse than that. The man threatened to make the whole story public unless Drusilla broke her engagement with Cyril and married himself. In this case, though of course the marriage would no more be legal than her mother's, he would allow the world to suppose it so. If she was docile and devoted, he would be generous enough to let the facts remain hidden. If she was rebellious—there was the auction block, for he was of course her owner, or would be, as the Colonel's rightful heir. . . . And her father was, and knew it, dying."

"So he asked you to be her rescuer?"

"There was no time to reach Cyril Eaton. He was hunting in the Canadian wilds and would not return to civilization for some weeks to come. Huntington could see to it, so close we were to the war's end. He used, I fear, his last vitality, summoning the Lieutenant Colonel, and seeing to it that I had a year's leave. He told him truthfully that I and I alone could handle his urgent private affairs. I had been close to him—his adjutant—and Lieutenant Colonel Waring was my good friend also." I remembered what I had heard of Mark's magnificent war record. Yes, they would give him anything they could: he was a man loved by men as well as women. He went on quietly, "I was in time. I do not know, love, whether you have heard of an organization known as the Underground Railroad, whose purpose is to assist runaway slaves to Canada. Your uncle belonged to it. So did a Quaker farmer some miles above Grandison. There was a Negro woman who if she had been white and a man might have been a famous general. This Harriet Tubman was reached, informed—God knows how—and brought Drusilla halfway from the Carolinas, cared for by stations of the Underground till I could reach her and bring her the rest of the way, or as much as was needful. I wrote to Eugenia to postpone our wedding. There was no time even to see her at the Red Castle and explain, even if I could have trusted to her being anti-slavery."

"I think she still regards Petronius as her slave, in spite of the New York laws," I said.

"So I thought. Well, you know the rest, my dear. I was to

116

put Drusilla in the hands of the Osgoods, the Quaker farmers who were the next station. I expected Mr. Van Dorn to take over, indeed: but as he was absent I had to carry on. When we reached the Osgood farm I found that Osgood, the only person there able to take her on, was too ill to travel. I had to escort her still, to the group upstate who were to take her on to Canada. And so I seemed a faithless knight to Eugenia—but you remember the rest."

"And is she safe now?" I asked breathlessly.

"Safe in the hands of her husband. They were married within a week of the time she found safety. They have written me."

With what gratitude, I could imagine. Knight-errant, indeed!

"It is a dreadful story, dearest. But it has ended well, remember. Has it tired you—after all the shopping?"

"Tired, indeed! No."

"Then," he said, "we will stop thinking or talking of serious things. The Opera House is practically next door: how long since you have seen a stage play?"

"Never at all," I said, delighted.

"There's also the Vauxhall Gardens. We'll dine there and go on to the Astor Place Opera House."

He hadn't played quite fair. There was another gown, rose taffeta this time, with a bertha of valenciennes lace lying atop the blue gown and *sortie du bal*. It seemed if you sat in a box you wore evening dress.

It was *Rigoletto*. I knew some of the arias, at least I'd heard and played them on the pianoforte: but I had not dreamed of the beauty and excitement of a real opera. A good many people knew Mark, or at least spoke to him as we promenaded between the acts: they looked at me curiously, I thought. I could scarcely sleep for the excitement of it all. Tomorrow there would be Laura, another of the great ladies

Mark belonged with . . . I felt a little afraid of her; if she did not think the beautiful and aristocratic Eugenia good enough for Mark, what would she think of me? And then, lying there in the dark, with Mark's sleeping hand still fast on mine, I remembered the story he had told me of his selfless and courageous deed for Miss Huntington. How could anyone, seeing and knowing him, have other than faith in him, honor in keeping his secret? It was so little a thing to have done . . . And yet Eugenia, who had known him long and well, and even Isobel a little, could doubt him . . . I must have made some ejaculation aloud, for he turned and half-woke; he said "Little love!" and his hand tightened as if to be sure I was there and I was drawn close against him once more. Suddenly, in the moment before I slept again, I knew a strange thing—that he had been lonely; and because of me was not now. It was a blessed thing to learn.

A pink, perfumed billet-doux from Laura, brought from Madison Square by her footman, lay on my breakfast tray next morning. Nothing, she wrote, in her pretty English hand, would keep her a moment longer than necessary from visiting her new *cousine*. She was calling at three that afternoon. Be absent at our peril!

She arrived, as Mark said, for her practically on time, that is, only a half hour later than she had appointed. She was not at all what I had, with terror, expected. He had said that she was nearing thirty, the mother of two boisterous little sons, and usually got her own way. But she looked not more than twenty-one or -two. She burst into our parlor, yellow curls, bonnet-plumes, lavender velvet skirts, all flying wide: a pretty blue-eyed blonde all vivacity and gayety. She was laughing as she ran to me and kissed me.

"Oh, she's lovely, Mark!" she cried, her plump little hands in their lavender chevrette gloves fast on mine. "She will be one of the sensations of the season. However you came by so much sense—"

"I told you so, Perdita," he said, shrugging, as she released me to kiss him in turn. "She's planning festivities already."

"Of course!" Laura said. "She reminds me of someone—some portrait—" she added, settling herself in the biggest armchair with a whirl of skirts.

"She is like one of the Romneys in the English National Portrait Gallery," Mark said quietly. But my heart leaped. Could this delightful lady perhaps hold a key to what I needed to know?

She shook her head. "But never mind," she said. "You must settle down for once in your life, cousin. I have completely exhausted myself getting the Grammercy Park mansion swept and garnished for your bride. You owe it to society to entertain . . . I'll launch her myself at a reception. After that the *beau monde* will take over without more done."

I rang for tea, and wine for Mark, and she went on chattering. She had planned a winter's gayeties before Mark laughingly stopped her.

"We haven't even planned our wedding journey yet," he said. "This was a mere stopping-place to look the landscape o'er. My liege lady there declines Niagara Falls, and has offered me no alternative so far."

"It's too late and cool for Saratoga," Laura said thoughtfully.

"True."

"And Newport—"

"Even colder." He was laughing at her; she laughed and pouted a little too.

"I see you have your mind all made up," she said. "The point is, when will you be settled in Grammercy Place for the winter?"

"And eligible for your campaign?"

119

"Exactly."

He looked over at me. "Perhaps, if Perdita agrees, we will be in the city a week longer. Time, if you will be so good a little cousin, to guide her as to campaign uniforms. After that we shall seek a mysterious locality where it is nearer summer still: we should return after the holidays."

Laura, pouting forgotten, clapped her little hands. "It will be wonderful—like dressing a doll—or a daughter! Consider yourself my youngest child from now on, Perdita."

Nobody could help liking Laura. She seemed to really like me. Before I knew what was happening, she had arranged to take me shopping again next morning, and meet Mark at the Grammercy Park house in the afternoon, to decide whether we would move into it for the week before we left the city. She went, saying that her Edgar must know the news immediately, setting a time for dining with them in two days. Then with another whirl of skirts and perfume she was gone.

"I told you she always got her way," Mark said when he had returned from escorting her to her carriage.

"But what a fascinating way!"

"I hoped you would like her. She is a good little soul under all the frivolity. And now . . . I have thought of St. Augustine. It will be like late Spring there; if we are fortunate, early summer. It is an old Spanish town on the sea which has belonged to America now for some years: I spent a couple of short leaves there when I was down in the Florida war. We'll come back after the holidays and let Laura do her worst."

I could see that he was pleased that his cousin's wife and I liked each other, and that she wished to introduce me. If he liked St. Augustine, why, so would I. We moved into the Grammercy Park house two days later.

I fell in love with it at first sight. Despite the height of the great hall, with its portraits of dead and gone Harradines, the double parlors stretching through from the street to the windows that overlooked a garden even now alive, with its asters and chrysanthemums, the great turning stair with its white statues gleaming from their niches, the rich lace curtains and fine tapestries, the velvet carpets one's feet sank in, the carved marble fireplaces, it was a kind house, a welcoming house. And in perfect condition.

"There's always been a caretaker," Laura said, "a good old housekeeper, half in love with Mark of course like most of us—her husband the butler, and a couple of people to wait on them. Actually there was little to do but to fill out the staff and set the Townes to taking the covers from the pictures and furniture and so on."

"It is perfection and I can't thank you enough."

"You needn't thank me at all—Mark will tell you, and Edgar too, the wretches, that I adore having fingers in pies!"

I had been looking out the long front windows on the park that centered the square of beautiful brownstone houses. It was still green underfoot; it was a sunny day, and there were nurses with little children: pretty, brightclad little boys and girls playing with their hoops and balls; and gamboling with their little dogs. They were like an illustration from a book. I spoke without turning.

"There's more to thank you for than that . . . Mark's people need not have welcomed so generously—Perdita of the ferry."

The rustling skirts rushed on me; Laura caught me in her arms.

"You little goosie! Didn't Cousin Abigail, that model of virtue and propriety, practically bring you up? And Mark says that your mother, that he and all the lads of his day— we're almost of an age, he and I—were romantical about, was a beautiful and elegant young lady. Her betrothal ring, he said, was the soberly valuable sort a man doesn't give a light o'love."

I said, "Her last words, Uncle Jacob told me, were that she was a wedded and widowed woman."

"I know the story—he stayed single all his life for her sake." Laura stood off and spoke with a seriousness I hadn't known she possessed. "But, dear little cousin, we love Mark. And we supposed that his exaggerated chivalry and sense of honor was dooming him to a marriage that could make no man happy. So if you were merely good and amiable and good-mannered, instead of all else you are also, we would be grateful." She pulled a note from her reticule and said, "Listen to this—it's Miss Abigail's hand."

" 'I cannot but be happy that Mark has married a pure, amiable and well-principled young woman who loves him unselfishly. If I may express myself without boasting, I have helped to form Perdita Van Dorn's character and manners since early childhood. Mark is safe in her hands, and if he gives her no more than respect and regard, it is a good beginning. I trust that he will learn to love her soon."

Laura thrust the note back in the reticule and giggled.

"I wonder where her eyesight was! The man's head over ears. So say no more about all that . . . Mark was to spend the afternoon tying up some dry business things, wasn't he? You're both dining with us tonight—just our four selves. You will like Edgar, once you can get him to talk. He says I never give him time, but that's a scandal . . . And now let's go upstairs to look at those preposterous fourposters and decide what's the *dernier cri* to put instead. I hear the newest things are brass beds, with scarcely any curtains, just lace draperies from a hook at the head."

CHAPTER TEN

Must I thus leave thee, Paradise? Thus leave
These happy shades and walks where I had hoped to spend
Quiet, though sad, the respite of that day
That must be mortal to us both . . .

MILTON

It was Mark's key; I thought I'd heard it. In another moment
he was standing behind us. He must have been there a little
longer than we knew, for he said, "I like fourposters better.
I am sure the glittering of the brass would keep us awake,
Laura."

"Oh, you're hopeless," she laughed, and then, "I must go.
Seven, remember—just ourselves. Wait, though, I must take
Perdita down to meet the rest of the staff. Will you come
with us, Mark?"

I was sufficiently used to dealing with the Red Castle
servants to see that Laura had done well. Towne and his
wife, a handsome upright elderly pair, marshaled the rest.
Laura had not, she said, engaged a ladies' maid for me, saying
that I might prefer to choose my own. I would do without
one till I returned from St. Augustine, I thought, and then

take Janet Mackenzie if she could be spared from the Red Castle.

After we had lingered a little longer in the great room with its pierglasses and sweeping velvet curtains that framed lace, sweet with Laura's hothouse flowers, it was time to dress and go to her. It was to be a family dinner only. But there was a white taffeta of Miss Abigail's choosing, with short sleeves that my white lace shawl would drape if I was overdressed. Mark fastened the white silk brodequins for me, and clasped on my bracelets and necklace. The footman came to tell us that the carriage waited.

Laura had been so gay and easy with me that I was not as much afraid as I would otherwise have been, even when we were announced formally by the powdered footman and led into a withdrawing room as elegant as our own . . . I hoped it was not *parvenu* to feel encouraged by that recollection. And Laura, so laughing and welcoming that all her jewels did not matter, was kissing us again; and her husband was behind her smiling and speaking in a voice not unlike Mark's, saying how pleased and happy he was to see us, and how charming a new cousin he was finding. He was not unlike Mark in other ways indeed, though heavier, of course older, shorter and a little more quiet. I liked him.

Their little sons came in for dessert. They were polite, and very neat in their roundabouts. But I thought the elder, who was fair like his mother, had, too, her glint of mischief in his eyes. They came and spoke to me like little gentlemen, and we made friends almost immediately. The dark-eyed seven-year-old, Alston, leaned against me and began talking to me and I to him. Suddenly I was aware of Mark's eyes on us as I sat with an arm round the child, and he looked up at me smiling and chattering. I thought I knew what Mark did not say, for his smile had something of tenderness in it, and I flushed high. And presently the nurse came in for the protest-

124

ing children. Then Laura asked if I sang, and I told them that I only knew the old songs my uncle had liked, and sang without sheet music. But Mark's look encouraged me, and Edgar led me to the piano.

"It's a relief to hear songs like that instead of those everlasting *roulades* of the Italian opera," Edgar said when I was done. "This little Perdita of ours can do everything, apparently."

I looked over at him: he was smiling as if he meant it. Laura, also—it was no pretense or mere politeness. It was true what Mark had said. They were pleased with me for his wife . . . Such kind, such dear people— I felt happy and at home, as I had not since Uncle Jacob died. I could see, too, that Mark, where he sat on the bergere by Laura, watching me quietly, was pleased too and proud of me. I had been afraid to visit these people. I need not have been: their welcome and liking was real. They were not just being kindly, like Miss Abigail and Isobel.

And then the footman entered, a little hurriedly, if so rigidly correct a servant could seem hurried.

"A lady to see Mrs. Mark Harradine," he said amazingly.

"Mrs. *Mark?*" Laura said, as surprised as I.

"Yes, madam. She said she had called at the Astor first, and been directed first to Grammercy Park and then here. Miss Isobel Somerwell, a relative."

Isobel! How had she come from the Red Castle at Grandison?

"The lady said that she would prefer to await Mrs. Harradine in the hall: she wishes to speak to her only for a moment, alone," the footman said, looking a little embarrassed. I thought I knew why. Isobel's everlasting self-hiding because of her scar!

"She is very shy of strangers," I said, with an imploring look at Mark, who could explain, I thought, with more grace than I. The Edgar Harradines, apparently, had not met her—as indeed it proved.

I wrapped my shawl about my shoulders against the colder hall, excused myself, and went.

Isobel was in carriage costume still, with the familiar black lace veil across her face, even now it was evening. She stood close against the wall, hands behind her, in the old shrinking position. Behind the veil I could see her frightened eyes.

"Dearest, what has happened?" I said. "How did you get here? But come in and speak to Mark's people." But she shook her head as I had thought she would.

"It's a little difficult to explain to strangers," she said. "That's why I wanted to see you alone. I came up with Cousin Abigail for our usual fall shopping. We're at the usual hotel. But she's ill—one of her migraines—and wants to see you. Frankly, I think she wants to be reassured about your being happy with Cousin Mark. She keeps fretting about it till the doctor said it would be better if you could see her as soon as possible. If you could . . ."

"We could come tomorrow," I said. "Dear Miss Abigail! She mustn't worry. If she sees us together, I am sure it will be all right. Oh Isobel, I am so happy!"

The great blue eyes behind the veil filled; but she smiled. "I am glad," she said. "You should be, you have given me what happiness I had. But—Perdita, that isn't all I had to say. Eugenia is there too, and I'm afraid on the edge of one of her tantrums. She heard Aunt Abigail asking for you, and she said that if Mark ever entered her house or anywhere she was, she would not answer for his safety . . . Oh, you know . . ."

"Mark, not me?"

"No, she said . . ." Isobel stopped herself. "Never mind . . . And—she'll be in her room—you won't have to see

126

her. That is if you could possibly come tonight, when Aunt Abigail wanted you."

"Are you sure?"

"She was fretting badly . . . but it is a good deal to ask, taking you away in the middle of a party. Only the doctor did say that it would quiet Aunt Abigail. It isn't far—"

I knew the hotel: it was only two blocks away. I could be there and back in a half hour. I said, "Wait, I must tell them. I think they will understand—"

I re-entered the drawing room. The three of them seemed happy enough. They were talking and laughing as old intimates talk, in a group by the fire. The golden hands of the black marble clock on the mantel above said incredibly that only seven minutes had passed since I left the room.

Mark demurred a little when I explained; but Laura said impulsively, "Poor soul, no wonder she's worried—jilted herself, and with that wild Eugenia on her hands, not to speak of living in that red mausoleum with the servants all remembering about the Indian that said none of the women would be happily married. Let Perdita go, Mark, and send a footman with her."

Isobel, who had plucked up courage to follow me, spoke now:

"My old Negro maid, Mr. Harradine—I am Isobel Somerwell, as you know—is with me in the carriage. My aunt would never allow me to be alone in the carriage at night."

Mark went with me to the carriage, and spoke to old Keziah. "Don't be long, my love," he said softly; and I said no, and presently was there at Miss Abigail's hotel with Isobel nervously beside me, as she had so often been. I heard a closing door, and knew it was Eugenia.

It did quiet Miss Abigail to see me. She lay high on her pillows, looking rather worn and tired. The doctor thanked me for coming. Eugenia might have done more than angrily

127

refuse to have Mark in the house, I thought. I kissed my old friend goodbye, told her again softly that Mark and I were very happy.

"And has he begun to learn to love you, my dear child?" she whispered.

"He says he loves me," I murmured back. "Everything is wonderful." I would tell her the rest, I thought, when she was well.

Then Isobel and I went downstairs and out with the doctor. His carriage and ours waited, and we got in. In the little pause before he started, she said, still nervously, "I wonder if I ought to tell you . . . but Eugenia lies so—"

My mind went as always to my mother's story. And I was right.

"Whatever it is, tell me," I said.

"I was going to write you and Mark, then it seemed futile—she's so untrustworthy—"

I stopped the coachman. "No, you are to tell me now. I don't have to believe it."

It took a little longer, but finally she spoke, still reluctantly.

"She said—but oh, dearest, you don't need to believe her, she was a little angry—she said that her New York guardian's housekeeper said when she was ill, and a little unstrung she thought, that she knew who your mother might be. You know Eugenia had been staying with the Olivers until they went South a little while ago."

I caught my breath. "Where is the housekeeper now?"

"Why, where would she be? At the Oliver mansion. The maids are looking after her. She's convalescing . . ."

I said, "Wait, we'll go back to Edgar's and get Mark . . ."

"Oh, Perdita, you can't do that! If Eugenia went back to the Oliver house and found Mark there, it would be what we're trying to avoid, one of her rages . . ." Isobel's voice dropped. "They are closer to insanity than we realized. The doctor says so—and Dr. De Witt back home."

"Was she going there?"

"She is sleeping there. She stays late with us and then is called for by a maid," she said.

I made up my mind. "There is time. Will you come with me? If not I will go alone. Now. Or lend me Keziah. It would only be another half hour, and I stayed a shorter time than I expected with Miss Abigail."

Isobel gave in suddenly. "I'll go with you. They know me, I can explain."

I spoke to the coachman. It was almost as near as our own house. The stalwart old Negress with us, the well-trained servants who knew Isobel: their waiter, in fact, whom I had known when the Olivers visited the Red Castle. The housekeeper was convalescent: it was still early; five minutes brought us there, five more saw us on the steps, entering as a tall liveried servant, handsome and nearly white, flung open the door and bowed us in. The house was as I had thought it, as stiff, elegant and mannered as its owners. Their man showed us and old Keziah into a small reception room off the front hall. I could see the Red Castle barouche, with its old known coachman, awaiting us under the window beyond the lawn.

Isobel spoke to the man. "My friend—my cousin, really, Mrs. Harradine, has been informed that she might have a few words with your housekeeper. It is quite important. We know she is convalescent, but if she is awake still may she? It will only take a few minutes."

Isobel could be very winning. The man hesitated, and I thought I knew what he wanted and came forward and slipped a goldpiece into his white-gloved hand. He bowed, seemed to demur a moment, and then said, "The housekeeper is ill, madame, or has been, but if the lady could be quick . . ."

I said, "I'll only take a few minutes. Come, Isobel." If she only told me that she did have information, I thought, and promised to give it me at length when she was well, I could turn the whole thing over to Mark . . .

The man shook his head. "Mrs. Humblethwaite can only see one person at a time," he said. "As it is, I may get into trouble with Miss Eugenia for letting this happen. But as Madame is a relative . . ."

"And as madame," I thought, "has given you money and may give you more—" I said aloud, "Very well." Isobel dropped into her armchair by the door reluctantly: Keziah stood behind her as I had seen her standing behind her mistress so many years. I followed the major-domo, for such he seemed, along the hall to a rear room at the lower end of the house, and quietly opened a door.

The old woman who half sat, half lay in a mahogany bed at the end of the room, dimly seen by a nightlight, seemed half asleep. It was a well-furnished room: they took good care of her, it seemed, for her white hair was gathered underneath a fine lace nightcap, and her arms, out on the honeycomb counterpane, were in a padded silk bedjacket. I wondered if I should disturb her. But at my step she began to move and mutter. She opened her eyes.

"I am sorry to intrude," I said timidly, "but I am told that you know something of my mother, whose identity we have sought for so long. She was Madame Honor, who lived at the Grandison ferryhouse. I will not disturb you now, more than to ask if this is so, and my husband and I could call on you at your convenience and learn more . . ."

Her eyes opened wider. "Madame Honor—Madame Honor? No, no, my dear, nobody like that . . ." Her eyes closed again. I turned to the major-domo by the door.

"Could you get her nurse?" I asked. "She seems so dazed."

"I am all the nurse she has," he said. "There is nobody else

130

in the house." Before I could cross the room he had left, shutting the door. I heard the click of its lock.

For a moment it seemed incredible. Then I remembered Eugenia's hatred of me, the wild temper that it was hinted made her irresponsible, the attack on my wedding day, only stopped by her collapse. Was it possible this man was under her orders? I stood for a moment. The old lady was dropped on her pillows, apparently fast asleep again. I made myself go quietly to the door and speak in as controlled a manner as I could.

"Do you know that you have locked me in?" I said. "Miss Isobel Somerwell is awaiting me, and my husband expects me."

"Miss Somerwell and her maid are gone," the man's voice said. "I told her you wanted her to go, and gave orders to the coachman."

"What is all this about?" I said. "If it is some performance of Miss Eugenia's, I can pay you more than she can. And my husband will see that you are punished for this."

The man's voice answered coolly, "The master and mistress won't be back for another week. There's a sofa in the room. Tomorrow you're going on a good long trip where your husband will have hard work finding you. The old lady's all right. She's full of laudanum, she can't help you. There's nobody else in the house. If your husband won't play our game, you're for the Argentine."

It was a nightmare. But the man did not sound crazy.

"What do you want? What is it all about?" I said. He did not answer. I began to call and cry out, and his voice came close to the door again.

"Yell all you like," he said. "The servants are all on leave." I heard his steps going away from the door. I ran to the windows, but they were not only high from the ground, but locked and shuttered. There was no other door. I ran wildly to the one he had locked, and began to beat on it and scream. He might be lying.

I was exhausted; for a while I lay there by the door, hopeless. Then I rose and tried again. There was a heavy poker by the dying fire of the grate, and I tried to break the lock with it. The arms that were strong from rowing finally had their way; the lock broke, and heedless of what the man might do to me I fled out.

Before I could gain the hall, I heard the front door crash: and then deliberate steps coming near. "What's all this?" a man's voice said sharply, "Hey you, come back!" There was a crash, and an angry exclamation. I saw what it was: Mr. and Mrs. Oliver, Eugenia's guardians, had unexpectedly returned. And the strange man we had thought a major-domo had knocked him down and run past him and was gone. Mr. Oliver, getting up slowly, was furious; his wife, standing against the wall, looked at me in shock.

"You're Isobel's little companion, Perdita," she said. "Who was that ruffian and what are you doing here?"

"Isobel and I, with her maid, came here to speak to your housekeeper," I said, trying to be steady-voiced. "I understood she knew something about—about my mother. That man took me to your housekeeper's room and locked me in. I had to break the lock—"

"You *did?*" Her voice was offended. "And what are you doing in those fancy clothes, Miss Van Dorn? What were you doing with that man and where is Isobel, if as you say she came with you?"

"I am not Miss Van Dorn now," I said. "I am dressed for evening because I am married to Major Harradine, and we were dining with his cousins. I was foolish enough to come here, as I have told you, because I was informed that the housekeeper—"

"Here, Annette," said Mr. Oliver, who had dusted himself

132

off and come to stand by his wife, "the child's on the edge of fainting." His arm came round me just in time, and followed by his wife, he steered me to the reception room sofa.

"But we have no housekeeper here," Mrs. Oliver said crossly. "She is on leave with the rest of the staff. Who—"

"I thought the old lady in bed in the room was the housekeeper," I managed to say. "He said so—"

"Cousin Letitia!" she said in surprise.

Mr. Oliver, who was apparently kinder than I had ever thought him, brought me a glass of water.

"Where is Isobel?" she demanded.

"The man said he told her I wanted her and Keziah to go home, and sent the coachman," I said.

"No use asking her questions—give her time to recover, my dear," Mr. Oliver said. "The man was obviously a burglar. The thing to do is to see if he got away with anything."

It was suddenly all so sane and ordinary that, though Mrs. Oliver eyed me still as if I had had something to do with the burglar, I stopped being shaken.

"My husband is still, I think, with the Edgar Harradines," I said. "And I am troubled about Isobel. Could you . . ."

"Yes, yes," she said still irritably. "But you can tell me first why you say that you're Major Harradine's wife. He was to have married our ward Eugenia just after we left for the South."

Her husband tried to hush her. I answered with what seemed my last bit of strength, leaning against the sofa's arm.

"Apparently you have not heard from your ward. She broke her engagement to him, not for the first time, he said. This time he held her to it. We . . . had known each other . . ."

"But how did you—"

133

Mr. Oliver drew his wife farther away and spoke low, but I could hear.

"If you don't know what a shrew Eugenia was, after having her here for years, I do. This girl's good tempered and good looking, and whether they knew who she was or not her mother was a lady, and so is she, ferryhouse or not. And if you want to be on bad terms with a wealthy aristocrat who was a hero in the last war, and his cousins who are leaders of society, not to say Edgar's a prominent Wall Street man and a philanthropist, I don't—"

Before she could answer the doorbell rang sharply, and the door, which must have been ajar, was flung open and heard Mark's step and angry voice.

"Where's my wife? Perdita, are you safe?" He was pushing the Olivers aside, and in two steps had me in his arms.

"I'm sure," said Mrs. Oliver still angrily also, "what with a strange Negro locking her up with my cousin Letitia, and those two girls intruding into my empty house, and breaking my lock . . ."

I had learned before that Mark's excellent self-control was a mask for the Somerwell temper. "When Mrs. Harradin has recovered from the obvious shock of what she has undergone, I will discuss this with you," he said in a voice like ice. "I will visit you tomorrow, Mr. Oliver."

I felt myself dizzying, and Mr. Oliver's answer was far off. "No, no, my dear sir, don't take it like that . . ." and then everything but the feel of Mark's hold was gone. When I could still think clearly again I was in his carriage, his arm still round me. "I—I must explain to Laura," I said vaguely.

"For once in your life think of yourself instead of every one else," he said. "Tomorrow you can go into all this." He stopped himself and said more gently, "Laura and I went to Cousin Abigail's hotel and I sent her, not to stir up that hellcat Eugenia, to see Isobel. She saw Keziah; Isobel was back in bed and asleep. Keziah told me where you were. Don't talk."

Mrs. Towne, the old housekeeper, put me to bed. "You shouldn't have to do this," I said drowsily, and was asleep.

I was none the worse the next day. In spite of Mark's protest I was up and dressed. Edgar and Laura came over in the afternoon, and almost on top of that Mr. Oliver, to hope, he said, that all was well with me.

"I must apologize again for our intrusion," I said.

"My dear," he said, "we can only be grateful that a change of plans brought us home a week earlier than we had planned. Also, if you had not been there, the house might have been looted. As it was, a careful search proves that the man had no time to take anything."

"But why did he say," I asked, "that if my husband did not play the game with them my journey would be longer yet, to the Argentine? What is the Argentine?"

Laura gave a gasp. The two men looked at each other: Mark's face was set hard, Edgar's as shocked as Laura's. Then Edgar said gently, "It is a term for the Argentine Republic, in South America. It is more properly called Argentina."

Laura asked quickly after the Cousin Letitia I had supposed a housekeeper, and was told she was still a little drowsy but otherwise well. Mr. Oliver expressed his pleasure at seeing me well again. The visit, as far as he was concerned, ended with great courtesy on both sides, and his hope that he and his wife might call and continue an acquaintance so romantically begun.

Nobody had said a word about Eugenia. It was not for me to accuse her. I only asked, "If Eugenia was always difficult to live with, why did the Olivers keep her as a ward?"

Laura laughed a little. "Because it is expensive to keep up with the *ton*, my dear, and the money the Olivers received for her by her grandfather's will was not inconsiderable. Poor Mr. Oliver—he feared Eugenia had something to do with it. Had she?"

The question came so quick that I answered before I thought, "Yes." And then—"Oh, I should not have told!"

"Go on," Mark said. He was not unkind, but it was a voice which demanded obedience.

I said reluctantly, "She told Isobel, not me—only that the old housekeeper remembered something about my mother. But Miss Letitia was not the housekeeper, you remember. She and all the other servants but one maid for Miss Letitia were on leave."

"A little more and Eugenia should be put in confinement," Edgar said sharply. "With her background do you think the child is safe from her?"

Mark said, "She will be safe from now on, because tomorrow I am taking her to St. Augustine for a month. Before I go I will talk to cousin Abigail, ill or well, and see that Eugenia is out of the country or at least the state before our return."

Laura kissed me goodbye. "Well, you're safe, thank heaven. It's dreadful to think that such things could come so near happening. But at least it isn't like . . ." she stopped herself. "Only remember that when you're back I shall present you to society at the most magnificent ball New York can imagine." Her voice was light again.

Once alone with him, I asked Mark what Laura's "it isn't like" had meant.

"Wait till you are more rested," he said.

Next morning, in comforting daylight, after we had breakfasted, he told me what the man might have meant. He came around from his seat at the foot of the little table where we sat in a window of the dining room, and kept an arm around me while he talked.

"You're not a child," he said. "I wish I need not talk to

you about such things, but I think it is better. To begin with, it does not seem likely that even Eugenia's temper or vindictiveness could let her have any part in this. I think we are both glad to believe this."

"Yes," I said sincerely.

"We have known of two other cases something like this," he went on. "In one case the young lady was never found. In the other she was found, poor girl, in a way too late . . . she is traveling abroad now with her parents: I think they hope to stay until the incident is forgotten. I do not suppose she will enter society again until she is a much older woman, if at all. The fact that Isobel was sent away is a clue," he added abruptly. "The poor child is disfigured; her servant is old. The people behind the attempt on you want beauty, young girlhood."

I shivered a little. "For—what?"

"For the vilest of purposes," he said gravely, "a cruel and evil thing of which it is hard to speak to a pure woman . . . We think the attempt to kidnap you has behind it a corps of wicked men and women who are paid to find fresh beauty and innocence to supply the houses of ill-fame that flourish in this city." His arm tightened about me.

I was safe at home. The morning sunlight made a broad band across the floor. It glittered on the ordered silver and damask, the bouquet in its epergne. His arm held me. Yet I lay back, faint for the moment.

"It is dreadful," I said, "but as you say I am glad to feel it is no doing of Eugenia's."

"Had you any reason to?"

"The reason was that Isobel told me, as I went to see Miss Abigail, that the housekeeper knew something of my mother—" I stopped. "But she wasn't the housekeeper—but Eugenia had said it—oh, it is all so tangled."

"They don't have one," he said thoughtfully. "I wonder—"

137

I watched him a moment, then said, "Mark, how could that man who pretended he was their major-domo know those things: that the Olivers were away, that we were coming there? He had drugged Miss Letitia and the maid."

"Who knows?" he said. And then, as though trying to explain away to himself any other possibility, he said, "A tradesman's helper, any servant in the Astor House or Miss Abigail's hotel. The thing has its evil meshes through the city. The poor girl who was retrieved from that life of shame by a chance I would rather not speak of—a young man who pitied and believed her—was returning from boarding school to be met at the station by her mother's maid. The woman who met her, she said, told her in pretty broken English that she was the latest engaged *fille de chambre;* the other was ill. The last she remembered was, after going with the woman to Delmonico's, feeling dizzy after one cup of coffee . . ."

"How dreadful!" I said. "How do you know?"

"Edgar is one of a committee of gentlemen who are trying to stamp it out," he said. "Laura, for all her light gayety, has helped more than one poor girl to lead a new life. There is an institution where they are given a second chance of goodness and decent self-support, if they are in need. Oh, little love, let us not speak of it again. Tomorrow, if you are rested enough—indeed, if you're not—we start for a month's second honeymoon in St. Augustine."

CHAPTER ELEVEN

Soft as the voice of an angel, —
Breathing a lesson unheard,
Hope, with her gentle persuasion
Whispers a comforting word.
ALICE HAWTHORNE

I remember St. Augustine as a place of soft winds and blue waves, of summer weather in November, of the friendliness and gayety of the young officers of the garrison who had known Mark in the Florida war. We left it reluctantly: we had stayed longer than we planned. But Laura wrote, "The season will be over if you keep on hiding in your honeymoon Paradise: I have promised my friends to show them my loveliest of new cousins: they will think me a deceiver!"

And it was good, after all, to be back in the beautiful old Grammercy Park house. And Laura, dining with us next evening, pointed out that the cards in the salver in the hall were piled high. "Practically all of the *ton* have left cards and invitations, and she's not even formally introduced yet!"

Mark said, "It sounds as if I'd have small chance of seeing anything of my wife. I must take measures."

Laura looked serious. "I know you too well," she said. "I hope you don't mean that."

"The Red Castle is empty, dearest Laura, and it is time its master and mistress took over, if only for a short while. The overseer has been writing me more and more plaintively." He smiled at my unprepared look, and said, "Do not look so troubled, my dear. Cousin Abigail will have left everything in excellent order, and has promised to return for a week to ceremonially hand the reins over to you, Perdita. For myself, I've come and gone there, of course, since my childhood; since the tragedy of my uncles' drowning off Long Island I have been more or less regarded as the heir to the place, I suppose. There's a good deal of business to discuss with old Van Brunt."

Laura took it easily. "What you will do you will, I suppose —you Harradines! You must be back, though, well before Lent. *Foi de gentilhomme?*"

"*Foi de gentilhomme,*" he repeated.

So, after a few days' rest in the city, our carriage, luxurious with fur rugs and footwarmers, came from the stables in the mews behind our house, and we were on our way back along the Bloomingdale Road to the Red Castle. I could not but remember the other drive with Mark after our marriage. I was no longer the rash child who had ventured her life and happiness on a man from whom she hoped, at best, to win kindness. I was a loved and guarded wife. And the Red Castle, where I had come, grateful to be half companion, half *souffre-douleur* for Isobel's moods, was mine now as mistress. I had done so little to deserve it all, I thought. But I would deserve it. I would try. I said the last words aloud, unwittingly, and heard my husband's soft laugh.

"Whatever it is," he said, "you are not to try. You are to be exactly what you are if you wish to please me."

Miss Abigail, of course, expected us. But I had not been prepared for our homecoming. As we entered the driveway we could see that the Red Castle was lighted from top to bottom. The great stone hall sconces, as we stood within the doors, were alight; so were the tall wax candles thick in the chandeliers. The servants were drawn up to welcome us; the butler and housekeeper, the other servants, in their liveries. And Cousin Abigail, gay for once in her wide hooped maroon taffeta with her gold chain and bracelets, came with hands out to us both, kissing and welcoming us. Isobel stood smiling beside her. My own Janet Mackenzie, too, smiled at me from among the maids, and followed us up presently with the footmen who carried our portmanteaux.

I forgot, and almost turned at my own room. But Mark's hand on my arm guided me in time to the master bedroom at the stairhead. It was a suite I had never entered, bright with astral lamps, warm with its great heaped hearthfire, luxurious with its brocaded chairs and *chaises longues*, its great bed with its satin counterpane. There were doors to dressing-room, bathroom and boudoir.

"You are tired," Mark said, untired himself as ever. He untied my bonnet, lifted my cloak from my shoulders, and established me on the *chaise longue* across the bedfoot. "I must go down to see if the horses are in the right place." He spoke to Janet, who stood waiting. "I am leaving your mistress in good hands, I know," he said.

Janet's friendly hands were about me again, changing my shoes for slippers, loosening my stays and wrapping me in my warm rose negligee with the swansdown trimmings. "The Major says if you want me I may come back with you," she said happily.

"I do want you," I said. "We spoke about it before we came." My eyelids drooped as I saw her face lighting. I was sleepy after the long drive. When I awakened, Janet had gone, my unpacking all done and a dinner dress she knew I liked laid out. Mark came in from his dressing-room, changed for evening. "Don't bother to call your maid back," he said.

"It's almost dinnertime. I'll help you with your fastenings and lacing if you need it, as I did in St. Augustine."

I could help myself, as he well knew. I smiled at him, and spoke drowsily without thinking.

"But you said Eugenia wouldn't be here—"

"Wake up, my dear! No more she is. Did you dream it?"

"No—yes—" I said. "What made me think so? Oh, I know—her footman Petronius was among the servants in the hall when we came."

"Possibly he's staying here to look after Miss Anna," he said. "She was his charge too, I think. I suppose by now she's pretty old and needs more attention."

"Miss Anna? But I didn't know we had any visitors. When did she come?" I was up now, slipping on my hoop and its covering silk petticoat, and lifting the blue taffeta. The gong for dinner rang just then: I hurried to fasten my bodice, and Mark laughed and took my hands away in a teasing way he had, and did it for me. As we came down the stair he answered me.

"Oh, didn't you know about her? Just one of Cousin Abigail's pensioners, a connection, I think. She was here, though, as far as I know, before my grandfather died. I think it was kept rather quiet because she was a little eccentric or something. One of those penniless elderly ladies prosperous families keep somewhere, poor thing. I don't believe she likes to see people. I saw her once in a while when I was a boy, exploring the top rooms. It seemed to frighten her rather. And Petronius—yes, that's why, I think, he's staying—was there waiting on her, and lectured me. So incidentally did my grandfather. You know how people are about kinfolk who are a little odd." We had reached the dining-room door. "Ask Cousin Abigail about her, why don't you?" he said. "You're one of the family now."

I did know how families were about such dependents. I

142

remembered a farmer whose place I had visited once or twice when the little daughter of the house was too ill to bring us butter and eggs. Eliza had sent me with a basket to be packed, and as I went with Dora's brother to get my pony from their barn somebody banged on an attic window. I looked up, to see a grinning face with a mop of tangled hair. I saw that the window was barred. "Oh," I said to Zach, "Oh, what was that?"

"Oh, that's only Obadiah," he said shamefacedly. "He haint no business at that window. Somebody must a' forgot to bring his dinner. Don't tell nobody you saw him, except your uncle, he knows. They might want to take him off to the poor farm. Dora says you always stick to what you promise."

"I promise not to tell," I said, but naturally I was curious, and asked my uncle next time I was alone with him.

"It's the Ebbitts' oldest son," he said. "Poor Obadiah is an idiot. People don't like it known when they have relations who are afflicted. It's partly shame and partly dread of how the boy might be treated in an asylum." My eyes must have widened, for he went on. "It's common enough, I'm sorry to say, dear. Every so often you find, or don't find, a crazy old Uncle Zeke or Aunt Elvira kept in some villager's attic room, and the family very silent about it till they die, and sometimes after. They are usually kindly treated."

It worried me a little. But the Ebbitts were kind people. When Dora was well and bringing the butter and eggs again I said nothing to her. . . .

The Somerwells had been like the rest, that was all. I thought of the great parties that had been held for Eugenia, the lighted towers one could see across the river, and all the time the poor woman, "a little odd," alone up there. . . .

Cousin Abigail's arm came round me, leading me to what had been her place at the table's head. I was laughing and protesting and she was insisting. "You're the mistress of the manor now," she said, smiling, and Mark, at the foot, nodded. Presently they were deep in matters of the estate, the tenants, the crops, the rentals, the prospects of the year. I had not realized before what a domain it was that I, too, had responsibility for in my way. After dinner the overseer was coming to talk the affairs of the place over with Mark.

"It will be a relief to have all this off my female shoulders," Cousin Abigail said. I thought she meant it. I thought, too, what a selfless person she was; a life given to taking charge of two high spirited girls and an estate not her own. Some women would have resented me. But neither she nor Isobel did.

Isobel seemed, indeed, for her lighthearted, and prettier than usual. Across from me, next to the candles, she sat in her pretty frock, pale blue to my dark blue. Only a little of the scar showed. She was covering it better than usual, I thought. Then I saw that her cheeks were a little pinker than usual, and that her eyes looked even larger and bluer because of their darkened lashes. She must have a new and very good maid. Surely, I thought, there might be gentlemen who would love her for her prettiness as well as her dowry.

She had seen my glance. We knew each other so well. She nodded and spoke under cover of the business talk. "Yes—I have a new maid," she said as if I had spoken. "She is good, don't you think? French."

"You were always pretty," I said sincerely, "but you are lovelier now than ever. And oh, darling, you've stopped brooding about it, haven't you, now that it scarcely shows? You are so beautiful!"

The blue eyes brightened. Was everything coming at once? For my Isobel was more a happy and carefree girl than I had ever seen her.

"No," she said. She dropped her voice. She leaned closer. "I met a gentleman when I was visiting Mrs. De Pauw in

144

Tarrytown. I think—I think he really likes me. I want to show you his daguerreotype."

Her hand came out of her pocket. "Oh, do show me," I murmured. She laid the small morocco case in my hand under the table, its fastening unhooked. I looked down at a man's face: dark as Mark's but unlike it in every other way. It was a long narrow face; there was a small pointed mustache and a goatee. The lips, thin and decided, smiled a little scornfully; so did the half-shut eyes. It charmed, but it looked also as if it judged arrogantly. Unmistakably a gentleman: foreign-looking, though that might have been because of the furred cloak across one shoulder.

"He is handsome," I said sincerely. "He looks like a Frenchman."

"No, he is American," she said. "But he is of French descent. His name is Etienne Ducross. And he says—he says that if I come to New York this winter he will accept the invitation of a bachelor friend to stay the winter with him. If we remain in Peekskill he will take lodgings in Tarrytown. He can go anywhere, of course; he has his own equipage, beautiful horses and traveling carriage . . . Oh, Dita, he is wealthy —I need not be afraid of *that*." I knew what she meant; the old fear of being courted only for her money.

And then we were moving back to the little withdrawing room as we had always done. Miss Abigail went on talking to Mark a little longer about the farms and the tenantry, before she summoned Isobel and me in the old way to the piano. I remember that we sang "Whispering Hope" at the end . . . the duet Miss Abigail liked best:

> *Soft as the voice of an angel,*
> *Breathing a lesson unheard,*
> *Hope, with her gentle persuasion*
> *Whispers a comforting word.*

145

Isobel had a lovely contralto, but till now she had never been willing to sing before anyone but her aunt and our teacher. She did now. Oh, I thought, she is really happy.

Then the bailiff came and Mark went to talk to him in the office, the little room where the business of the estate had been conducted since time immemorial. Presently Isobel said she was sleepy and summoned Keziah and went upstairs to bed. I took the opportunity to ask Miss Abigail, as Mark had suggested, about the woman housed, nearly unknown, high in the Red Castle. I think I was a little selfishly afraid she might be my responsibility now. But Miss Abigail, when I asked her, said not: Petronius took complete care of her. She was, as Mark had supposed, a connection of the Somerwells. "Her mind is a little strange, I think from being too much alone," Miss Abigail said. "Though now I think of it, I was told that she had suffered a severe shock before she came here, and that at one time she was considered talented as a sculptress, and had been a pupil of Hiram Powers."

I had seen Mr. Powers' famous statue *The Greek Slave*, of course.

"But she must have been good, then," I said. "Could nothing be done to make her keep on having an interest in it?"

"Old Eugenius Somerwell left orders in his will that she should be kept supplied with clay and wax for modeling," Miss Abigail said. "I remember that now. And there was a sum for her support. He never forgot anything. When the slaves were freed, I remember hearing, a number of women ran off and left their babies. He left money to have them cared for, also. That was—let me see—1826. I think Miss Anna does some modeling. I remember some charming statuettes under glass in one of the guest rooms. When Mark takes you over the Castle you must look for them. But I don't think she has gone on doing it. When I see her she always seems very sad and quiet."

146

"Oh," I said impulsively, "it seems such a monotonous life. Could she not be given rooms nearer the rest of the family, and have something to do with people?"

"I don't think she would want to. She has become the complete recluse," Miss Abigail said. "She has depressed moods, I understand from Dr. De Witt and Petronius. And—well, till now, we have felt it was best to keep any knowledge of her from Isobel. She is so sensitive herself, remember. Indeed, I think old Mr. Somerwell felt that the less known of Miss Anna the better. After all she is a Somerwell. You know that quotation, 'Do good by stealth and blush to find it fame!'"

From what little I had heard of Mark's grandfather, he had been a harsh and domineering old gentleman, and it seemed to me much more likely that if Miss Anna's shock had brought on permanent fits of depression and inability to earn her living, he wanted it kept quiet as a small blot on the scutcheon. But it was not my affair; though I confess it seemed to me too bad that she was kept such a secret. The Red Castle had enough stories about it already. But I could scarcely keep my eyes open, and Miss Abigail saw it.

"Go on to bed, dear child," she said. "I'll tell Mark I sent you when he is through with Van Brunt."

But when Mark came upstairs I wakened enough to ask him the one thing I hadn't asked Miss Abigail. "What shall you do about Miss Anna?" I said. "Is it in your grandfather's will that she always has a home here?"

"No," he said. "And I may say that I do not approve of the custom of housing eccentric connections. Dr. De Witt and I have talked it over, before there was any question of its being my responsibility. We agreed that a trustworthy retreat where Miss Anna could have modern medical care was better than the most luxurious solitude like hers. But don't worry

147

about the poor old soul tonight, my love; she's usually gloomily content enough among her waxwork."

As always, his swift mind had dealt with the problem wisely. The fire sprang up a little and was low again: its warmth made the room nearly like summer. The wind made only a delighting background for my comfort. I sank deep in our luxurious bed, and hoped sleepily that poor Miss Anna, alone upstairs with her modeling, was not too unhappy. Out of my happiness I began to pray for her. But I was asleep before the end of the prayer.

Next morning Mark took me with him, riding the estate. The tenants must know their little mistress, he said. Many of them, naturally, I had already known from my earlier stay. Mark they had of course known. I was glad to see how they liked him: and I think me. As I rode down a narrow lane between two of the meadows ahead of him he said from behind me, "That's a new habit, isn't it, darling? Not the fatal one you lent poor Drusilla, that Eugenia used as a pretext for her temper?"

"Oh yes," I said over my shoulder, "we had been holding a review of my wardrobe, and Cousin Abigail and the seamstress both said it was past praying for."

"I almost feel like praying about it!" he said. "If Eugenia hadn't made her scene over it, where would you and I be now?"

"If I know you, you would be back among the Apaches, having done your duty by Eugenia," I said, "and I would be Isobel's companion, and trying to get over being in love with you. I think I would have asked to go back to the ferryhouse . . . Mark! Presently I must cross to it: I want to see them all again."

"Why not go tomorrow?" he said. "And I will escort you if I may."

"Oh would you, Mark? I would be so glad, and so would they."

"It's a reward of merit, darling. We are taking the keys to your safe, and going through every inch of the things your mother left. My military mind may see or find something you have overlooked. Seriously, dear, I want you to feel that everything has been done that can be."

"It's very good of you," I said sincerely.

"No—it's a sensible thing to do. You were in grief when you looked before. We may find something: if not, as I said, you won't awake at night wondering."

I had done just that. I wondered how he knew. And then we were at the overseer's house, and his wife and children were running out to greet us and group round us in great excitement at seeing me again, married and chatelaine now.

CHAPTER TWELVE

♖

Fold carefully the broidered wool,
Its silken wreaths will ne'er grow old,
And lay the linen, soft and cool
Above it gently, fold on fold,
So lie the snows on that soft breast
Where mortal garb will never rest.
ROSE TERRY COOKE

So it was that next morning we summoned the ferryman. It was Andy who came for us, glad enough to see me to break from his usual taciturnity. Lorena's welcome at the dock, and Eliza's rushing from her kitchen in the old way, kept us for a little while before Mark could state our errand. Even young Joseph, shyly coming up to make his bow, rather terrified at the Major, had to be praised, and his share of bringing him over that first night, thanked. Mark never forgot anybody or anything.

My room and Isobel's were unchanged; I was touched to see how carefully they had ordered and kept everything of mine as it had been. Only the little safe that had been locked behind old Mr. Van Dorn's picture was double-locked in Isobel's room now.

"You want everything, sir?" Andy asked.

"Everything."

Andy brought the little trunk and portmanteau which had been my mother's, setting them by my bed. I opened them and spread their contents on the counterpane and he went. We began with what jewelry I had left in its case on my last visit, beyond wedding and betrothal rings, which I'd kept. They were not here; I had them with my own jewels. We lifted out and carefully looked at everything that was left. We reread her husband's letter, which I had kept locked there, but discovered nothing new.

"It is the letter of a man," Mark said, "who had some strong reason for keeping his marriage a secret. Possibly he was dependent financially on his father or some older relative."

His quick, thorough hands went deftly all through her other possessions: reticules, handkerchief boxes, trinket boxes, daintily folded veils and gloves and ribbons. He even pulled her little prayerbook and hymnal apart from their slip-fastening together, and shook them.

It had not occurred to me to go through her clothes before. Mark told me to do it, saying that a woman would know more about their ins and outs than a man. But he watched me carefully: cloaks, sacques, shawls, finally the gowns. I was nearly done when we came to a garment of somewhat older fashion than the rest: a morning gown of heavy changeable silk in rose and violet. It was buttoned from throat to hem, with a delicate lace fichu. I shook it out, and as the easiest way of searching it slipped it on, sliding my hands into its gathered pockets. My right hand touched something smooth and hard, and I pulled it out with a little cry.

It was a red-colored ivory chessman. I laid it in Mark's hand. "That's all," I said, and slid my hand down again—and

151

brought it out. It had not been all. Under it had been a piece of crumpled paper.

"It's a red castle," he said. "Is there anything on that bit of paper?"

I stared at it and took it to the window. "Get the magnifying glass from my uncle's desk," I said. He was back with it quickly, and held it. "Queen of the red CASTLE," I made it out to read. "Come."

"Don't you understand?" he said. "She came, that wild night, and brought you and her possessions. She had been summoned to the Red Castle!"

"But, Mark, it doesn't make sense! The letter begs her to be patient a little longer, and the chessman and the note send for her!"

"It makes sense," he said, "if the letter was written first and kept, and then she was summoned."

"But—" I said. "Why in the world the token, instead of another letter?"

"My darling, the answer to that lies in what we do not know. The next thing to do is to finish our search: after that to find out if your uncle's servants knew anything about the token and its significance if any."

I curbed my impatience and slipped off the pretty, faded garment, and we went on till the search was done. Finally everything was back in safe, trunk and portmanteau except the letter and the red ivory castle.

But Andy, Lorena and Eliza, questioned, knew nothing of the chess castle. Madame Honor, they said, did not know how to play chess. And the only chessmen that had ever been in the ferryhouse were of black and white wood. I remembered them, of course. My uncle and I used to play with them in the winter evenings.

So there was no more to do than to return to the Red

Castle, our own Red Castle that was so lighted and friendly now. After dinner was over, and Isobel and I were at the piano, I heard Mark say, beneath the music of the "Dying Poet," "Cousin Abigail, who resided here, or visited here, the year that Madame Honor came to the ferryhouse?"

She laid down her crewelwork. Isobel went on playing— she had come to the third variation—but I listened hard. "I cannot remember accurately," Miss Abigail said. "I did not come here to stay, you remember, until after the little girls were orphaned. I was with my mother in our house in Peekskill. I—there was quite a time when I did not visit here; my mother was ailing."

I remembered Eliza's story of the jilting which had taken place when Miss Abigail first visited the Red Castle. She went on speaking quietly; "Petronius or old Keziah might remember. Would you ring the bell, my dear boy?"

The footman came and was sent for Petronius, who came promptly and stood bowing in the door, dignified and elegant as ever. I glanced at him and remembered that I had been told he came of aristocratic white stock on one side.

"Many guests came and went, of course, madam," he said. "We did not have house guests who stayed long that year," when the question was put to him.

"Who lived here?" Mark asked. The man looked a little surprised. "Only Miss Eugenia's parents, Mr. Eugenius and Mrs. Juliana Somerwell," he said. "From time to time Miss Isobel's father and mother, Mr. Nicholas and Mrs. Sibylla Somerwell. And of course, their daughters," he said. "The Nicholases had a home on Long Island, you remember."

"And of course my grandfather," Mark said.

"Of course the older Mr. Eugenius," Petronius amended. "I took him for granted, sir. Miss Eleanor—your mother, Major, Mrs. Harradine—was the eldest, as of course you

153

know. She had been married and living in the city at least ten years then. Your own parents came and went also, though not frequently."

"And you do not remember the names of any house guests."

"No, Major. Mr. Van Brunt might possibly."

The family, and a small train of anonymous guests . . .

We were back in the city in another fortnight. Miss Abigail and Isobel had returned to Peekskill, leaving us the Castle to ourselves, nearly two weeks before we returned. I would have liked to stay longer: after all, it was my own country; but once in the Grammercy Park house there was a strange sense of relief, of lightheartedness, as if I had moved to a new chapter of my life. I locked the red chessman and its scrawled note into my mother's jewelcase, which I had brought back in toto, and put it out of my mind.

That was one part of the relief. The other was that Isobel loved and was loved. I realized now that under everything I had felt worried and perhaps a little guilty, because of my fear that she had loved Mark. I had not wanted to admit this to myself, but the prick of distress had been there in my mind. Now it was gone. And everything was as light and bright and luxurious as always, from the glittering chandelier in the wide hall with its statues and portraits, to the shining mahoganies and sweeping velvet curtains of our bedroom, with the plate glass windows framing the brightclad children in the park.

Mark came upstairs and stood by me, as I stood by the window on a morning. He too had been a little troubled about Isobel, I thought, for he said, "This suitor of Isobel's seems in earnest. He is apparently a close friend of young Arthur Lawrence, who was a lieutenant in my battalion, and like me is back at his home in the city here. The Lawrences are connections of ours, you know. I understand Lawrence is to have him as a more or less permanent house guest this winter, if Isobel and Cousin Abigail are in town."

I said thankfully, "Yes, Isobel said as much. I am so glad."

"And I," Mark said quietly, "am doubly glad. My too conscientious little girl, I won't have to see your bright face turn grave over those long, crossed, close-written epistles of my grievous cousin's any more—or at least I hope not. She'll be writing loveletters to Ducross instead. Also"—by now he had pulled me back against him and the rest of what he was saying was with his cheek against mine—"I can say now what would have seemed jealous to say before. My dear, from what I can see and have been told, you have felt yourself responsible for Isobel's moods, Isobel's supposed tragedy, since you were both seven years old. No money or protection could pay for the devotion, the companionship, the patience, you have given her. As the saying is, you have carried her on your hands. Heaven only knows"—his hold tightened—"how it is you are lighthearted and loving, unscarred in soul and mind, after half a lifetime with that little female misanthrope!"

"But, dearest—" I faltered, turning from the laughing children below to look into his eyes, "they have done so much for me, Cousin Abigail and Isobel. They have shared Isobel's education with me. They have taken me into their household and given me love—"

"Who that knew you wouldn't give you love?"

"It has been done," I said demurely. He smiled, and then went on seriously again. "Perdita, your belief in your duty to Isobel is of such long standing that you may find it difficult to alter. Yet I ask you to."

"Why, my first love and duty are to you, of course," I said. "But why should I alter my feeling to Isobel?"

"Because long habit has made you feel that whatever she demands of you must be given. My dearest, she is spoiled because of that scar, which scarcely shows today, and which has not hindered her being loved and sought. Her demands on your love and time and sympathy, I tell you again, are excessive. Abigail, you, her nurse, have all spoiled her. I don't blame you, child, it was made your religion when you were very young. Your very sweetness and unselfishness have victimized you. You have a right to your own life. Moreover, she needs you no longer."

It was a strange idea to me. It was like one of those moments when suddenly a wrongly seen street's direction moves from right to left, from east to west, in the mind. I was silent; my world had turned.

"But Mark—there's nothing *you* could ask of me I wouldn't do. And that can't be wrong—"

"It can be wrong," he said. "I can only tell you that it is my hope and pleasure to think of your welfare before my own, my wife; which balances the fact that you think of mine before yours, as well. That is the proof of actual love, Perdita. Isobel does not give it to you. My little love, I ask an alteration in your whole thought and feeling, but it is for your good and mine, your right and mine."

I stood there shaken. It was a reversal of lifelong feeling and belief; the road I had thought went immutably east had whirled to west. It was right to be what I had thought selfish.

"You are right," I said. "But it will take time."

He smiled. I knew him wise, and that it was mine to obey. "Yes, it will take time," he said. "I am afraid you'll feel guilty toward Isobel for a while. But rather that than endanger again something more dear to me than anything else in the world."

It came clearer. I had unwittingly been sharing my allegiance. I found I could smile up, answering his smile. I remembered a new book he had given me, a strange wild poem called "Maud," by the English poet Tennyson, and what it said:

> *"If I be dear to someone else*
> *Then I should be to myself more dear,"*

I said the words aloud.

"Thank you for understanding," he said. "And now we'll forget all this lecturing. You're not a battalion, to be ruled! And I came up, actually, to bring you this letter from Laura."

I took the scented gilt-edged note. It was, as I had thought, about her plans for introducing me into society.

I was a little frightened, of course, and a good deal excited. The others laughed at me. I would enjoy it, and so would everybody who knew me, Laura added encouragingly. And the evening came, with that swiftness evenings one dreads a little do come.

I should, I suppose, being a bride, have worn my wedding gown. But as it had only been the white muslin like Isobel's, its black ribbons hastily changed for rose, Laura decreed otherwise. The gown she and the mantua-maker created together was of heavy white satin. It had an overskirt draped above the wide-flowing skirt, of point lace, looped with orange blossoms. Orange blossoms caught back my curls. Just before Janet was through with me, Mark entered with his hands full of velvet boxes. I had expected to wear the emeralds he had bought at Tiffany's when we first came to the city. But these jewels were, though suited to my youth, more beautiful. An opal necklace framed, jewel by jewel, with diamonds; earrings, parure and bracelets matching, flashing their strange colors on my hair and neck and arms. Gesturing Janet aside, he arrayed me in them himself, and in spite of her presence bent and kissed me, and led me down to the waiting carriage, my cloak held close.

We were early, of course: but the musicians were beginning to play as we entered Laura's ballroom. Laura, dazzling in violet velvet and draping laces, as gay and careless as if she was receiving us for an evening alone, her diamonds only saved from too much glitter by the amethysts they surrounded, stood to meet us. Edgar, smiling and unmoved as always, stood behind her.

We had come, as Laura asked, a half hour before the guests were to come. I suppose I should have been frightened, but suddenly I felt lifted above the terror of my *debut*. Everything was wonderful: it would go on being wonderful.

The ballroom was on the second floor, the length of the house. The garlanded walls, heavy with roses, the scent of the flowers and of perfumed powder, the gay leaping music, the brilliant lights, made it fairyland. I was introduced to beautiful girls, jeweled matrons, bowing smiling gentlemen. But presently I was led to a tall elderly lady with sweeping black velvets about her, and a tiara on her high-piled white hair.

"Mrs. Harper, this is our new cousin, our little debutante . . ." I scarcely recall the rest of the introduction: I was so held by the strength of personality, the dominant charm, of the old lady. She greeted me with warm kindness; her eyes looked me through and through and seemed satisfied by what she saw.

"I am sure she is as charming as she is lovely to look at," she said. "You must see to it that I see more of her, dear Laura. We are happy for our war hero."

Mark, behind me, bowed. "You cannot be happier than I am," he said lightly, and she smiled as he led me away.

We were, I realized as we took our places, the leading couple of the first quadrille; the dance was begun. But it was not, as I had feared it would be, hard. Tonight everything seemed easy and right; the dream would not break.

It did not. When we returned to Laura, looking childlike among the row of chaperones, she said, "Bravo, my ingenue!"

I sank down by her, puzzled. "What do you mean?" I asked. "I was a little afraid at first, but the quadrilles went well."

"I mean that you're among the chosen, my child. Madame Harper is our arbiter of fashion as her father was before her. You have passed with flying colors. You will be in the height of the *ton*, my dear."

Before I could ask more or reply, a gentleman was bowing before me and being introduced, and asking my hand for the lancers. When they ended there was a touch on my shoulder that I knew, and Mark was laughing as he swept me into the waltz.

"I'm making sure that I'm the first to waltz with you," he said. "Indeed, I'm not sure that I want anyone else to."

I was not sure that I did either, as I was swept along in his embrace to the music. It was like flying to heaven. His arms tightened. The lights, the perfumes, the music, the floating in loved arms . . . "Oh, I wish it would never cease!" I said before I thought: and then flushing at my own boldness, I looked up and saw the wish in his eyes too.

The next was a redowa, gay and quick, more like playing a game than dancing; I do not know who was my partner, one of the young gentlemen I had met at one of Laura's parties. I was glad I could work off my excitement, more glad that the close hold of the waltz was not repeated. When it was done I was a little tired, and Mark, who, I had learned, saw everything about me, was near again. "Would you like to rest in the conservatory through the next quadrille?" he said. I nodded, and he led me out to where Laura's conservatory blossomed along the ballroom's side. There was a seat under one of the low flowering trees. He said, "Do you know that everyone is asking who you are? Laura is right, you are the belle of the evening! I am hiding you a little. There were too many gentlemen crowding near you."

I had scarcely noticed it. I had, indeed, thought that this was the way it always happened; that it was only a part of courtesy that the gentlemen had clustered round me at the end of each dance. "I am glad," I said. "I want you to be proud of me."

"I couldn't be more than I was before!" But I knew that I had something now to bring him. Madame Harper's accolade, the admiration, they were what his wife should have, should be. His choice was being justified.

We were happily silent for a short time, there among the flowers and tropical sweetness. Mark was just rising and laying my hand on his arm when a footman entered and spoke to him.

"My help is needed, it seems, love," he said. "Madame Harper asks for me. It's nothing important, I'll be back shortly. Wait for me in Emily's garden."

I walked slowly to what looked like the conservatory's end. But what looked like a curtain of vines was actually hiding a little door. Only the family knew of it. I opened it and went in, greeted by a breath of lilac. Edgar's mother, who had been Emily, had made it or had it made when she was a bride. I went down steps to the ground floor, which I knew was level with the lawn.

"It's well enough to have conservatories that are scenes from the tropics," she had said when she came back from her wedding journey, all magnolias and strange heavy scents. "But I want one secret part where there's country spring and summer in winter!"

And so—at more expense, I was told, than the tropical trees and blossoms had meant, it was done, for the Harradine men were like that. How I do not know, except that mould was brought from the country and somehow the soil beneath it protected from winter cold. And there still, watched by careful florists, lilacs and syringas bloomed, monthly roses and bridal wreath. There were strips of lawn and beds of violets and pansies in their turn. Only close friends and relatives knew it existed. Only a few of these had keys. Above an invisible glass roof were the winter stars. I stood there, drawing a long breath of pleasure in the faint moonlight. Then I moved a little way to find a rustic bench I knew was there. It was not empty.

A slender, slightly bowed gentleman in point-device evening dress which had something strange about it rose and bowed deeply to me in the half light. As my eyes grew used, I saw that he was old and frail, and had been very handsome once, for his features were delicate, and his white hair, longer than today's fashion, still curled thickly. The hand he held out to me, smiling as at an old friend, was half hidden by a ruffle, and his stock had something lacy about it. He was dressed, indeed, as one's grandfather might have been in youth; like a portrait of President Jefferson's time. For a moment I started back, almost thinking this was a ghost from the youth of that willful Emily Harradine whose garden out of time and space it was still. He spoke softly.

"But, my dear lady, what a pleasure and surprise to find you here! in our dear Emily's garden after losing you so long!" he said. He gestured to the seat beside him, and mechanically I sat down. I knew I had never seen him before. But he was speaking eagerly, and smiling, leaning toward me. He was very, very old, I could see now; his voice, elegant and soft, was an old man's. "My dear Melinda and I wondered so often what had become of you. The little cottage *ornee* was empty when we returned to our summer home in Hoboken, that last June. You had all been gone, the neighbors said, since the early winter before. We supposed you had joined, Edward, with your little girl, was it in New York? We thought you would have written . . ."

He stopped and drew back. I had, I suppose, stared instead of replying. "But dear Honor, have you forgotten us? It is so long . . . time is so strange . . ."

My heart beat violently. He was so old that time meant little to him. He took me—oh, it must be—for my mother.

"I am her daughter—Honor's daughter—" I said. "I am the little girl you remember—oh, tell me what her name was, who Edward was—" Before I had done I knew that my violent tone had disturbed the delicate balance of his memory. He moved back and gasped a little. He spoke, as I heard steps behind us.

"But surely you are Honor—"

I turned; it was Mark, and with him a man who was obviously a valet. The servant moved forward, and in an accustomed way bent over the old gentleman, an arm behind him.

"Oh, Mr. Harper," he said, "this is too much for you. The doctor said you were not to rise—"

His face flushed. "Not arise and dress when I was due to lead the cotillion?" he said. "I came here to Mrs. Addington Harradine's private garden to rest. I have found an old friend," he went on, unheeding. "Young gentleman—you must be a Harradine, to have entrance here—will you tell this officious servant of mine to remove himself. I am about to lead the cotillion with, yes, it must be this lady, my wife's young friend. My daughter-in-law will tell you . . ." As he spoke his head fell back.

The valet said, alarmed, "I was only out of his rooms a short while, sir: Madame Harper—he sent me to her with a message"—he had smelling salts in his hand: he held them to the old gentleman's face. They seemed to have no effect.

"Dr. Van Andem is among the guests, Perdita," Mark said. "Will you wait here with them a few minutes, my dear?"

He was back in less time than seemed possible, with the doctor, and Laura. It was a prolonged fainting fit; the frail old head lay on his servant's shoulder. Presently Mr. Harper was carried out through the gardener's entrance, and to a room on the ground floor, out of sight and hearing of the ballroom. Laura summoned Madame Harper: there was a cot found from somewhere. It was all done quietly and swiftly: I could hear the music, now, from upstairs, as the three men carried the old gentleman, still unconscious, into a servants' carryall from the stables behind, where he could be laid stretched out on the long side seat. His daughter-in-law followed. She turned, a foot on the step, to say graciously, "You were wonderful, my dear Mrs. Harradine. My poor old father-in-law—he was the *arbiter elegantiaum* in his day. We did not dream he could hear the music."

"I suppose it was like the scent of the battle to the war-horse."

Old Mr. Harper wakened a little as he was carried into the vehicle. His eyes turned on me, where I stood heedless of the cold, a cloak I had snatched from the hall over my shoulders. "Honor, child—" he called feebly. I set a foot on the step; but the coachman, who could not see me, started the horses, and Mark caught me just in time.

"I must go with him—he wanted me—" I gasped. "He knows."

But the carryall was halfway down the square. "Come in, my darling," Mark said. "Their house is nearby. He will be better off in his own bed."

Laura had gone already. The music was louder, as we entered again, the lights raying out on us.

"Old Peter Harper—you must have heard of him," my husband said. I shook my head. "He must be nearly ninety.

163

He ruled society in his day. His daughter-in-law has his mantle to an extent. Nobody realized he was able to leave his rooms. He had not been himself for a long time now. He must have always kept Aunt Emily's key to her garden."

The waltz was continuing: an encore, I supposed. We mounted the wide staircase to the ballroom, and Mark swept me into his arms, and we were moving to the music again.

"You were disturbed, love," he said. "What did the old man say that made you try to follow him into the carryall?"

"He spoke—of something I promised to forget," I said.

"But if I ask you will you not tell me?"

"He called me—Honor. He asked why we had left the cottage *ornee* next to his country place. He spoke of Edward —of the child." I stopped—in another moment I would be crying.

"But this is important, love. You must not be shut off from any road to actual knowledge of your identity. I've been concerned only to keep you from feeling that it mattered, when there seemed no road. We will follow this up tomorrow."

And then the waltz was done, and the gentleman whose name was next on my *carnet de bal* was bowing before me, I heard myself speaking lightly, moving away with him, racing through the polka which was next. But the music and the colorful dancers and the glittering rooms were like a bright mist, behind which was the reality of what old Mr. Harper would tell me.

CHAPTER THIRTEEN

Love rules the court, the camp, the grove,
And men below, and saints above,
For love is heaven, and heaven is love.
SIR WALTER SCOTT

After what seemed too long a time I made the gentleman of the moment bring me back to Laura. As I dropped into my seat beside her I saw something I could scarcely believe among the moving bright-colored dancers. A girl with yellow hair flying out behind her, brushing the wide skirts of an exquisite blue gown: a girl with great blue eyes, as she whirled, that laughed. As they swung closer, I knew her partner's face from somewhere. Of all people, Isobel! Isobel, who hated crowds, groups, anything public! The gentleman with her—yes, I recalled his face in her daguerrotype, now. The sleepy eyes, the smartly pointed mustache, the picturesque narrow pointed goatee. He was handsome, foreign looking, I thought, a little scornful looking even, as they came nearer in the pretty high-stepping dance, and paused before us.

"This is Mr. Ducross!" she said breathlessly. "We didn't tell you we were coming, dear Mrs. Edgar, it was to be a wonderful surprise. Oh, what a delightful ball! Mr. Ducross is staying with Mark's friend Mr. Lawrence here. They came together with me—"

Mr. Ducross bowed deeply, first to Laura, then to me. "It is shocking boldness," he said, smiling. "Miss Isobel tells me that hers heretofore has been a blanket refusal of all dances. But learning that this was the *debut* of her friend and almost sister, I persuaded her to take for granted that she would be welcome, refusal or none. Also Lieutenant Lawrence, Major Harradine's distant cousin and favorite subaltern, my host, was coming. Otherwise, dear ladies, I would have let Miss Isobel have her way."

It *was* shocking boldness in a way. But we could not do less than welcome them. As Laura said later, though Isobel had declined, she was not an extra young lady, but had brought an escort, guaranteed by a close friend. Presently Mark, courteous though a little less cordial than we women had known him to be, was dancing with Isobel and I with her suitor.

Later young Mr. Lawrence approached. I liked him: he was evidently devoted to Mark, and Mark seemed fond of him. He was a fresh-faced, half shy, half gay young man who, when we danced, spent most of the time talking about Mark. I had been told that his subalterns worshipped him, and evidently from what Arthur Lawrence said it was true. Like Mark, now the Mexican War was over he had a long furlough.

"I hope we shall see a good deal of you," I said sincerely. "My husband has spoken of you with affection."

He smiled with pleasure as he answered, "The Major has said that I am to haunt your door." He seemed almost immediately a friend.

When Isobel came back to me she said with that new brightness, "I knew it would be all right if I stayed with you

166

tonight. Aunt Abigail and I are coming up for the rest of the winter, but you know how long it takes her to pack and what she calls locking up. She'll be up in a couple of days, the suite is engaged at the same hotel. I knew it would be all right if I came to you. I sent old Keziah ahead: I have the red guest room."

It would have been a matter of course before Mark's talk with me. As it was, there was nothing to do but to say that I hoped Keziah had a comfortable room in the servants' quarters. After all, Isobel was still my friend and companion of a lifetime. And I was glad that things were becoming natural and happy for her.

"Come, talk to me while I undress," she said, when at last we were at home. After seeing us within, Mark had gone to send a servant to the Harper's house, to see if there was anything he could do for them: Madame Harper was a widow, and had lived alone with the old father-in-law. So I followed Isobel into her room, where her old nurse waited, nodding asleep in the rocker by the window. Now that the ball was over, my mind had fled back to old Mr. Harper and his words. So near the knowledge! I realized that I had not pushed very far down my desire to know. . . .

"Strange to go to my room, not yours," Isobel was saying as, leaving Keziah unwakened, she sat down on the bed and kicked off her slippers. "Do unhook my gown and corsets, dear," she added, as she had often. "You're so much quicker than Keziah." I stooped to do it for her. I found myself bringing her nightgown and dressing gown in the old way, as she sat down before the glass. She handed me a comb, and I began combing her curls out for the night. Her lace night-cap lay ready. "It's strange, too," she went on, "to think that this time next year it may be I who cannot ask you to talk in my bedroom, for fear of the impending gentleman!"

"Oh, then, everything is settled," I said happily.

"Nearly," she said. "There is something or other Etienne must finish, business connected with the late war, I think, before we can give it out."

"That should not be long, then," I said. I had her ready for bed: I kissed her goodnight and returned to my own room. Mark had not returned. Despite the thoughts that I could not change from the strange half-knowledge of the old gentleman's words, I was so tired from the unaccustomed long hours of dancing that I sank into a deep sleep almost at once: a sleep that lasted longer than I supposed it would. It had been past three when we returned.

I was awakened by Mark's lowered voice. He was dressed and standing by the door with Janet.

"No, don't wake her," he said. "Let her sleep the afternoon through if she will."

But I was awake. I turned to the watch that hung in its velvet case, as always, by my pillow. It was two in the afternoon.

"I'm awake, and it's time," I said to them, sitting up against my pillows. "I don't want you just yet, Janet. I'll rest a little longer." She curtsied and went, and I beckoned my husband. "Have you—" I asked, and could get no further. He came over and sat down on the bed by me, an arm round me.

"I went to the Harpers' house myself, dear," he said gently. "Madame Harper was alone with him excepting for the servants and I thought she might need me. I learned a little from her, but old Mr. Harper cannot tell you anything more, sweet."

I knew. I sat up against the pillows. "He is dead," I said.

"Yes," Mark said, "he was a very old man."

I was quiet for a long time, or what seemed so. Finally, because I thought Mark's face showed concern for me, I spoke.

"I think I understand. It isn't meant that I should know. I

168

promised before to put it all away from me, and I mean it still, my dear. And now—good heaven—I must rise and dress. You put me to shame—you have had so much less sleep than I, and you look untired. But you must be."

He shook his head. "It takes a good deal of lost sleep to tire me. I didn't sleep to speak of in Mexico and I was none the worse." I thought we had stopped talking about Mr. Harper, but he went on. "Now I will tell you what I know. As I think he said to you, he did own a summer estate in Hoboken, when it was a country place. When his wife died he sold it, against the wishes of his neighbors—for the new possessors took advantage of a street going through; and put up a row of brownstones. There's no such place any more, estate or cottage."

That door, too, was locked. So I accepted it . . .

After that the New York season caught us. We did—what did we not do? I remember one delightful evening of tableaux from the poets at Laura's: Mark, rather unwillingly, as the Corsair: Laura as Longfellow's Evangeline: I in a nun's robe as Constance de Beverley, about to be walled up for running off with Scott's Marmion: Isobel and Ducross as Geraint and Enid.

For Isobel and Ducross were asked to most of the parties that we were: the *soirees*, the musical evenings. And she did not seem to mind that it was because she was our cousin and I could chaperone her. Miss Abigail passed Isobel's responsibility to me, the old way, but it was nominal. There were no moods; she was gay: we still went pleasuring together, but with groups of other young men and girls.

There was enough to go pleasuring for. Ole Bull, the violinist, was performing in New York City that winter, and a young girl they called the Swedish Nightingale, a singer named Jenny Lind, with the gentlest of girlish manners and an exquisite voice, and two dazzling actors, the English

169

William Macready and the American Edwin Forrest, who were rivals for fame at the Astor Place Opera House. It was as if everything one could ask to see and hear was piled up for our pleasure, that wonderful shining snowy winter in the city.

Laura, presently, was planning a fancy ball, and had demanded our presence to discuss the details. I went to their house early, for Edgar and Mark had some business to discuss together at Edgar's office, and I liked playing with the children. They came in almost as I did, ruddy and muffled up in their scarfs, clinking their skates, and making a rush for me when they saw me alighting from my carriage. I went up to their playroom with them, and had to be summoned down by Laura. The gentlemen had come in together, and were having a cigar in the smoking room before they joined us where we sat in the drawing room with our tea. Laura and I had been talking, I remember, about the Rochester knockings as they were called. Some little country girls named Fox had insisted that there was a ghost in their cellar, a pedlar who said he had been murdered there. And Mr. Horace Greeley, who was the editor of the *Tribune*, believed it, and was bringing one of them on to the city to meet all sorts of people and be investigated. It was very exciting, though it did not seem as impossible to me as to Laura. I had heard too much of the Red Castle's strange legends to quite disbelieve. And then the gentlemen came in, still discussing politics. They both looked grave. "I am with Henry Clay," I remember Mark was saying. "Why not let the Southern states depart in peace?"

And Edgar, rather crossly, "Oh, that's a soldier, all for peace. The financial confusion—the crisis—"

Laura laughed and ran over to her husband. "That's enough, you old bear," she said, flinging her arms round him. "We have a crisis of our own to handle just now. How to tuck my fancy-dress ball into the busiest season I've ever known since

170

I made my *debut*. And Perdita must appear as Undine and ravish everyone!"

Mark smiled. "She was nearly Undine the first night I met her," he said. "She, and her young servant, who was doubtless a mask of Kuhleborn, rowed across the Hudson on the worst storm possible."

He had never before spoken of that wild night when he brought Drusilla Huntington across to the ferryhouse, and I caught my breath. And then Edgar said calmly, "I remember." And I realized that he too must know: that his philanthropies included the Underground Railroad as well as the rescue of lost women. Presently it was time to return: we were attending the Philharmonic that evening.

"And I hope it will cheer you up, dear boy," Laura said. "Some of the Corsair's gloom from the other night seems to have rubbed off on you."

He smiled and made some light reply. But it was true. He had seemed quieter than usual. I said so as we drove home, slipping my hand through his arm as we sat in the carriage. "Is there anything wrong except politics?" I asked, "or can't you tell me?"

"Nothing exactly wrong," he said, "except that I am afraid I must go on an unexpected mission."

"Military? Or may I go too?"

"I shall say so," he said. "And I can't take you. As a matter of fact, it is more trouble, in a minor way, about Drusilla Huntington—or Drusilla Eaton as she is now."

I shivered a little. I had hoped that all that was over. "I thought that she was safe in Canada now, and a married woman."

"So she is. This is not as much of a problem, love. It merely means a journey; and secrecy on your part and mine. Drusilla has written me, enclosing in a letter from Lieutenant Colonel Waring, who is Colonel of my regiment now. It

171

seems that Colonel Huntington left a considerable sum of money deposited in a Washington bank, in Drusilla's name.

"It is Drusilla's, of course; but as Washington City is slave-holding, in strict legality it belongs to her cur of a cousin. Waring cannot leave his military duties. Colonel Huntington's will, probated in the West, leaves everything to his daughter: I have only to present the power of attorney, draw the money and take it to them in Canada. It is hers by right, legal or not. She has sent me the power of attorney. She adds that they are in need of it. Her husband, who was a younger son, is settled with her in Canada, where he had purchased land, and is growing wheat. I imagine he has invested too deeply."

"But why doesn't her husband come for the money?"

"Because Stephen Huntington knew Cyril's name and engagement to her. She does not want him to know where she is or anything about her. She has an exaggerated fear of him."

I shook my head. "I don't think she could be too much afraid of a man who would treat her as he has threatened to—I think tried to—demand that she be his mistress, under threat of exposing her and perhaps selling her if she displeased him!"

"It isn't a question of his ill treatment, which I agree with you would be dastardly. She seems to me safe enough in Canada. But one cannot argue with terror: and the poor girl went through a terrible disillusionment and shock. Huntington is still administering the estate as for Drusilla. I agree that it looks as if he still desired to force her to live with him. I suppose it would give him the social recognition he has apparently lacked."

"How did she know that? Or did you?"

"No, how should I? One of her slaves from her plantation had been run to Canada and told her, she said."

We had returned from the concert—to which I am afraid

after all this I paid little attention—when we spoke of it again. We were still alone: I was sitting at the foot of the bed in negligee and slippers, finishing the cup of chocolate Janet had brought me: Mark in a dressing gown leaning by the window, with the emptied glass that had held wine. We had had a little midnight luncheon, hungry after the drive in the cold air. The room was softly candlelit; everything was warm and lovely and content: we smiled across at each other.

"Everything has been so wonderful," I said. "It is still. You here with me, the fire burning so bright; our happiness together. I shouldn't begrudge your knight-errantry to Drusilla, after all. If it hadn't been, before, we wouldn't be married now."

He laughed, and came to sit beside me. "I like it a little too," he said. His arm went around me and tightened. "There won't be any more of it," he said. He leaned a little from me and gave me a long look as if he wanted to remember me. It frightened me a little. "After that business at the Olivers' house I feel as if I wanted to keep you in a locked glass box I carried with me, like the Arabian Nights' genie. But I won't be more than a week or two away. I wish I could take you, but Waring has given me some sort of military pretext which prevents, confound him! I want you to stay with Laura while I am away, love. If you can't do that, Cousin Abigail had better come be with you. Incidentally I am detailing young Arthur Lawrence to more or less guard and escort you. He is a good lad, and I know you like him."

I smiled and nodded. With that arm round me, everything but love and safety seemed so unreal.

"It's so *silly*," I said impulsively, "that delicate, refined young lady, fairer actually than either of us! One sixteenth Negro blood! If she were a dog or a cat they wouldn't count it at all!"

"As a matter of fact, I believe that it does not count legally

173

in some of the states. But she is illegitimate, unfortunately, in any. Her mother could not legally marry."

"I still say it's silly. And—oh Mark, I'm ashamed of all the trouble I've made about just being a foundling."

He laughed aloud at this. "That's a romantic name for a little girl whose mother was married and a lady, and lived at the ferryhouse for three years in the face of the congregation!" he said. "But you *are* a romantic little goose." He rose and pulled me up with him. "And now, my love, we are going to have the good night's sleep we should have begun an hour ago. That is, sooner or later. Come along."

CHAPTER FOURTEEN

The road is winding and long,
With many a turn and twist,
And one could easy go wrong
Or ever one thought or list.

NORA PERRY

Miss Abigail—I still thought of her so—and, of course, Isobel were my guardian housemates after all. For Laura's boys, or rather one, which would eventually mean the other, came down with scarlatina. Though I'd had it, and Laura told me to come to her anyway, as the children had their own quarters, I knew it would be an imposition, not to say that Miss Abigail apparently took it for granted that she would come to me while I was alone. And after all Isobel and I had been together so many years that being with her and her aunt was a natural thing enough: I was neither guest nor hostess any more than I had been, as far as I felt. And after Mark's little lecture about my taking too much responsibility for Isobel, I took pains to go my way and let her go hers, now that she had Etienne Ducross for her companion.

Presently, indeed, Mr. Ducross and young Arthur Lawrence were almost as much at home as she was. Also it was worth a good deal to see Miss Abigail's face, her increased cheerfulness. Altogether, except that I missed Mark badly, things went easily and pleasantly. Isobel's engagement seemed in an informal way a *fait accompli*. Lawrence and Ducross began by giving us a delightful little bachelor dinner at their house, chaperoned of course by Cousin Abigail and graced by a charming elderly gentleman whose wife had been her closest friend until her death a couple of years before. Laura, always under her casual gay manner thoughtful for me, was seeing to it, had it been needful, that I was amused and distracted for the fortnight or less Mark would be gone. I had made friends already with a group of girls and young married women of my age, giving and receiving little luncheons and parties. I called on Laura, as well, every other day, to get news of the children, and to give her and Edgar mine of Mark. He wrote me daily; I could not write him, but it would not be long—long as it seemed. The letters came under cover to Edgar.

There had been, he wrote, no trouble about drawing the money from the bank in Washington. Guarding, I thought, too carefully his whereabouts, he was carrying it in cash in a money belt. When he was asked after, I answered as I had been told that his Colonel in the West had sent him on a military errand which was, naturally, something he could not tell me about. It was common knowledge that President Taylor was having trouble adjusting the spoils of the Mexican War, so people—especially the gentlemen—looked wise and said nothing more. As a matter of fact I could have followed his route to Canada.

"Thank heaven," he wrote, "my darling, this will be my last involvement with the matter. Fond as I was of my late Colonel, and deeply as I still feel gratitude for his having saved me on the battlefield, I shall be glad when this errand and its need for secrecy is done. But shortly now the money will be in the Eatons' hands, and then I shall come straight home to you—not to part, I hope, for a long time again."

A week was eventually gone. In four more days at the most he would be with me. Laura's younger boy, my especial pet Stanford, had not taken the scarlatina after all and the doctor thought would not; Laura herself was freed enough to go out once more, and, always thoughtful, gave a ladies' luncheon for me at Delmonico's. I remember enjoying it more than I had expected to. He would be back soon now.

The principal talk at the table over the dessert was of a wonderful fortuneteller, a real gypsy. Three or four of the young ladies had been to her already, and were full of the things she had told them. Some of them had come true already, one of the girls said.

"Oh, we must all go," Laura said. "Just where is she located?"

It seemed it was Church Street. She looked a little more serious. "That isn't a very good neighborhood."

"Oh, we needn't meet them socially!" Lucy Van Vooren laughed.

Anna Archinard, one of the young ladies who had visited the gypsy, said, "The street was quiet, and the house was clean enough. My brother waited for me outside in the carriage, and nothing much was going on, he said."

We went on talking and laughing, over the charlotte russes, which were especially good there. The cousin of another of the group had gone out, against his parents' wishes, to the California gold fields, and returned home—at nineteen!—with a fortune. It was even more exciting than the fortune-tellers. After that we made up a party to go to the matinee of *Maritana*.

As we left the restaurant, a bouquet of rustling hoops and laughing voices, the arias from the opera went through my mind. Mark had brought me home a handful of sheet music

177

a little before he left, and the songs from it were among the pile. One of them echoed still in my mind as I was driven home, dropping some of my friends on the way:

Scenes that are brightest may please awhile
Hearts that are lightest and eyes that smile,
But o'er us, above us, though bright nature gleam
With none to love us, how sad they seem!

It haunted my mind. I thought how silly I was; it was only a few days more. His last letter was safe in my reticule, and it was a loveletter . . . Oh, poor Eugenia, who could have had that love, or could have won it, losing her chance in a fit of disbelief and jealousy! And yet—I knew that the night he had brought Drusilla across the river, though I did not admit it to myself, I too had been jealous—and that there had been an undertone with the music in my mind, today, that wondered if Mark's care of Drusilla had been more than his gratitude and chivalry . . . If it had been, I told myself, surely it was not now! Words and looks of Isobel's came to me with it. She had, unknowingly, or in fear and love for me, sowed the thing in my mind, writing me that frantic letter the day of our marriage. And Isobel even now saw many things too darkly . . . I wondered if her presence, close once more, was awakening its old spell, the sadness and the fear of being unloved I had to fight in her always . . .

She sat beside me. I turned to look, for she had sighed. She had lost the look of gayety I had seen across our luncheon table. She had pushed up the Chantilly veil with its pink illusion lining that hid all but her prettiness, and in doing so she wiped the covering wash from the scar. She was suddenly the old tragic Isobel.

"Oh, what is it, dear?" I said, involuntarily the comforter as of old.

"How do I know if I am loved?" she said. It was the old

fear of lovelessness that had struck across my own mood, as I had thought.

"It's chilly, dear," I said. "Pull down your veil. Of course you are loved, silly!"

"Pull it down—because of the coachman, and the footman when we re-enter! Oh I suppose so . . . But . . . I cannot cover my face all day and all night. He might look and see the paint come off on the pillow, his kiss might uncover it."

I said sharply, "If his kiss uncovered it, it would be to show you that his love made nothing of it . . . I know. Mark Harradine, whose ancestry goes back to the Conqueror, married me, a nameless girl, and because he loves me it is nothing to him. If your lover kisses your scar it will be as the children say to make it well, to show you you are the dearer to him."

"And—you never doubt?"

I said, "No." And then we were at home. It was sunset. A nurse with two little children were coming sedately from the Park. As I looked the little girl laughed happily. She knew she was loved. So did I. So must poor Isobel.

As we mounted the stair when the footman had taken our wraps, she said low, "Perdita, when we were all last at the Red Castle, you and Mark and Aunt Abigail and I, did you hear nothing, see nothing of the Leaf? Or—of anything, anyone else? Do you know that the servants say that it isn't only her spirit, her curse, that is about the Castle, that the slaves the first Eugenius threw overboard when he was making the money to build the Castle—they moan sometimes at night . . . that the poor Chinese people he mistreated walk softly upstairs, sometimes whispering among themselves . . . that even my father and mother, Nicholas and Sibylla, and the other two—Eugenia's parents—come back to their old rooms sometimes, because they were drowned so young . . . There is a portrait of Eugenius, Eugenia's young father, in

179

one of the rooms: alive and handsome and as if he was stepping out of the canvas to court you. They said he could win any woman . . . They say he does not rest either, or his wife Juliana. They come in, their clothes all drenched with the salt water of the Sound. Once someone found a spray of seaweed on the floor, damp still."

"Isobel," I said, "much as I love you, I feel like forbidding you ever to set foot in the Red Castle again: and besides that, finding out which of the servants told you those tales and sending them flying. I have never seen or felt anything of the sort . . ."

"Not Onnorate?"

I caught my breath. How did she know of my Achilles heel? Of the brown leaves that blew against the window of my bridal night, the leaf that touched me like a caress when the rest were afraid, the leaves that blew near, but always kind: always as if a little love came with them . . . always, yes always, with protection. I could not lie to Isobel; but I could tell her a misleading truth. "Brown leaves blow where there are trees to drop them from and winds to carry them, never with any terror, and I have felt and seen them," I said. "For the rest—the stories are memories of actual cruelties, built into ghost stories: remember the generations of poor blacks who had no revenge but weaving those tales in a sort of vengeance. It is their thoughts and fears, my darling, that if you are sensitive you feel, if anything at all. And those four young people, your parents and Eugenia's, who were drowned twenty-five years or so ago; it was such a tragedy that more tales were built."

"And my mother and Eugenia's were not cursed, then?" she looked at me in mockery.

"No. They were all four as far as we know good and fine Christians. Sibylla and Juliana Somerwell were not the only women drowned on that yacht—or in that same storm."

"And there was no damp spot and no seaweed that was miles from the sea . . ."

"No, there was not." By now we were in her room and I was mechanically undressing her to replace the walking suit with an evening frock, and in any case I wanted no part of old Keziah, who was greatly to blame for all this.

Isobel turned on me and spoke sharply. "You fear nothing. Then you would not be afraid to go with me to the fortune-teller."

"Not afraid," I said. "Why should I be? But there isn't anything I want to know."

"I do—oh, I do," she said tensely. "And you know Aunt Abigail wouldn't let me go alone. She is so used to feeling you take good care of me that if you went I could."

"But everything is going well with you, Isobel!"

"No," she said. "Oh, you do not know . . . Oh Perdita, he has not spoken!"

I stared at her, aghast. We had all supposed it to be the case, down to the very maids and footmen. She answered my look.

"Everything but that—but the actual offer. Yes—he has kissed and embraced me—he has used endearing terms—"

"And you have permitted it, Isobel, before he made his intentions known?" I said, surprised.

"Yes!" she said. "I am not cold and prim like you—"

I let it pass. "When Mark returns," I said, "as your nearest male relative, I think if you wished he would speak to Mr. Ducross."

"No!" she said. "Do you think I have no pride?"

I did think so from what she had just confessed, but it was not a thing to say.

"I wish there was some way in which I could help," I said.

"I have told you. Come with me to the fortuneteller. If she could tell Anna and Lizzie things that came true, she could

181

tell me. It would set my mind at rest even if it broke my heart."

"But if you wait a little longer—"

"I have waited till I can stand it no longer."

I knew Isobel: till she had her way her unhappiness would persist. Finally I went to Miss Abigail.

"I knew something was troubling her," she said. "But, my dear, Church and Leonard Streets! They are places where no virtuous lady should enter, at least not unless chaperoned and on an errand of mercy."

"But if you chaperoned us?" I said. "And if Arthur and Mr. Ducross went as escorts also?"

She continued to disapprove. But the end was, as I had known it would be, that we went: she had consented to be with us.

That is, the gentlemen went with us. For at the last moment, the engagement made—for the gypsy woman was popular, and we had to write ahead and hear from her—a delayed scrawled "yes" with the hours set—Miss Abigail had one of her sick headaches. I was all for putting it off, but it seemed that the gypsy was so crowded with engagements that if we did not go then we might not for heaven knew when. Our own engagement books were crowded, also. I tried to call it off. But Isobel was desperate.

"If you loved a man as I do, you would fly to any help to soothe your pain! Do not be cruel! This old hag may tell me just what the delay is! If I don't go I may always, always, feel that I may have lost what means most to me in the world!"

She was shaking from head to foot: she was on the verge of weeping violently. I pressed my handkerchief to her eyes and said, "Very well, Isobel. After all, two stalwart gentlemen are enough of a guard, without one frail elderly lady to support them!"

She laughed a little at that, as I had intended, and we went down to the waiting gentlemen and the waiting carriage.

Isobel kept hurrying the coachman. "If we are late," she said, "she won't have us. Anna said her waiting room was always crowded."

The coachman, who of course knew Isobel almost as well as he did me, demurred at first. "The traffic grows thicker here," he said, "and the street is narrower." We were on muddy Broadway by now, but she insisted, her voice raised; he shrugged and flicked the leader. We dashed ahead.

As we did so, a troop of ragged girls and boys, pauper and vagrant children unmistakably, ran shrieking and shouting from a side street. The coachman reined up with something closer to strong language than he should have used before ladies. "Police can't do nothin' with them," he muttered. His slowing down had been too late. He had knocked down a small girl who had run before the horses. A somewhat older boy, a bootblack by the box strapped to his thin little back, ran to her. He lifted her with an effort and swore at the coachman.

I was out of the carriage in a moment, and had the child in my arms and in the carriage with me. In spite of the coachman's demurral I beckoned the boy to follow. Both children were cleaner than I had supposed they would be; he was bright-eyed and looked intelligent.

"Is she your sister?" I asked the boy. He nodded. His clothes were worn and patched; his trousers looked to have been cut down from a larger pair. Her frock was cobbled down the front as if by an unaccustomed hand, and she wore a boy's jacket too large for her, worn also. But she had a pretty bright little face, and curly hair which had been combed not too long ago.

"I make her hold my hand when we go places," he said, "but she runs away, don't you, Annabel?"

183

She laughed; apparently she had not been hurt, or she was very courageous. "Yes, I does!" she said. "I like it."

"Perdita, we'll be late for our appointment!" Isobel interrupted.

"I can't help that," I said. "Children, where do you live? Does your mother know you are out without her?"

"We ain't got people," the boy said. "They died with smallpox last time, and Jim. We live with each other an' I take care of her."

I beckoned to the policeman who, attracted by the accident, had come near. Lieutenant Lawrence was giving him the details he asked. "Do you know anything about these children?" I asked. "I would like to do what I can to make up to them for this."

"Sure, they're all right, ma'am, as these young rascals down here go. They live in a room in a decent enough tenement, and he takes good care of her. Them bootblacks that works hard makes good money, some of 'em. This lad Rufus, matter of fact, I think nigh supported his mother—Dad wasn't much good. The last smallpox epidemic wiped out father and mother and one kid. The charities wanted to take these away for paupers, but the mission visitor she spoke up for 'em and got a stay—I dunno how much longer they got."

Annabel pulled my sleeve.

"Couldn't you get us another stay? Rich ladies can. We'd be awful good. I'd hold his hand when we went places."

"You better," Rufus said to her grimly. His eyes fixed on mine hungrily. "You don't look old enough to get people stays," he said. "Maybe them dandies with you might—"

Isobel pulled my other sleeve. "Perdita! We'll be late!"

Perdita! My very name reminded me. These were lost ones, too. Suddenly I had an idea. "Do you know the name of Mr. Edgar Harradine, officer? He is on a good many committees—he works with people in trouble—"

184

"Sure, he's a big bug in the stock market, and he has a finger in some sort of city rescue work," the policeman said to my relief. "Has a cousin was a hero in Chapultepec, handsome feller—seen him marchin' when the Mex War was over."

I pulled out my cardcase and showed him my name. "I am married to your hero," I said, smiling. "This gentleman, Lieutenant Lawrence, was in his regiment."

Rufus cried out, before the policeman could answer, "Oh lady, you *could* git a stay—"

We meant so much to these waifs; we must have seemed so happy and powerful . . . "Arthur," I said impulsively, "can't you get a hack and take these children up to Edgar's house? He'd be home by the time you got there."

"That would leave you and Miss Somerwell with only Etienne," he said, half laughing. "What would Miss Abigail say? It's like the Ten Little Injuns."

But Ducross, laughing too, said that he thought he was adequate to guard the fair seekers after good fortune. And as Isobel continued to fret about the delay, the policeman, who had by now entered into the spirit of it completely, signaled a hack, and the children, excited and almost unbelieving, got in.

"Now, on to the Gypsy's Warning on Church Street," I said lightly. Little Rufus turned round in the hack and said, "Aw, no, Lady, that ain't a nice street for swells."

"Just like Aunt Abigail!" Isobel said, shrugging, and told the coachman to go on.

It did not seem like a bad street. Common perhaps: windows with pillows along the sills where women leaned and looked out. There were other women, nicely clad, some of them very pretty and quite young, strolling up and down.

"So far not very exciting," Isobel said as we rang and were admitted, by a turbaned colored girl. She led us up what seemed an everlasting number of stairs; the fortuneteller apparently lived at the very top of the house. The girl went downstairs again after knocking.

The woman who opened to us was unquestionably a gypsy: tall, dark, harsh-featured, turbaned like her servant, and clad in gaudy sweeping hoopless garments.

"Miss Anna Archinard sent us," Isobel said. "You gave us an appointment—I am Miss Somerwell; this is Mrs. Harradine. Mr. Ducross here is our escort."

"Yes, pretty ladies," the woman said. "But I can only take one at a time. I have no anteroom."

"Wait where, then?" Ducross asked.

"Outside in your carriage," she said calmly, "or in the hall."

"Oh, not in the hall," Isobel said. "There is nothing to sit on!" And, she could have added, it was narrow and darkening already.

"I will stand guard in the hall," Ducross said, smiling. "And Mrs. Harradine can wait below in the carriage if she doesn't mind descending and ascending again."

It seemed the only way to do. He escorted me down to the carriage, and I settled myself to wait while he went back up as he had said. The passing girls glanced at us; the passersby in general paid little attention. Carriages in front of the gypsy's were of course a common sight.

The wait seemed long—it was, indeed; it was all of an hour by the little gold watch looped by its long chain at my breast. Finally they descended. Isobel ran to the side of the carriage, flushed and radiant.

"Oh, she was wonderful," she whispered. "She told me what I wanted to know. She told me about a beautiful wonderful future—"

It had been worth coming down, then, I thought, and then smiled a little at myself—it would take some time for

186

me to make the street go right instead of left: I still watched Isobel's moods in spite of myself . . . Well, it was a little thing after all. Ducross so unmistakably had intentions, so frankly shown before the *ton* these weeks now: but if she had to be told so by a fortuneteller, well, now she knew.

But it was getting late, and it was a good thing there was nothing I actually wanted to hear; I could cut my time short, I thought as I stepped from the carriage to lay my hand on Etienne's arm—he would have to be Etienne to us all soon, of course. The old lamplighter was moving up and down now, touching the gas lamps with his fire, one by one. He seemed a comfortingly homely sort of person, where the street was so strange.

I took a last look at Isobel established in her seat, and we turned and remounted the narrow dark stair. There was, finally, the lighted lantern, smoking a little, hanging beside the gypsy's room. I hadn't noticed before the name rather badly printed on a tacked-up card, MADAME ESMERELDA. A song ran through my head as they were apt to do, this time a gay little parlor piece:

> *Where is the little gypsy's home?*
> *Under the spreading greenwood tree!*
> *Wherever she may roam*
> *Where'er that tree may be—*

that ended: "Esmerelda—Esmerelda Zingara!" I wondered if this woman were really named that or had taken her name from the song. My mind was trying to catch at everything passing—why did I dislike coming so much, I wondered? I realized that I had wanted underneath to stay home not to miss Mark's possible return. And Ducross was bowing and holding the door for me to pass in: as I stood in it, he made a mock-salute, and sang softly underbreath a line from another of the parlor songs, "Thy sentinel am I!"

187

We both laughed a little as the door closed between us.

It was a rather large, ill-lighted room under the skylight of a rickety old house that had seen better days. There was one large well-cushioned chair, with a small table and stool near it. Esmerelda motioned me to it and took the stool beside the table.

"I cannot stay long," I said. "But I will pay you as if for a full-length sitting."

"So kind and pretty a young lady need not think of that," she said, her deep-lined brown face wreathing itself into a professional smile. She pulled the stool closer and took the hand I ungloved. "Will the lady have her palm read, or learn what my crystal ball tells?" she asked.

Suddenly I didn't want to have her touch me. "The crystal ball," I said.

She lifted a glass ball, laid a piece of black velvet under it, and set it on the table. There were two tall candles on the table; she lighted them, and moved them so that the ball was illuminated. Her voice began, moving on monotonously, as she stared down into the ball's heart.

"You are married," she said. "You have your ring, but I should have known without that, young as you seem to be a wife. I see water—flowing water—always around you. You left the water—but you will return to it. You had best return. When you married you took love from another woman, one who had never wished you ill—"

I said, "But this is past. I know my past. I am not sure you are right about the lady whom, you say, wished me well. But what of the future?"

She said, "You may choose your future. The man you trust now is unworthy of your trust; he gave you a little love, yes, but today he is with the woman he loves truly, the woman for whom he has deceived you . . . You think yourself a wife—

188

perhaps you are no wife. Perhaps the other woman he is with now was his bride all the time."

I rose and said, "That is enough, thank you. I will hear no more. Tell me what I owe you."

Her hand reached out and gripped my wrist like a glove. "You must hear the rest. He will not come back. Another, better life awaits you, jewels, satins, gentlemen at your feet—"

I wrenched my wrist away and ran to the door, flinging a gold coin I had held behind me. I pulled at the doorknob and called "Mr. Ducross—Mr. Ducross—"

There was no answer; the door would not move. Behind me the woman laughed. There was no accent in her speech now, it was the voice of a lower-class American woman. She said, "He is gone. You sent him a message that he was to drive your friend home and return for you, as you wanted a longer fortune told. Before he is back you will be gone."

As I tried vainly to open the door her arms, strong as a man's, came round me from behind. Strong as I was myself I was nothing beside her. She dragged me inside, across the room, and as suddenly had unlocked the door and shut me in. I heard the lock click. It all seemed mad. It was like that other dreadful time when I was trapped at the Olivers' . . . Was it the same people?

I stood by the window, too small to escape from I saw now, and tried to be calm and get my breath.

I heard the door click again, and saw that it was, it must be. For the same elegant, fairskinned quadroon man, the one who had named himself the Olivers' major-domo, dressed now as a gentleman would dress, had come quickly and silently in and stood against the locked door. It was like a nightmare that one dreams twice.

"I am sorry, madame, that we were interrupted last time," he said. "It will not happen this."

I made myself speak steadily. "What is all this for? Why do

189

you do this? Why do you persecute me? I do not even know you."

He spoke in the same slow, wellbred Southern accent I remembered. "Because you are a pawn on our chessboard," he said. "No, that rates you too low; you are one of its queens. You are the queen of the Red Castle, the chessman of the red towers. You must know, you received its sign as your mother did before you; it is not a fortunate sign. And the player is exchanging queens."

I almost forgot my own terror. "How do you know—what do you know—who are you?"

"My name is Cassius Huntington," he said, "that is, if we blacks have any right to names. And I am the half brother, also of course illegally, of Stephen Huntington; like him—also by the left hand of course—Drusilla Huntington's cousin. Poor Drusilla and I are Negroid."

That cold steadiness which is the ultimate of dread came over me. "What have I to do with all that?" I said.

He smiled, and was silent for a long moment, his eyes fixed on me. My mind, tangential as it sometimes is in shock, thought how sad it was that so intelligent and strong and able a man should be so completely corrupt and evil. He spoke slowly, still with that softness and courtesy which made it more dreadful.

"You are Major Harradine's wife," he said. "It is probable—almost certain—that you know of his commerce with Drusilla. You may not have known that theirs was a love affair: that does not interest my good brother, whose valet and property I am, or myself . . . Will Madame allow me to sit while I explain further?" I mechanically gestured him to the nearest chair, the client's armchair. He said, "My master is annoyed that Drusilla has vanished. He faced her, and her father, which was his mistake, with the facts, giving them a month in which to decide. I do not know how much you know of his plans. He dislikes changing plans. He explained that he would assume that she was his wife. It was known that he had been her suitor. She was much loved in the neighborhood: I fear he was not. He felt, I fear rightly, that, disliked as he is, and loved as she has been, his social life might not be improved if the actual facts were known as to his rightful possession of the demesne, and making Drusilla publicly his slave. He is still believed to be taking charge for her, and she to be in the West, for her period of mourning.

"You must know the rest, I suppose: for old Harriet Tubman, the Negro woman who has stolen at least a half million dollars' worth of slave flesh and blood from owners, was alerted, God knows how. And the next we knew young Major Harradine came East posthaste, not, as was supposed, to marry Miss Eugenia Somerwell, but to carry Drusilla to Canada. This was seen. When he returned to the Red Castle he married instead of his lifelong sweetheart a girl he scarcely knew, niece or come-by-chance of one of the worst old Abolitionists, and a pillar of the Underground. Obviously it was the price Harradine had to pay for saving Drusilla. For the rest, all we know is that he has left the ferry girl, gone to Washington, and vanished in the direction of Canada. We know you have heard from him; a servant in Edgar Harradine's house has informed us, let us say."

I caught my breath. If this was all they knew . . .

"I do not know where he is," I said truthfully, "or when he will return."

"We do, as it happens. He returns today. What we do not know is where in the great country of Canada he has met Drusilla, and with whom she is. He was, we think, given an authentic secret military mission as camouflage—and our spy lost him when he could no longer follow, barred by the military secrecy."

"How do you know he went to Drusilla at all—that it was not an actually military erand?" I said desperately.

He smiled. "Her handwriting on her Canadian letter to Colonel Waring was known. His letter to Mark Harradine was known. We know Harradine went to Washington; thence to Canada. He knows where she is; that is all we need from him. We have those who can do the rest: put her in her cousin's hands. Write your note to him. There is pen and ink. The gypsy will come for it and add that when we have Drusilla we will set you free. If you or he refuse this, our good Gitana will turn you over to friends of hers who will, as they have other ladies as good and lovely, send you to an address in the Argentine Republic. Even if Harradine has become attached to you he will not want you back from that voyage. Tell him we give him two days to consider. After dark tonight we move you to a safer place." He bowed. "You will not escape: my freedom is promised for what I am doing. Good afternoon, Madame." He had leaned against the door as he talked: he turned swiftly; the door was opened and locked behind him before I could run across the room.

CHAPTER FIFTEEN

I knew a gypsy, a vile shameless bawd
Whose craft was to betray the young and fair . . .
H. W. LONGFELLOW

I do not know how long I stood, frozen, against the wall. I know that presently I made myself move and stare round me. I prayed—I prayed hard. "Show me a way out—send rescuers!" I prayed over and over again. I got hold of myself after a little and investigated my surroundings. There might be something—oh surely some help, some way!

There was air enough in the room. It came from the bottom of the barred window. So this room had been used as a prison before. The skylight, daubed over with paint, was far above my reach. Piling the two chairs and standing on them I could not touch it. The table was too small to put chairs on. The door was of course locked. The awful feeling that this was a nightmare repeated paralyzed me for a moment. The slave-valet's words, that Mark would not want me after I had been in the hands of the procurers, came sickeningly to me. And Mark's story of the girl who had been found months later in a house of shame, whose parents had taken her abroad and never returned—I tried to stop thinking of that and think clearly of this situation. I prayed again; locked doors, unknown hiding places, were nothing to God. I must know that He was help . . .

But why, why was all this loosed upon me? I was a pawn on the chessboard where Drusilla was a queen; but there was more to it than that. There was hatred somewhere, and there was someone helping these men in their designs on Drusilla. Eugenia. Eugenia's hating eyes on me, always. Eugenia, she of insane furies and jealousies, they said, on her mother's side, whose lover I had taken from her . . . That was useless. I tried to think of other things. My people would come to look for me, I knew, if I did not return within an hour of Isobel's returning . . . They would move me, these Huntington men, as soon as it was dark enough to be safe for them . . . It would be dark sooner than the time I was supposed to have told Ducross and Isobel . . . I found myself running wildly about the room, pushing against the walls, trying to escape as a bird or animal does . . .

I must have fainted; I came to my senses in a heap on the floor, awakened by the sound of pounding blows above me. There was a light above the skylight . . . the blows came harder; someone was trying to break the glass. Then I heard the shatter; a rain of slivers came from the skylight, and I cowered to the side of the room. I heard steps, now the glass was broken above me, and a rush of cool air came through. Men's voices: and the high triumphant voice of the boy Rufus I had sent to Edgar's house: "I see her! She's there in the corner!"

A man was swinging himself down by his hands, dropping on the floor and turning to catch me in his arms . . . Mark! Mark, dusty, panting, gripping me. "Are you safe, darling—are you all right?"

The Irish policemen were following him down, and the boy. "Is she all right, sir?" the nearest one said. Mark lifted

194

his head from where he knelt by me and said briefly, "I think so—Perdita, are you hurt, ill-treated . . ."

"No, no," I gasped. "I was frightened and fainted, that was all. They only locked me in."

He lifted me to the chair, and the policeman with the lantern stood beside us, while the other, a light in his hand, hunted for the door, which was nearly invisible, flush with the wall. Presently he had the lock broken and the door pushed open. They swept me through and, Mark holding fast to me as if I might still be snatched away, we went down the long flights of stairs. There was a queer silence all over the house.

"Where are all the people?" I asked.

"Sure the rats are in their holes," my policeman growled. There had been other policemen outside the door, I realized now. The boy Rufus got into the carriage with us with no words said. It was Edgar's carriage, I saw.

"I'm goin' up to get my sister," Rufus volunteered. "She's with your folks, the ones you sent us to that run committees." He sat back, at ease on the cushions.

Presently I had breath enough to ask him, "Why did you come?"

"I knew where you had to be," he said. "A lot of us fellers my age knew about it. The old woman's son was locked up there onct. He'd stole a lot of money and he was wanted. He had to have whiskey, and us fellers used to take turns bringing it to him, crawling over the roofs. The old woman never knew. I told you, lady, it wasn't no place to be. So I told your folks."

Mark's arm tightened round me. "A street of fallen women and thieves," he said. "How on earth your friends who had gone down there to the fortuneteller should not have known—"

"Young girls are never told about things like that," I said.

195

I remembered what Cassius Huntington had said, what would befall me unless Mark gave up Drusilla's whereabouts. "What about Isobel and Mr. Ducross?" I thought to ask. "The gypsy said she gave them a message from me to return in an hour; why, they should have been here by now—"

"It is not an hour," Mark said. "But they had no business to take her word, or leave you at all. I shall not trust you with Ducross again, nor, I think, with Isobel." His face set.

And then we were stopping at our own house. Our carriage, with our policeman and Rufus, went on to Edgar's. After all that had come and gone, it was scarcely seven o'clock. The fresh air, with its hint of snow, seemed like heaven after what I had been through. Mark's arm supporting me, we went in.

Isobel, her face stained and smeared with tears, rushed to me as we came in. She was sobbing. "Oh, I shall never forgive myself!" she gasped, coming to throw her arms around me. Mark fended her off.

"I am not sure that I shall ever forgive you," he said harshly. "Your selfish wilfulness, your insistence, are to blame for all this. Where is Ducross?"

"He went to the police station," she said. "When he had left me here he drove back to the gypsy's place, and she said—she said Perdita had taken a hack and was driving home now . . . When he came back here and found she was not here yet, after waiting a little he went out again—"

"That will do," Mark said. He half led, half carried me to our rooms, throwing an order to the footman as he passed him.

"Tell Mr. Ducross he need not trouble himself further; Mrs. Harradine is returned," he said. I could hear Isobel sobbing aloud in the lower hall.

Mark undressed me and put me to bed himself, as if I were a baby. He sat by me holding my hand; I gripped it as if I were lost still. Janet, controlling herself Scottish fashion, came and went, bringing me first the water I asked for, then the tray of food the footman carried up. I found I could eat, after a moment, and begged Mark to go down and dine himself. He left me reluctantly and was back in a short time.

"You are tired, you are fresh from your journey," I said when Janet was gone. "Lie down by me and tell me what happened."

He flung off coat and shoes and lay down in his dressing gown. I think he would have anyway; he did not want me out of his sight, nor indeed I him.

"What has happened to you is more important, if you feel able to tell me now," he said. "I only know what the boy could tell us; you almost ran over the little sister, and sent them under Arthur's care to Edgar's. He made Edgar believe you were in a dangerous place; indeed, when Edgar knew where you were he knew it. I had come home, to find Cousin Abigail worried because the party was late returning. Isobel came in as we talked, and was chattering about her fortune—little fool! As for Ducross he hasn't been heard from yet."

"I suppose he is hunting for me as she said. Yes, I feel able to talk, indeed I want to. The wine and food have made me feel almost all right—along with having you here."

The black head on the pillow turned. "You are very brave," he said. "Most women would have been weeping and reproaching me for leaving you to look after another woman's affairs."

I laughed a little. I was so lighthearted to think it was over and Mark back again! "The gypsy said so too," I reminded him. "She hinted that it was Drusilla you loved, not me. She wasn't sure you hadn't married her!"

"And you can laugh about it!" His arm tightened round me. "You mean she knew there was such a person as Drusilla?

But no, darling, it will keep. If you're too tired, wait till tomorrow."

"You don't have to go anywhere else, do you?" I said, and suddenly I was crying. He soothed me and whispered words I loved hearing and presently I was quiet again. After all everything was right. "No, I'd like to tell you," I said. "The gypsy may or may not have been in league with Huntington. But when she left me alone in the locked room the same man who tried to kidnap me at the Olivers came in."

"Perdita!" The strong bridle-hardened hand gripped mine as if I might fly away. I went on quietly. I knew the sooner he knew all this, the better for us all—the Eatons, the law, ourselves. I repeated what the man who called himself Cassius Huntington had said: that he was the slave half brother of Stephen Huntington who was Drusilla's cousin and enemy. That their plan was to exchange me for Drusilla. That they would hold me so that Huntington could carry out his plan to keep Drusilla as his pretended wife and actual mistress, so that her friends and social circle would accept him also.

"I wonder how long she would have lived after that happened," Mark said quietly. I shivered in his arms.

"Is there nothing you can do to punish them?" I asked.

"I hope so, God knows. Is that all?"

"I was to write a note—you would be given two days to decide—"

"And then?"

"Unless you submitted—the Argentine."

"The fiends! Edgar was right; they did have a link of some sort with that trade. He thought so before. Perdita, I shall not let you out of my sight again."

"That will be good," I said drowsily. "Did you get the money safe to Drusilla?"

"Oh, yes. Twenty-five thousand. A small fortune. And

that's the end. I think my debt to Colonel Huntington is more than paid."

I could not help being glad he felt this. And then, as he stood up, saying that he had given orders that we were seeing nobody tonight, I realized that he had come straight from his journey in search of me. "Do you really want to sit up any longer?" I said.

"Considering that I am still dusty and disheveled from my journey, no." He locked the door and crossed to the bathroom. "I was really in no state to kiss you even," he said.

I was so tired, and so relieved to have him at home and be there myself, that I was asleep when he returned, and I think he went to sleep almost immediately himself. For two people who had been through what we had, I thought dimly the next day, we had made a good recovery. I was only a little languid: and as for Mark, he seemed rested and even gay. I think the feeling that Drusilla's affairs were no longer his responsibility had something to do with it.

Edgar and Laura, naturally, came over the following evening. Laura said what I had been thinking.

"I don't know what the two of you are made of," she said. "You should be swooning at the least, Perdita. Of course Mark always was made of iron, it runs in the Harradine family. But a slight failure of energy, my dear boy, would be only correct."

"I have her back," he said briefly.

After we had dined, I had to tell the story for them.

"The worst of it is," Edgar said in his calm way, "that there is nothing we can do, at least at present, as regards Stephen Huntington. Apparently he has remained out of reach, and made his slave Cassius commit the actual crimes. Of course if and when we can get hold of Cassius, if he can be brought to confession, we might have something."

"You mean that after these two attempts on Perdita we have no case against that villain?" Mark said angrily.

"Consider," Edgar said. "It would mean stirring up the whole matter of Mrs. Eaton's story. I do not know how she feels about it."

"In her place," I said, "I would tell the truth. From the point of view of the Canadians among whom her life will be spent—or even the English—she is legally married, and white and a lady."

"Her husband agrees with you," Mark said. "But she herself would not. Remember that her whole life has been spent looking at women like herself from the point of view of those around her. I am afraid that she still feels deeply shamed by the fact of her actual birth and background."

I thought that there was a likeness between my case and hers. But I had faced and accepted my unknown origin. And I was liked and accepted for what I was.

"I talked to our lawyer this morning," Edgar said. "He reminded me that in the present stormy state of the South a story like this, told by a Northern officer, would have little credit. And of course the Eatons' true story would have to come out, which you say she would deplore. After all, she is happily married, and in no case can she return to claim her estate. She is provided for. Her cousin will probably put about the news that she has died. By the way, the gypsy woman was jailed. She was found tied up in a corner of the building, but we have enough against her to send her down for a long term, which should please you, Mark. Perdita is not her first victim."

"It does."

"Also we are, with your permission, Mark, about to employ a very intelligent detective named Allan Pinkerton, who has hopes of tying up Cassius Huntington with the trade in young girls for the Argentine, as well as this city."

"Is there any clue to his whereabouts?"

"At present, no. Pinkerton's employees are on the way to Charleston to see what they can find there. The man may have returned to his master; probably has. Or he may have disguised himself: he could pass for a Spaniard or Italian, with a little stain."

It was left at that. I asked about the boy who had been instrumental in saving me, and his little sister.

"They're country children originally," Laura said. "Rufus is a couple of years older than my Stanford and they are great friends. It seems the mother married again, a ne'er-do-well, who brought them all to the city, where the mother and he died. Rufus is a capable intelligent child, and is delighted at the idea of being given an education. His only fear was that he might be separated from Annabel, for whom he apparently felt as responsible as if he had been a man. Edgar has even, already, remembered a kindly and childless couple who would be willing to board the children and see to their schooling, for which Mark would pay."

"So some good is coming out of it all," I said. "But it seems incredible that a man like Stephen Huntington could exist. His slave was evil; but there was some excuse for him: he was intelligent, and strangely enough, well-mannered and educated, and the prize was his freedom."

"Probably educated by their father along with Stephen Huntington," Edgar said. "I have known of such cases. It makes it doubly cruel for them. Not that that excuses them."

"And yet," Mark said, "there are none finer than the finest of the Southern gentlemen. Chivalrous, honorable, kind. But the possession of absolute power over human beings is a thing some men cannot stand without deterioration into absolute unfeelingness. Drusilla's cousin is apparently one of those so corrupted."

"I suppose spending his life in dependent poverty and be-

201

ing the next heir was too much for him," Laura said. "And then he was perhaps actually in love with Drusilla too, to begin with. Well, let's talk about more important things. Mrs. Harper can't, as usual, give *the* ball of the season, because of being in mourning. She has passed it on to Almira Willesdon, so to speak her vice-regent, to handle, and is compromising on a series of at-homes. I suppose you've had your invitations."

I nodded. "Yes, and too many more! The table in the hall is heaped high with invitations I've scarcely had courage to open."

"I'll weed them out for you," she said gayly, and when she came to luncheon next day was as good as her word. But even when she had helped me mark two-thirds for refusal there was a shocking pile.

Mark, entering my boudoir a couple of weeks later, fresh from what was one of a series of business talks with Edgar, found me, he said, at my desk with a look of desperation. "What is all this?" he said. "You seem knee-deep."

"I am," I said, half laughing, half dismayed. "Parties and parties and parties that are, according to Laura, most important. And oh, I'm so tired!"

"You're thinner, love," he said, "and that color—it isn't as bright. We must do something—or rather, not do something."

"I suppose I could use rouge like old Madame van Raade," I said.

He smiled. He knew I wouldn't do anything so fast, at my age.

"That won't be quite enough," he said. "I think I must carry you off somewhere. I wish it could be this minute, to St. Augustine again, or even Italy: but this business of my downtown property is rather complicated."

"That would be wonderful—what is the trouble?"

"I have, with Edgar's help and his lawyer's been trying to

make the houses more habitable. We plan running water in the halls, new roofs, and even kitchen stoves, repairs straight through—"

"But why not?"

"Why not? Because of our neighboring landlords. It seems it is most subversive, especially as I am not raising the rents, merely introducing a little comfort and cleanliness. Trinity Corporation, which is powerful, seems to be trying to pull various political wires against it, not to say others of our acquaintance. We shall continue. But we both have to be in the city for the next two weeks. I would like to take you away sooner than that to where you could recover from the circles under those great eyes."

I thought a moment. "Mark, how far is it to the Red Castle?"

"By stagecoach most of the day. By the Hudson River steamboats, which are floating palaces, if their captains weren't so fond of dangerous racing, two hours perhaps. By the steamcars less still. Or we could drive."

"Everybody says the steamcars are horrid: all packed together with everybody having lapfuls of bundles and bags, and whiskey-smelling Irishmen and gentlemen going to and from the smoking-car—"

"What a proud little lady! What are you thinking of? Driving?"

"Well, anything but the cars! The Red Castle, unless—"

"Unless what?"

"Well—the possibility of Eugenia. Aside from that, it is after all our own; the servants are there, and nobody else but your old dependent spinster in the top story rooms, and it is lovely and I love it. And . . . we were married there . . ."

"As far as I know," he said, "there is no possibility of Eugenia. Cousin Abigail tells me she is with a colleague of

Dr. De Witt's, who has some sort of convalescent home. I hope she is having her temper removed!"

"If I were safe from her—" I said.

"My dear child! What can she do except make herself unpleasant?"

"You have forgotten," I said, "that it was Eugenia, Isobel said, who told her that the housekeeper at the Olivers' knew my story. And . . . Cassius Huntington, at the gypsy's tenement, used the same phrase that was with the castle that summoned my mother—do you not remember? He said that they were exchanging the queens on the chessboard—that I was the queen of the Red Castle. And she hates me still. And she loves you."

"If this is so, nothing of her sex or her relationship shall spare her," he said. "She shall end her days in a jail or an asylum—for good God, it is close to madness if you are right. And surely she couldn't suppose that if you were out of the way, I would marry her. Why did you not tell me about what Huntington said before?"

"There was so much to tell—" I said weakly. "And if you know anyone hates you, you are apt to suspect them. And Cassius Huntington said—and indeed I think you said—after he had trapped me at the Olivers', that a servant in Edgar's house told me that Edgar gave me letters from you—in the first case, you thought a servant might have spied for the Huntingtons also."

"It must be reported to the proper authorities and to the Pinkerton man," he said.

"I suppose so," I agreed.

"In any case," he went on, "I am taking you out of New York City for a while. If you still feel that you would be safe in the Red Castle, Edgar can reach me there by telegram if anything comes up which requires my signature or decision, and I can return easily. Edgar, being a lawyer and

204

a philanthropist, rather likes rows; being a mere military man I don't." He was smiling down at me now. "You are sure you don't think Eugenia can emerge from her convalescent home or whatever it is, or Onnorate the Iroquois send her message of brown leaves?"

I smiled too. "Do you know, Mark, I have always rather liked the idea of Onnorate—as if she were my friend, not an evil warning. You remember the evening of our marriage?"

"Naturally." His eyes said more than that.

"There were leaves which blew against the pane that night. There shouldn't have been leaves near the Astor that night, but there were."

"And we were happy. And we are happy. You are a superstitious child, but you have made your point. Myself, I don't believe in curses—that avaricious wretch of a Huntington and his minion are enough, and we're free of them, thank Heaven. Huntington must be somewhere, and the old gypsy, if she is actually a gypsy, will probably turn states' evidence: meanwhile we will forget about it as much as we can. I've always liked the old Red Castle myself; after all, it is my heritage."

"I love it too," I said.

I had not seen much of Isobel or Cousin Abigail or of Ducross and Lawrence. That is, we met at the same affairs and Ducross had finally come and apologized for taking the gypsy woman's word that I had sent them away, and been forgiven. Mark had not let me see much of Isobel. Indeed, I did not want to. And presently my social obligations had been either met or canceled; Mark and I had gone to the last ball, and his tenements were on their way to being improved despite Trinity Corporation. Laura and Edgar and the children were to try to find a long free week to visit us. If the men had any news of Huntington or his slave-brother, they did not tell us. We left the Townes in charge of the Grammercy Square house, with a skeleton staff.

Mark put an arm around me in the carriage, for we drove after all, and said, "It never happened!"

I laughed. "It never happened at all," I said. The horses went at a lively trot up the Bloomingdale Road. I did not know till long after that Allan Pinkerton's men, armed, went before and behind us, nor that the new grooms, following us with our riding-horses, were armed men from Mark's old troop.

CHAPTER SIXTEEN

The past walks here, unseen forevermore
Save by some heart who, in her half-closed door
Looks forth and sighs—with candle held above
"It is too late for laughter—or for love."
VIRGINIA WOODWARD CLOUD

We went back to the Red Castle this time, as Mark said, like children returning home. I had not known how deep its roots had gone with us.

Enough of the staff, I knew, always remained to keep the place in running order; it was an old custom, it seemed. Of course, the laborers on the grounds, including Mackenzie the gardener and his assistants, lived near enough to be there at work. So, I found, did Petronius. He had been here on our first visit, and I remembered now that I had been surprised, thinking him Eugenia's personal footman, and had been told that he was also old Miss Anna's, the recluse cousin or connection far upstairs, old Mr. Somerwell's protégée. Miss Anna was a fixture also, but Dr. De Witt and Mark, it seemed, planned to place her elsewhere.

"Are you sure you should?" I asked Mark. "After all, for

all we see or know of her she might almost not be here at all. And she has lived here practically forever, hasn't she?"

He frowned a little. We were alone in the great stone hall, by the fireplace, waiting for our horses to be brought around; we were going riding along the river. I remember how he looked, standing with one booted foot on the fender, restlessly playing with his riding-whip; strong, vivid, darkly handsome. He was like something in leash. I was suddenly a little afraid of him.

He shrugged, answering my question. "Actually, I don't know how long," he said. "I didn't ask questions of my grandfather, who was responsible for her being here. He was a tyrannical old gentleman. I don't think I cared enough to ask. You know how children are; everything in their house is taken for granted and nothing is stranger than anything else. Frankly, Dr. De Witt thinks that she would be better off elsewhere than in abnormal solitude upstairs. And quite as frankly, my love, I don't want our home to house old ladies who like abnormal solitude." Suddenly the leash broke. "I haven't forgotten that because of my too swift claiming you for my wife Eugenia tried to strike you down the day we were married. Nor the dreadful peril that has come to you twice because of my quixotry as regards Drusilla. Even our first meeting put you in danger on a stormy river. I wonder that you do not fear the sight of any Somerwell or one of the Somerwell blood! I won't risk even the presence of that melancholic old woman in a house you are in!"

He faced me with a look I did not know, alive with the desperate Somerwell anger. It was a felt vibration in the great old place. But my fear went; the tie between us was too strong for fear. I felt a cool, almost impassive calm rising to meet it as if I was upheld by the spell of that long-dead Onnorate whom strangely I had always felt my friend, and I laughed and leaned against him. For the moment I had

208

strength to counsel and reassure the man I had sometimes been in awe of.

"My darling, you will be a knight-errant to the end—the knight-errant who lifted a waif to your saddle-bow and made her your princess! The knight-errant who risked belief and reputation to succour that poor Drusilla you did not love, who stand now against your caste to help and protect the poor you have not even known. If Somerwells are like that, never ask me to stop loving them!"

Under my touch I felt the wild mood steady: the Somerwell violence was in leash, gone. He smiled, and spoke lightly once more.

"I hear the horses. Come, my dear—and we'll forget it, out in the sunlight."

And in the sunlight, in the fresh river wind, gay with the gait of the spirited horse, I dared speak of it again. "I wish you, or Dr. De Witt, would take me to see the poor woman. She can't be difficult, for Cousin Abigail, I remember, visited her periodically. I couldn't get much of an idea of her from Abigail's description, not even what relation she is to the family."

"They have lived here long enough to have uncounted cousins and kinfolk," he said. "I don't know, either. I will, if you insist, Perdita. I suppose she is amiable and harmless enough: she was when I remember meeting her. A rather mournful lady, who would have been stately if she had not been drooping. But she is not staying here."

It was Miss Anna herself who took the matter out of our hands. Before Dr. De Witt, who was away, could return and handle the matter with us, I met her.

I had been going over the third-story rooms, where guests were usually placed. It was a tradition, I had learned from Cousin Abigail, to keep them in order and ready. Accordingly, escorted by an elderly housemaid who knew much more about it all, I couldn't help seeing, than I did, I was standing in the first of these, watching her as she dusted the mantel. Fires had been built in all the rooms I was inspecting, also as a matter of routine, and some fine ash had blown up over the stone. It was somewhat larger than most, and a more charming room. The walls were hung with a tapestry which I was told, reverently, was of Queen Anne's day. There were comfortable deep-cushioned armchairs, seeming freshly done, in dark velvets, a great canopied double bed, a bureau-desk, and tall cases of books on the mantel's either side. Above the mantel hung the portrait of a young man, which by his dress, had been done perhaps twenty-five years back. I remembered, suddenly, Isobel's stories, the day in New York when we had come home from the luncheon at Delmonico's. She had talked of the ghosts that walked in the Red Castle. There was a portrait, she had said, of the younger Eugenius, Eugenia's young father, in one of the rooms kept for guests, young and vivid, and winning even in the painting. And, because the brothers, Eugenius and Nicholas, and their wives, had drowned so young, they walked.

"They say they come back to their rooms, with their clothes all drenched with the salt water," she had said: "Once someone found a spray of seaweed on one of the floors, damp still."

It was daylight, and the room was warm and orderly and bright with lighted candles. Yet I shivered, and scolded myself for it. There was a heavy Brussels carpet on the floor, unstained . . . of course it would be unstained! Isobel loved telling such stories. The portrait must be the one she had told me of, Eugenia's young father. Yes—those were Eugenia's long beautiful hands, her dark handsome features in a masculine mold. But the vividness, the bright winningness, the look as if he loved you and wished you well—the willed

210

charm that appeared even in a painting—were his alone. I remembered Isobel's "They say he could win any woman."

I stood, fascinated, a moment, and turned to the woman. "Do you know the subject of this painting? Would it be Miss Eugenia's father?"

"I believe so, ma'am," she said. "But I am not sure: I have only been here since the tragedy, when Miss Abigail came to take charge of the little girls."

He seemed too alive and gay for it all to have happened: the picnic on the younger brother's yacht on Long Island Sound, the sudden storm that wrecked the boat, the loss of all aboard.

I voiced my thought: "He looks so alive to have died so young," I said.

The maid was a rather wooden person. "It must have been all very sad, ma'am," she said. "Let us hope they are happy in Heaven."

"You can never tell that," said a lady's quiet voice from the doorway. I turned in surprise. Then I knew it must be poor Miss Anna, not only because she was in a handsome, somewhat old-fashioned indoor dress, but because behind her, deferential but not too far away, stood Petronius, a covered basket on his arm. He greeted me with his usual unsurprised deference.

Miss Anna looked sad. But she looked and spoke, otherwise, like anybody else. She was a tall woman, dignified, with masses of graying hair worn in an old-fashioned coiffure of high braidings and loopings, and had a sunken face which had, I thought, once been handsome in a strong-featured fashion.

"You are Miss Anna?" I said. "I am Mrs. Harradine. My husband says he knew you when he was a boy. His mother was Eleanor Somerwell."

"And you were—" she said, a bit vaguely. "Surely I have seen you somewhere. . . ."

"My name was Van Dorn," I said. "I have been Miss Isobel's friend since we were little, and lived here with her for a time till I married, so probably you have."

She shook her head. "But it does not matter. Yes, Miss Anna is what they call me. I did not know anyone had come back to the Red Castle. I live very much alone."

I wondered why Petronius had told her nothing; but then his ways were always a mystery to me. I said, "Cousin Abigail told me. She says you do beautiful work, modeling in wax and clay."

"It was considered promising once," she said. "I do it now only for my own amusement. I thought"—she stopped— "that perhaps I might adorn the mantel there. Miss Abigail has allowed it. I think your housekeeper must have put my vases away—"

"Oh, by all means do," I said. I could not have hurt this forlorn woman by a refusal.

She beckoned Petronius near, and drew out two beautiful and delicate waxen statuettes—a Spring and a Summer by the wreaths in their hands—and set them at the ends of the mantel. "They have a hard glaze," she said. "The heat will not hurt them." She knew the room, for she went to a closet I had not seen. The housemaid had curtsied and gone when she came in. She drew out a pair of Sèvres vases and set in them, under Eugenius Somerwell's portrait, a cluster each of white roses and orange blossoms that could only be known to be waxen by the way she lifted them and set them in, like a votive offering.

"Oh, did you know him?" I asked impulsively. "It is young Eugenius Somerwell, isn't it?"

"Yes, I knew him," she said. "This was—his room."

The way she spoke told me something. Poor woman, she

212

had loved him. Probably he had never known she existed except as a shadowy dependent of the Somerwell family, but her voice rang when she said his name. She said no more after that. Followed by Petronius, who bowed his farewell as always, she turned and went along the hall to the upper stair.

Mark was outdoors a good deal, I with him most of the time. It was near enough spring so that he was needed about the estate. He said that though Cousin Abigail had done her best, and a good best for a woman, there was a good deal to be pulled into shape still. It was a great possession: a half mile of territory up to the highway with orchards, gardens, the tenant farms. The old red stone castle, larger than any family today, or indeed in the first Somerwell day, could need, with its legends and terrors and luxury and loneliness, dominated all. I think that in spite of my fondness for it, it frightened me a little.

Mark was neither frightened nor romantic about it. There were generations of landowners behind him. He had still the better part of his year of leave free to put the place into shape. He approved the bailiff, who had been a top sergeant in the regular army, and also had as many generations of dirt farmers behind him as Mark had estated gentry. The combination pleased Mark, who said that a man with a sergeant's discipline and efficiency, combined with a liking for the land, could not be bettered. Especially, of course, with Mark's rule behind him. Mark was beginning to wonder if he wouldn't resign from the army when his year was up.

We were on one of our rides through the estate one morning soon after I had met Miss Anna, and I reminded him that he had said he would escort me to see her if I insisted. Which I was doing now.

He finally gave in. For, poor soul, if she was anything like content up there with her modeling materials and Petronius to serve her, it seemed to me that uprooting her would be hard on her after all these years, and I thought if he saw and talked to her he might agree with me.

He shook his head when I said so, but he replied, "We'll get it over this afternoon, after we've told Petronius to give her warning." I laughed at his military promptness, but he said if it had to be done it was best to get it over quickly. So when we returned to the house we sent word to her, and she said she was glad to see us at any time, and set four o'clock.

The Red Castle had five stories. We climbed stone stair after stone stair, each one narrower and darker than the other. Mark, who had been to the top of the Castle before, brought a lighted lantern, which had seemed absurd in the fresh daylight below, but which I was glad of in the gloom— almost as glad as I was of his guiding arm. Finally he came to the landing with no stairs beyond. Sunk in the wall to the right was a heavy door with a great keyhole. "They can't hear you through it," he explained. "There's a sort of hall before you reach her apartments."

I began to be very glad I had never ventured up here by myself. Mark took my hand and led me in.

If he had not I should have run back with a cry; as it was I did scream a little. In the dim light we seemed to be in the midst of a crowd of vague people, surrounding us along the walls. Mark said calmly, "Now you can see where the legend of the ghostly Chinese people came from."

As my eyes became accustomed to the dimness I realized that all the wall space was papered with scene after scene in the life of a Chinese village. It was in color and the people were nearly life size.

"If these could be stripped from the wall," he said calmly, "they could be sold for any amount of money. Old Edward

214

Eugenius who built the castle—remember, the supposed pirate?—brought them when he came. He was supposed to have robbed a Chinese temple of them. I think he spread or allowed it to be spread that they were victims of his who haunted the place. As a matter of fact, my grandfather said, he did have a crew of Chinamen to whom he wasn't too merciful, or smuggled them in in some unpleasant way. He was a good deal of a brute from all accounts."

The door at the other end of the room was closed also, but not locked. Mark knocked on it lightly.

Miss Anna had a suite, it seemed, though indeed she could have occupied the whole floor without discommoding anyone. Petronius opened to us; it was, it seemed, her living room or workroom, for there were statuettes and busts, and two larger figures at the sides of the window that faced the river . . . Hers had been the little light I had often watched from the ferryhouse, high up, and thought then how lonely it seemed. She welcomed us quietly, with dignity. She was dressed in a handsome dark satin gown which like her other gown was pathetically of a fashion twenty years ago. It was somehow as if she and all her surroundings had stopped, run down like a clock, when gown and coiffure and furniture were new. She had been remote and unchanged while the world had gone on.

But her work was alive. Statuettes like those she had set in young Eugenius' room on the mantel were in cabinets and on shelves. There was a head of Caesar, copies of other Roman and Greek art. She was unquestionably talented; it seemed a waste that she should do nothing with it all. I dared not say anything of the sort, of course, but I could admire and praise. Presently Petronius entered again with a tray, a cobwebbed bottle and glasses and delicate hors d'oeuvres. The wine, from Mark's expression, was excellent. We might have

215

been being entertained by any wellbred, rather quiet and withdrawn maiden lady. Pleased, I could see, by our praise, she unwrapped the damp cloths from the figures by the window: they were nearly finished, she said, an Astrea and a Hecate; the one sternly beautiful, the other with a Fury's face. Her final work was usually in wax, she said.

"May we, then, see the other covered figure?" Mark asked. I had not realized there was one, and saw, against the wall, an oblong box with a white shawl obviously covering a recumbent figure. Miss Anna shook her head.

"That is not far enough on to mean anything to anyone but myself," she said. She moved over to the cabinet and began to give us a detailed description of the groups of statuettes; Autumn and Winter, the rest of the set now in Eugenius' room; Cupids, graceful figures that could have had their inspiration in Tanagras, a child's head repeated over and over.

When we had left her, I said, "It's rather heartbreaking, isn't it? I wonder what would happen if we found her rooms in a city, and friends for her among other artists and sculptors? Laura knows everybody—"

Mark said, rather sternly, "My dear child, if Dr. De Witt, who has apparently looked after her for some time, hasn't decided that such a life would be best for her, he probably knows better than we do. From what Cousin Abigail has said, some severe shock made her retire from the world of her own volition. But when he gets back you shall talk it over with us."

"I didn't mean—"

We were standing on the top step; he slipped an arm around me. "You never mean anything but what is most generous, my little love," he said, and kissed me lightly. There was a slight noise, and I turned to look. Miss Anna had followed us to the outer door. She had caught her breath, and was staring at us in the dim light, her face tense. As she saw me turn she turned away, and went back into the Chinese room.

"I think she was in love with young Eugenius," I said. "Perhaps, perhaps it hurt her to see you kiss me."

"Then she shouldn't slip out and watch us," he said lightly. The soft dark mustache and smiling lips brushed my cheek again, and we went on down together.

Dr. De Witt got back a week later and came to dine with us and discuss the matter of Miss Anna.

"The situation is," Mark said over the wine, "that my softhearted little wife here encountered Miss Anna on the third floor, decking the apartment of my late uncle Eugenius with wax flowers and so on. She coaxed me to make a domiciliary visit with her after that. I am bound to admit that, except for a certain gloom often seen in maiden ladies, there seemed nothing unusual about her. Perdita, I think, would like to have her left here if she prefers: next to that, established in New York with introductions to other artists. Her work does seem to me excellent. I can't say that I prefer to have her left here. But we want your opinion."

Dr. De Witt's small wise gray eyes looked at me keenly. "My dear Perdita—forgive me, Mrs. Harradine—I've known the child always, Major—however harmless and content Miss Anna seems, if she has been so much a melancholic as to prefer years of this entire retreat, well—one never knows. You saw nothing strange about her, then?"

I flushed. "Well, all I remember—" I stopped short.

Mark picked it up, laughing a little. "Well—you've known me, too, since I was pretty young, Doctor . . . I'd almost scolded my girl here as we went, after which I kissed her. And Miss Anna, who had come out to watch us away without notice, gasped, and was staring down as shocked as if kissing one's wife was improper and depressing!"

"And you were saying nothing to upset her?"

"I think I was telling Honor here that she was too generous for her own good, or something like that."

"Honor?"

It was Mark's turn to color a little. "It's a pet name I use sometimes when she has been especially good," he said, smiling still.

Dr. De Witt did not answer directly.

"My dear boy, I still agree with you that Miss Anna will be better off, at least for a time, in the charge of an intelligent mental specialist; and fortunately my friend Dr. Reading has pleasant and ample quarters, to which her work and statuary can be transported. She is not too far from here to be checked on from time to time, and even, if he agrees, planned for as your wife suggests, eventually."

"And our Red Castle," Mark said, "will not be haunted by a prowling if harmless elderly lady. Onnorate the Oneida, my dear, and Isobel's Chinese friends are really enough!"

I was not convinced; but they were the two people in the world whose judgment I most respected. I said, "Very well. But you will really let her take her statues and materials with her?"

"Dr. Reading thinks it a good idea," Dr. De Witt said.

"Even," Mark said, "those lifesize ladies glowering at each other across the window, Astrea and Hecate?"

"Justice and Vengeance," the doctor said thoughtfully. "It might do her good to leave them behind."

"Well, you and Dr. Reading can decide those minor matters between you," Mark said cheerfully. "Shall we go into the small withdrawing room where the piano is, and let Perdita give you some music? You asked for it last time, I remember."

218

The doctor had always liked my singing. He and Uncle Jacob both loved the songs of their own day. I had sung a half dozen of such things, when my fingers slipped into Uncle Jacob's most loved song.

"*Near the lake where drooped the willow*
     Long time ago,
Where the rock threw back the billow
     Whiter than snow,
Dwelt a maiden loved and cherished
     By high and low,
But with Autumn's leaf she perished
     Long time ago."

I stopped short. In the mirror that reflected the door behind me I could see someone standing. Miss Anna, still in her outmoded elegance, listening intently.

"This is too much!" Mark said under his breath, and rose. But before he could move to the door a figure behind her moved also; Petronius, her shadow.

He spoke softly. "Miss Anna, you know you shouldn't come downstairs. Miss Anna—"

Without struggling he was turning her, quietly steering her away, along the hall, and apparently up the stone stair again.

"That settles it," Mark said harshly. "Out of our house she goes whether your Dr. Reading approves or not."

But Petronius was entering, bowing with his usual reverence. "Major Mark," he said, "please, sir, forgive her. She has a sort of interest in Mrs. Harradine. She couldn't talk of anything else. It shall not happen again."

"It shall not, indeed," Mark said, "or I shall provide for her immediately in a place she will like less than Dr. Reading's home."

Petronius only bowed deeply and was gone.

I began playing softly again. Presently Dr. De Witt made his *adieux*. He had a hard day ahead tomorrow, he said.

"Don't let poor Miss Anna weigh on you, Major Harradine," he said. "This time next week Reading will have her safe, and if I know him, content in his retreat."

Our peace and gayety, our placid routine of rides over the estate, visits to and from our neighbors, evenings together of plans for the place, books and music and content together, went on for a little while. But not for long.

We had just risen from the table one of these quiet spring evenings, looking forward to the hours together when we should talk over our redoing of the old place, when someone rang the bell sharply. I can see it now, swinging on its coiled wire above the door. The butler's quick steps down the hall were followed by footsteps that hurried, almost ran, entering and turning to where we had just crossed near the drawing-room fire. I had dropped into my own chair, I remember, and Mark was about to pick up the last monthly part of *Pendennis*, which he was reading aloud to me as it arrived. The door flew open. And of all people, it was staid quiet Cousin Abigail, all the way from Peekskill, her bonnet flung back from her tossed side-curls and her shawl awry on her shoulder.

"Children—oh, children! What is wrong?" she said. "Tell me—tell me!"

Mark put an arm round her and guided her to an armchair near us by the fire.

"Why, cousin, nothing whatever!" he said. "Everything is all right. Even the novel we are about to read is a trifle dull in parts!" I bent over to untie her bonnet-string and lift her shawl from her shoulders.

"Stop!" she said sharply to Mark. Mark, undisturbed, rang for a servant and ordered her wine.

"Stop," she said again. "You can't make light of what you did. You sent me the token."

"Token?" we both echoed in surprise. I wondered if she was unbalanced—which seemed to be the one thing impossible. She was deeply disturbed. "Don't try to explain till you're rested," I said, and poured the wine for her. She drank it slowly, set down the empty glass, and spoke more collectedly.

"You are the only members of the family here. Who else would have sent me the red castle?" she said, bewildered. Mark and I looked at each other in what was nearly dismay. She opened her reticule and lifted out a small thing wrapped in tissue paper. She held it to us, stripped. It was a red chess castle, smaller than the one we had found among my mother's things. Mark spoke with careful control. "Well?" he said.

"Do you mean that you have never known that it has always been a token of the Somerwell message—Come, because of deep need or trouble, to this place?"

I started to speak, but he stopped me. "I had never been told that a red chessman was anything but a part of a set of chess. I had nothing to do with it, Cousin Abigail. Nor, naturally, had Perdita."

"You mean there is nothing wrong?" She was white.

"Nothing is wrong."

We glanced at each other. Miss Anna?

He rang for the housekeeper, and had Petronius summoned. Without mentioning the chessman, he cross-questioned them. But nobody—not Miss Anna, not Petronius—had been to or from the post office within the week, except the man who always had that duty, Junius, the footman. And Junius, like the rest, had not left Grandison that winter.

She shook her head. "There is no way he could have known about it," she said. "Are you sure, Mark, that your mother never told you about it?"

221

"Quite sure. It seems a futile sort of way of sending word, at that."

"It began in the Revolution or earlier," she said. She had control of herself now. "If an enemy got possession of it it meant nothing to him: the Red Castle was a center of secret action for the patriots, from what I heard. But the tradition has always been carried on."

I had never heard much good of the earlier Somerwells. I wondered if the old pirate who built the house had not needed such secrecy for his messages . . . But my mother! The message had been sent to her, too . . .

Mark's hand lay on mine warningly . . . "Somebody has been playing a very unkind practical joke on you, cousin," he said. "Did I understand that the postmark was Grandison?"

"The postmark was illegible," she said faintly.

She looked worn out; she looked really sick.

"Well, you are in no state to worry about it tonight," he said gently. "Your room is I think ready for you always—isn't it, Perdita? We'll sleep on it."

She was exhausted, it was plain. She had come the fastest way, which was also the most tiring and the dirtiest, the steamcars. She could not bear the thought of anything to eat, she said. I went with her to her room, and saw to it that the fire was burning well, coaxed her to take a cup of hot milk, and sat with her till she fell asleep, which was soon, so tired she was.

"Well!" Mark said when I rejoined him. "Eugenia—or even Isobel?"

"You can't send chessmen if you are ill in bed," I said. "Cousin Abigail says Isobel has been in bed with a hard cold for a week: and besides, it is so pointless! We are both fond of Cousin Abigail. She could have come without a summons at any time, and knows it. As for Eugenia—"

But, to say what we learned later from Dr. De Witt,

222

Eugenia, too, had not gone out from the religious retreat where it seems she was staying now, for several days.

"It is the doing, probably, of some half-crazy servant or servant's friend, who had picked up the story while in the house."

When we were alone in our own room Mark spoke again, slowly. "There is always the possibility that it is tied up in some way with the Huntingtons."

"What good would it do them to send Abigail here, poor lady?"

"Perhaps to frighten—which it has not done. As you say, pointless."

"But—it summoned my mother."

"But what—why?"

There was no answer to that.

CHAPTER SEVENTEEN

♜

Silence and horror brood on the walls,
Through every crevice a little voice calls,
"Quicken, mad footsteps on pavement and stair:
Look not behind thee: the chamber is there!"
ROSE TERRY COOKE

It seemed that Dr. Reading could not receive Miss Anna for another couple of weeks. Mark was content, now it was settled that she was going. Both doctors said it was best not to tell her so far ahead. It did not seem to me especially important. Cousin Abigail, as I was learning to call her most of the time, visited her and reported that she was well and hard at work. Then Cousin Abigail herself fell ill, the second day. The doctor, who had come to tell us of the delay, was fortunately there. It was nothing either new or serious. It seemed she could never tolerate without cramps and difficulty in breathing something she had eaten before she came—I think it was strawberries or tomatoes. She denied having anything of the sort but nevertheless had a sharp attack.

So I wrote to Isobel at Peekskill to explain why she had not returned, only to have Isobel, frantic with worry, flutter down by the next stage from Peekskill. Mark and I were a little rueful—our second honeymoon surrounded! And I knew Mark was not too fond of her. But at least we knew that it would only be until Cousin Abigail got over the attack. They usually lasted a week or ten days. And the Castle, after all, was a Castle; its actual original, as Mark philosophically said, had been built to be packed with knights and ladies and all sorts of henchmen, without crowding, instead of five people and their necessary servants.

Also, Isobel had reverted to her calmer self. When I asked her if all was going well with her love affair, she brightened, and said, "That dreadful Meg Merrillies creature that they have put in jail for trying to kidnap you at least did tell me a good fortune! I think it is coming true."

It was so like the old childish, self-centered Isobel! I was beginning to realize that she would always be like a little girl in some ways. Well, many gentlemen liked pretty childlike little wives like Dickens' Dora; it was fortunate that Etienne Ducross was one of them. He was, it seemed, settled in his earlier lodgings in Tarrytown, carriages and all, and apparently there was, from Isobel's manner, a satisfactory understanding. Cousin Abigail must be satisfied also, I thought; when she was better I would ask her.

Meanwhile, Mark said that we would do well to make a last check on Eugenia's whereabouts at the ferryhouse and at the religious retreat; a group of high church ladies who had become a sisterhood too much like those of the Roman Catholics to please our old rector, Dr. Van Alstyne. The people at the ferry, where there was always coming and going, were always well informed about everybody's whereabouts. I was glad he wanted to. The affair, as far as Cousin Abigail went, might, as we said, have been a pointless trick. But the fact that it had happened as well to my mother, and perhaps had something to do with her accident, though that seemed an extravagant guess, Mark said, made it more important.

Eliza at the ferryhouse, her greetings and excitement over, knew little more of Eugenia than the others had. Some friends of the Blackwaters, farming folk, had seen her driving in a surrey with an older gentleman, and a lady in a black dress. They were going in the direction of New York. The Blackwaters had little more to tell. The surrey had stopped at that new house beside the Episcopal church—not Dr. Van Alstyne's, but the church further down toward New York, St. Maura's.

"It is not too far. Do you mind staying here till I return?" Mark asked, and when I assented, went. I went to see my old garden. There were snowdrops in the grass already. I ran across to the wood, where I knew the dark early violets grew at the wood's edge and came back with a handful. It was a warm, sunny day. There was a log where I had been used to sit, close by the road: I sat down there and lost myself in dreaming of the old days, my girlhood that was so close in time and was so far away: I could hear Uncle Jacob, in my mind, and his voice reading to me at night as we sat by the hearthfire . . .

> *"Where through groves deep and high*
> *Sounds the far billow,*
> *Where early violets die*
> *Under the willow . . ."*

Those had been such gentle and peaceful times.

And then I looked up and saw that Mark had returned and was standing watching me. He crossed to me, and I knew I would not change this time for that.

"This is where I met you first," he said, smiling at me. "You were a baby, running along beside your mother unafraid. You're unafraid still, bless you, my Honor. Come home now."

He held his hand out, and we went back through my garden and the ferryhouse again. I think for the moment we

226

had both forgotten our errand, and remembered that stormy night last November, when we had taken hands, not expecting to meet again, when he went away with Drusilla and I went in, facing the fact that he was Eugenia's. Andy Blackwater was waiting to row us back to the carriage on the other side. There was a fresh wind rising. It stirred the leaves under our feet as we stepped ashore and set them blowing.

"I love the wind and the leaves," I said. "You'll never make quite a city lady of me, Mark."

"Then you're not afraid of what Onnorate may do to you because you were brought to the Red Castle, when her brown leaves blow?"

"Not I!" I said. "When I first heard of Onnorate, I prayed for her. I felt we were friends, because we both loved unloved. You can't fear people you pray for."

"And when you found you were wrong did you still pray?"

"I think she needed it the more," I said, smiling. The horses had brought us within sight of our gates. "You were not long away," I said. "What did you learn if anything?"

"I learned that Eugenia *was* with the Anglican sisterhood," he said. "She went there the day the Blackwaters' friends saw her: the gentleman with her was Dr. Reading. And unless the Mother Superior is lying, which I think close to impossible, she has not left the house since. She does not contemplate joining the order. She is resting and studying only, or that was what the Mother stated. She did not wish to see me."

"It sounds as if she was doing what you once said in joke," I said, "trying, with this Dr. Reading's help, to get rid of her insane temper."

"You are my wise little girl," he said. "I think so, too. More power to her. Well, we have ruled out everything but the possibility of some villager who knows the old story of the chess token and wants to annoy us. I think we'll call in Mr. Pinkerton and his men if it happens again."

Miss Abigail was getting better. As for Miss Anna, I had nearly forgotten her: she had never troubled me much anyway, except that Mark disliked having her in the Castle. As for Isobel, though I could not help knowing that Mark preferred her absence also, and that her possessiveness fretted him a little, she would go when Cousin Abigail went, which would be shortly now.

It was a matter of a distant tenant farm and Mark's necessity for spending the day with Van Brunt dealing with it, which made me realize that Isobel's attitude to me was not only unchanged, but held a little resentment because Mark came first now. As he rode off directly after breakfast, she threw her arms around me. "We have a whole day for just us," she said. "Oh, Dita, I have so missed having you all to myself! Let the silly housekeeping go; I have so much to talk about."

"You won't want me all to yourself when you're married to Ducross," I said, smiling. But after I had seen the housekeeper, in spite of Isobel, I returned to her and the old attitude of care and protection—and loving service, though I had not known it for that before my marriage—was there again.

She followed me around like a kitten. She was a little fretful. When something came up—some matter of the maid's duties—she strayed off with something very like a flounce. "If you can't stay with me more than an hour at a time," she said petulantly, "I'm going to explore by myself. I've never really been all over the Red Castle."

"Shall I send for Petronius to accompany you?" I asked. "You will need a little help; think of those four flights of steep stairs!"

I was not quite ingenuous. She could know nothing of Miss

Anna, which I still thought foolish. But as long as it was Cousin Abigail's desire, it was for me to see that she did not discover the poor woman for herself. But there were the two locked doors, I remembered, the one that led through the hall with the Chinese papering, and Miss Anna's own.

"I don't want anybody," she said, still crossly.

I dealt with the quarreling maids satisfactorily, and after I had visited Cousin Abigail, who was now sitting up by her old window in a wrapper and deciding that she could come down to dinner that night, went up the Castle stairs in search of Isobel. I was pretty sure that frail as she was, she would not be able to make it to the very top without resting, and I was right. She was coiled on the bottom step of the second flight. "Oh, go back to your wifely duties as queen and chatelaine of the Red Castle!" she said as angrily as she sometimes had at seven. And I decided to treat her as if she *was* seven.

"I will," I said. "I owe Laura a letter I haven't had time to finish. Junius has gone to the post office already. I shall go and finish the letter and take it myself. The ride in the fresh air will do me good."

I turned and went down the hall before she could answer.

The ride in the fresh air refreshed and quieted me. Which was as well, for on my return, my face flushed and my hair loosened by the wind and the gallop, the first thing I saw was a still unhappy Isobel, sobbing this time, her face buried in the tall chair beside the doors.

"What on earth is the matter?" I said, putting a hand on her shaking shoulder. "Cousin Abigail is almost well, and you had a letter from Mr. Ducross yesterday, because I saw his name on the envelope in your hand."

She threw out a hand. "It's Eugenia! That dreadful Eugenia! You're letting her come and go in this house! She was here yesterday!"

229

"I have heard nothing of it," I said. "Are you sure?"

"You're as calm as that about it! Have Petronius up—he let her in. I tell you I saw them. She stayed a long time. She may be here now."

"You should have told me before," I said. "But don't you remember that your grandfather's will gave her the privilege of coming and going here still?"

"It shows she has no proper pride or sense of what a bold intrusion it is!" Isobel said angrily. I could but agree with her, though I did not say it. It seemed unlike her, I thought, to come in without telling anyone: bold and arrogant as she had always been.

"Oh, I am sure that she is gone," I said. "What would she stay for? Well, I suppose to see Cousin Abigail—but she would have said so."

"I asked Aunt Abigail. She knew nothing about it."

And it probably upset her, I thought. Isobel, certainly, was upset; her hand had gone up to her scarred cheek, as it always did when she was frightened. "I'll send for Petronius," I said.

He came, elegant and unmoved as always.

"Yes, madam," he replied to my question. "Madam has not forgotten that she may do so by her grandfather's will?"

"I remember. But in courtesy to the mistress of the house I should have been notified of her presence."

"Yes, madam. But the matter was too pressing to allow of it."

He had always belonged to Eugenia primarily. There was no use arguing with him, or inquiring. I said, "Where is Miss Eugenia now?"

"I believe, madam, that she is residing with a group of religious ladies who live near St. Maura's Episcopal Church."

"You won't get anything out of him," Isobel said angrily. "Oh, leave us!"

230

Before I could ask or say more he had slipped away.

"I don't believe a word of it. I'm going to find out if she's here still," Isobel said, and began running up the stair.

I thought that if Isobel got as far as Miss Anna's quarters it would be a shock she should not face, and as I followed hastily, catching up my trailing habit, I wished for the tenth time that the silly secret hadn't been kept from her. I called her, but she fled on. She had gained Miss Anna's floor before I had caught up with her. I called to her.

"No—there's music—there's something up here—" She turned her head to listen. It was, of all things, Miss Anna's aeolian harp. The doors through must both be open. The wind was high and strong, and carried the wailing music to us. The harp was fastened across a tall window in the Chinese room masked from outside by a treetop. I had never heard it so plainly. Rain was beginning to dash against the closed windows. There was going to be a storm. I stood between Isobel and the great door to the Chinese room that masked Miss Anna's.

"It's only an aeolian harp," I said. "I've seen it before, when Mark and I came up here." I put a hand on her shoulder to turn her.

"It's the ghosts crying—it's the ghosts!" Isobel wailed. She sank down, clinging to my skirts.

I lost patience. I cast a hasty glance back at the door to Miss Anna's workroom. It was almost closed, and there was no light there; she must be in the rooms behind, behind the closed bedroom door. I stood over the crouched sobbing little figure and thought of all the years I had petted and soothed her out of her weeping ways and dreads: and how useless it had been. And I remembered what Mark had said: and I was suddenly through spoiling her. It had not been for her good or mine. I was stronger than she was, of course. I pulled her to her feet and spoke sharply.

231

"There are no ghosts. That is an aeolian harp, as I told you. It's inside there, in the corner of the Chinese room. And the Chinese ghosts are a legend, too; made up or scared up because the room is all papered with pictures of a Chinese village. The people on the walls probably looked real to some frightened servant in the twilight some time or other, and the story grew from that. You are going to get up and see for yourself."

She said "No! No!" But I half pulled, half dragged her into the dim room. The daylight was going; the storm had darkened everything. The people on the walls—I did not wonder that in the half light they had made some frightened maidservant believe them real. It was too dark: there were lucifer matches on the sill, and I hastily lighted the candles in their sconces. They did not do enough to the light; it was blowing up a violent storm; the high stone walls still made a gloom. The wires that made the harp were fastened across the bottom of the window, and it was opened at the bottom, about a handsbreadth up, for them. I tried to close it and found it was immovable. A bough lay against the glass. I gave up the effort, and crossed to Isobel, standing where I had left her against the wall. She clung to me, burying her head on my shoulder. I tried to turn to lead her out. There was a slight noise, and she shrieked.

"Let me go! Let me go! It is Onnorate, come to haunt us!"

I let her go and turned to see. Miss Anna's workroom door was opening. Miss Anna herself stood there, her dressing gown open above her nightdress. She spoke, gasping:

"No, no! She died long ago of fever, Isobel! I tell you she died! I tried to kill her, but she lay there alive, I thought she was dead—but she did die afterwards, too late! She did! Why do you stand there in your habit, with your hair pulled loose by the fall, as if you were alive, Honor Leighton—Onnorate Leighton! Go back to your grave!"

I was as paralyzed as Isobel for the moment, but the woman staggered and fell backward into the inner room for the moment, grasped the doorjamb and moved forward. What she had said appalled me. She was calling me by a name that must be my mother's. She took me for my dead mother.

Isobel stood motionless. There was no time to wonder how she knew who Isobel was. The woman was delirious or insane, whether she spoke incredible truth or wild fantasy. I moved nearer her.

"I am not Honor Leighton. I am Perdita Harradine," I said as quietly as I could. "You are ill, Miss Anna. You had better go back to bed."

She backed and backed into the dusk of her workroom, the look of drawn horror on her face still. There were two candles in their sconces, giving a faint light only. She was standing now behind something that was between us. Presently I saw that it was the thing that had been against the wall, that Mark had called the croquet box. It was open now and set on two chairs. She bent to reach into it and take something out, and straightened herself. This time it was I who screamed.

For the moment I had thought it a dead woman, lying there in a rough coffin. When I got my breath I saw that it was one of Miss Anna's waxen statues. A girl with a faint flush on her cheeks, with long brown curls; a girl in an old-fashioned riding habit, with exquisitely made hands spread on her breast as if they guarded something. For a moment she was frighteningly real.

Miss Anna was out from behind the coffin, gripping my wrist with a strength I had not known she possessed. Her voice rose to a shriek again, that could be heard above the storm.

"You are dead, I tell you! How dare you come back! I have done everything! I gave the image of you back everything I took when you fell, all the papers, there in your hands! They can't say I didn't! You've no right to haunt me, it wasn't you I killed, you didn't die then! I didn't mean to kill Eugenius, the knife was there and I struck and it went too deep, I loved him, I did love him, I was only angry because he tricked me—Everyone knew I was his wife, they didn't know about your hole-and-corner marriage . . . Stop standing there, staring at me across your own coffin! Stop—"

She sprang around it. The terror that had frozen me broke; it was a knife in her uplifted hand. I ran from her room into the Chinese room: I was fleet, but the habit tangled round my feet. She was on me, nearly, there in the dark with the shrieking wind; then there was a crash, and the sound of a fall. Something brushed my feet. It lay long and dark between me and Miss Anna's prostrate body. I caught my breath and dared to stand still, and my eyes got used to the dim light.

The bough against the pane had been smashed through the glass by the tempest. It lay on the floor between us like a barrier. It lay heavy and broad across Miss Anna's ankle, pinning her down, if she had not already been motionless in a faint. Her knife had flung across the room. I saw Isobel stare at it a moment, then bend and pick it up.

"It is all right, Isobel," I said. "She's in a faint, and the bough is holding her down. Hurry out; she's insane; she may come to—" I broke off. I heard footsteps up the stone stair, and voices, and thanked heaven.

But Isobel screamed. "It's Eugenia! It's Eugenia!" she cried, and, terror making her lose her head, flung the heavy door shut.

I ran to the door and tried to push it open. "Eugenia isn't as dangerous as a homicidal maniac, you fool!" I called, struggling against the door.

Someone bent and called through the keyhole, "It's a spring lock. We have to get the key." Oh, blessed sound, it was

234

Mark's voice. I heard quick steps down the stairs: Mark's voice, raised clear in an order, "The keys in the second righthand drawer of the library desk, Petronius! Hurry, man, for God's sake! Perdita, stay close to the wall, barricade yourself with that chest in the corner, girls."

Isobel was crouched in the corner, but I managed to pull the chest before us, thankful for the arms that rowing had strengthened. I had scarcely done it when Petronius' flying feet came up the stair again; there was a clash of keys: I had just time to spring away before it flew open and Mark had me fast. Isobel was clutching his shoulder: he pushed her to Petronius.

Then I saw, holding high the lighted lantern, that Eugenia was actually there. Isobel's fear-sharpened ears had been right. She was pallid, set-faced and plainly clad as I had never seen her. And I saw that there was another person behind her. Only Dr. De Witt. He moved toward the room. "Let me pass, Perdita," he said. "Come, Eugenia."

Both Eugenia and Petronius quietly followed him in, to where the bough lay straight across the floor with its heavy end holding Miss Anna's ankle fast. Eugenia stood, silent as ice, the lantern high. The men gently lifted the bough and began to raise the prostrate woman as gently, but the motion made her conscious, and she spoke faintly.

"Eugenia—Eugenia dearest! I tried again to kill Honor Leighton, indeed I did . . . but she—was a ghost, you can't . . . She's over there . . . Eleanor's boy had her in his arms . . . I knew who she was awhile back . . . He loved her too. He called her by her name . . . Eugenia, try to kill her! You're strong and young . . ." Eugenia stepped back, horror on her face. The woman on the floor flung herself from the men's hold in a wild effort, and fell back, gasping. The doctor knelt and held her again.

"I was afraid of this, Eugenia, yesterday," he said. "Your

235

mother is dying." Eugenia's face did not change from its set severity.

"We had better take her back to her bedroom," she said coldly. She crossed to the inner room and flung the bedroom door wide. The two men lifted her, and I followed.

"Is there anything I can do, Dr. De Witt, or anyone I can send for?" I said. I could not understand what he had said, that Miss Anna was Eugenia's mother. But this was no time to ask questions. I looked around for Isobel, only to see her disappearing toward the staircase, and hear her feet running down. It was a relief to have her out of the way.

The doctor had not taken time to turn in my direction, where I had stood in the shadow of the outside door with Mark. He turned his head and started back.

"Perdita! No wonder the poor woman was in terror!" he said.

"What do you mean?" Mark said, coming over to stand with me.

"Can't you see, man?" He halted, with the woman in his arms; Petronius of course stopped too. "You're old enough to remember. She's Madame Honor as I saw her first, when she had been carried into the ferryhouse, in her riding habit with those curls loose. . . ." They laid Miss Anna on her bed. Dr. De Witt turned to face us.

"She called me that," I said, "Honor Leighton—and then Onnorate Leighton. It must have been the same name—" I felt dazed.

"Good God, what stupid fools we have been!" the doctor said. "It must have been Juliana, then, who stunned Honor—"

"*Juliana!*" I repeated, and then I understood, partly. "You mean—" He had said 'your mother' to Eugenia. He must mean that Miss Anna was Juliana Somerwell, who had been young Eugenius' wife and Eugenia's mother. "But—but she was drowned! She and her husband were drowned with the others . . ." I said.

"That was what they told us all," Eugenia said stonily, from where she stood now at the foot of the bed. "That was our dear grandfather's lie. She sent for me by Petronius yesterday. She told me who she was because she knew she was near dying."

"But why, in God's name?" Mark asked.

Eugenia's face wrenched. "Do not ask me—"

Dr. De Witt put a protective arm around Eugenia. "My poor girl, you have had enough. Let Petronius take you back to St. Maura's now."

"No! Tell them—they'll have to know sooner or later—" she said. "My cousin I think will keep quiet for the honor of the name; he'll keep the ferry girl quiet—"

"If you knew that our grandfather was keeping my uncle Eugenius' widow here under another name," Mark said sharply, "you should at least have informed me, when I took possession of the Red Castle, Doctor."

"I came here yesterday with Eugenia, when Juliana sent Petronius for her," the doctor answered. "We did not learn of her identity until then. She kept her secret well, poor woman."

"She tried to kill my mother," I said. "And she tried to kill me. And she said—she said—" I remembered. "She said, 'I did not mean to kill Eugenius!'"

"And you pity her!" Mark said. "That's enough, Doctor—"

"I pity her," Dr. De Witt said quietly, "because she inherited homicidal mania from her father's people, and because her husband let himself be pushed into marrying her when he was already married to another woman, whom he loved. He was too weak to confess the marriage to his father: he may have been driven into telling Juliana: we may never

237

know how she found out. She came to the Red Castle first to visit her sister Sibylla, who had married Eugenius' younger brother: that we know. He was the sort—Eugenius—women go mad over. It was said that old Somerwell made the match. The Vincent girls were wealthy independently, and he'd never let his heir have a profession as he did the younger brother . . . We envied him, we young bucks with our livings to earn; handsome, brilliant, fascinating to any woman he made a gesture toward—heir to the fine estate—"

"But they were all drowned together!" I said again. I clung to Mark; he seemed the only sane thing in a nightmare.

"Juliana did go out of her head and stab her husband," the doctor said as if it was a small matter. I suppose he was used to it. "His father covered it up rather than have a scandal. You can't do anything here, either of you—take her downstairs, Mark. Even her courage probably has its limits. There's no time to go into it. Juliana is there with only Petronius to look after her. Go with them, Eugenia. Juliana won't come out of her coma."

"No," Eugenia said stonily. She stood, looking nearly as frozen as the dying woman on the bed, one hand on the footboard.

"Come, Perdita," Mark said. His strong grasp drew me from the room and the deathbed. "Come!" he said again, as I stopped in the workroom, where the image of my mother lay. I had remembered what Juliana said about the papers being under its hands. Suddenly I did not mind the waxen figure. Juliana's hate had not made it anything but quiet and innocent, lying there. I gently moved the wax hands away from what they had sheltered. Under them lay, as Juliana had said, a flat long parcel wrapped in discolored brown paper and sealed across a tear. And then for the first time I shrieked; Eugenia's hand fell on my shoulder, chill even through the cloth of my habit. I winced and moved closer to Mark.

"You need not be afraid," she said slowly. "Onnorate the Leaf has protected her daughter."

"Perdita! You shall not look at her or speak to her!" Mark said. "She has been your enemy—and mine—from the beginning."

"Your tie was, you admit, as close as that?" she said mockingly.

"From our meeting," he said coolly. "But I gave you fidelity until you publicly broke our engagement. Eugenia, you tried to strike Perdita down the day I married her, and threatened to ruin her reputation before the world. That we know and remember. What I believe also, though as yet it is not proven, is that you have conspired with Stephen Huntington twice through his servant to kidnap her as a hostage for Drusilla Huntington—and worse. Give me your word never to come near her again, or I shall make public what I know and do my utmost to prove what I suspect."

Her stern face altered to a faint bitter half smile. "I will not defend myself against your irrational suspicions," she said. "But she has been my enemy, not I hers. I know now that her very existence wrongs me. Her coming to the Red Castle robbed me of all that remained to me; the marriage our grandfather planned, to restore me what should have been my right. But you need not threaten or fear, Cousin Mark. I am learning to shut weak human emotions away. It is the only answer to the heritage my mother, who was wronged too, has left me. I no longer hate her or love you. Nor do I, thank God, any longer desire the Red Castle and all it brings. You have my word of honor for this: the word of honor of— I suppose still, a Somerwell of the Red Castle."

She spoke again, still with that bitter half smile: "Goodbye, my sister."

239

We heard her steps cross the stone floor through the room with the image of my mother Honor to the inner room where her mother Juliana lay. "Come," Mark said, and guided me toward the stair. At the landing he paused a moment and took a brown leaf from my skirt.

Once in our room he put me on the bed and rang for Janet. The civilized pattern of our life closed around us again. He was saying as if nothing had happened, "Get Mrs. Harradine into something more comfortable, Janet. I'll come back to you when I've changed, Perdita." He went into the dressing room, and Janet moved quietly about me, wrapping me into a negligee, and laying out a demi-toilette and saying that here was the bell-pull by the bed, and when I decided whether I wanted dinner up here or felt well enough to dress and go down, would I ring for her.

I had been gripping the yellowed packet with one hand or another all this time. I pushed it under the pillow now, and thought to ask Janet where Isobel was. In her room, she said with a little surprise at the question. Getting ready to dine, she supposed.

I must have slept a little then, for when I opened my eyes someone was knocking, and Mark, changed, was sitting by the bed. He rose and opened the door: it was Dr. De Witt.

"Eugenia has returned to the Sisters' house," he said. "Juliana is dead. Eugenia asks me to obtain your permission to take her up the hill after dark tonight to the family burying ground near the Post Road. She and the clergyman will meet there."

Mark gave the permission, of course. He said then, "I think, Doctor, that you owe it to us to explain what we do not know of all this. From what you said up there in the Chinese room, Miss Anna was the Juliana Vincent who was supposed to have drowned with her husband, when Nicholas and Sibylla, their brother and sister, drowned. You said that

240

Juliana went insane and stabbed her husband and that his father covered it up to save scandal. How long have you known all this? And how do you reconcile with your conscience exposing the inhabitants of the Castle to a woman who has killed and might—indeed nearly did—again?"

"I have known it just two days," the doctor said. "Eugenia came to me as soon as her mother told her. And as I told you when you escorted us to her rooms, Petronius and I were about to take her away, to Dr. Reading's. I did not feel it necessary to inform you of her real identity: I did not know then, any more than you did, that she had killed her husband, nor that Madame Honor was his actual wife—if that was not a delusion of her insanity. From what she said, before we carried her into her bedroom, she did try to kill Madame Honor, and succeeded in stunning her and making her fall from her horse. Perdita's survival, as we have always said, was a miracle . . . The shipwreck of Nicholas' yacht, which drowned himself and his wife Sibylla and the rest on board, was close enough to Juliana's fatal attack of mania for an old gentleman with power and pride to cover it up, and I suppose terrify Miss Anna into obeying him. . . . The meekest, most frightened creature . . . even for me it is hard to believe."

"How much has Petronius had to do with it all?" Mark asked abruptly. "We have all been at the mercy, actually, of a Negro servant's fidelity or lack of it, for a generation . . . He at least should have told the authorities—"

"That," Dr. De Witt said, "I do not know. I suppose the explanation is in his family feeling. You are right; since the New York slaves were freed, they can legally bear witness . . . But—there it is—the Somerwell pride and the Somerwell loyalties—the man—well, he is old Eugenius' son as much as the other two, by the left hand of course. The girls are his nieces, and you his nephew, as much as you all were to young Eugenius and young Nicholas. I think that's all."

I saw that he looked very tired and pale . . . But I was tired too; so was Mark. It was best to finish it, I thought.

"No," I said, "it isn't quite all, Doctor. She spoke to me before you came. She did think I was my mother Honor. She said, 'I gave you back everything I took when you fell, there under your hands—you've no right to haunt me.' She meant the image in the box—"

"Where are they?" the men spoke together.

I reached under my pillow and laid the packet in Dr. De Witt's hands.

CHAPTER EIGHTEEN

> *The sickness, the nausea,*
> *The pitiless pain,*
> *Have ceased, with the fever*
> *That maddened my brain—*
> *With the fever called "Living"*
> *That maddened my brain . . .*
>
> EDGAR ALLAN POE

We watched him break the battered seal. There were three papers. He took them out slowly and read them over.

"One of these," he said, lifting his head, "is the marriage certificate of Onnorate Leighton to Edward Eugenius Somerwell. The date"—he caught his breath—"is one year earlier than that of his marriage, which I attended, to Juliana Vincent. The second, dated a little more than fifteen months later, is a copy of a christening register of a Reverend George Whitney: the christening of Onnorate Somerwell, aged six weeks, daughter of Eugenius and Onnorate Somerwell. His rectory was on Madison Avenue in New York City."

"And the third paper?" Mark asked as he hesitated.

"A letter beginning 'My dearest Honor,' and signed 'Your loving mother always, Elizabeth Leighton.' The address is a street in Canandaigua, New York."

"As simple as that!" Mark said.

"The red castle—the chess castle, I mean," I said, "that was in my mother's pocket—Miss Anna—Juliana—must have sent it and the message, when she learned of the prior marriage." I shivered, lying there. "And she has been harbored here all these years—a meek, melancholy dependent— What sort of man was young Eugenius to submit when he was already married?"

"Old Eugenius had an iron hand," Dr. De Witt said. "And I suppose he knew little and cared less about hereditary insanity. The Vincents were very rich. Young Eugenius was helpless as regards money. Juliana fell wildly in love with him; he was a most fascinating and handsome young man. Your mother, Mark, the eldest child, was married and gone: Nicholas' marriage to Juliana's sister Sibylla was a happy one, and her money naturally had freed Nicholas from the parental tyranny. The full focus of the old man's will fell on Eugenius. He had always been away from the Red Castle a great deal, traveling, it was supposed. I do remember that Juliana was very frail, and it was supposed not long for this world: Eugenius may have given in to a marriage to what he thought a dying girl. He paid for his weakness, poor fellow."

"And so," said Mark, steel in his voice, "did his true wife, beautiful, loyal Madame Honor. So did my own Perdita, nameless until now."

"I am not Perdita," I said. "I am Onnorate—" Suddenly the meaning of what I had said came to me—and to the others.

"*Onnorate!*" Mark repeated, and his eyes met Dr. De Witt's equally shocked eyes across me. "And so was Honor Onnorate. My God—!"

"It could be a coincidence—" I said. But I did not think so.

"You say Eugenius traveled a good deal," I said. "He must

244

have known the story of the Oneida girl—the Iroquois girl. Could he have gone upstate to the Oneida reservation—"

"And found Madame Honor?" Mark shook his head. "She was not an Indian; the picture of her mother in your locket is unmistakably of a white woman. And yet—"

"He did know the story, of course," Dr. De Witt said quietly, "and he did say once, I remember now, that someone should investigate it. If he did, himself—"

There was a knock on the door: the doctor pushed the papers back into their envelope as I said, "Come in." I knew Janet's knock.

She stood there, a visitor from the normal world. "Mrs. Harradine, Miss Abigail says she feels well enough to come down to dinner. The gong will ring in ten minutes. If I might help you—"

"You will stay, of course, Doctor. We may need you," Mark said, and as the doctor assented, they rose, and left Janet to help me into the gown she had made ready. As the gentlemen went, I heard Dr. De Witt saying, "I do not approve of the extreme repression Eugenia is practising: I understand the ladies of the sisterhood believe it to be a necessary stage of self-control, which will pass into something more normal. Dominie Van Alstyne has visited her, and agrees with me: Dr. Reading seems to feel that it is a result of her intensity of temperament; but what this last shock will do . . ."

I joined them in time to go into the dining room when the second gong rang: Isobel and Miss Abigail, both looking nearly as usual, were there already. My rest, in spite of the shock of what we had learned from the documents, enabled me, I think, to seem as usual throughout dinner. Isobel, also, was normal enough, though a little sharp-voiced when she spoke, as if it was hard to carry on. When we had finished and removed to the small withdrawing room, for the men did

245

not linger over their wine but accompanied us, Dr. De Witt spoke, in response to a questioning look from Mark.

"Miss Abigail, perhaps you may be prepared for what I am about to say. An old pensioner of this family, Miss Anna, has died, more or less suddenly, this afternoon."

I was watching Isobel. Had she poured out the wild scenes of the afternoon to her aunt? Her face did not change; nor did Miss Abigail's, excepting to show a kind concern. Isobel had not spoken then. I wondered why.

"Ah, poor Miss Anna," Cousin Abigail said. "Yes, in a way; her heart was in bad condition. She did not have much to live for. I will take old Keziah, by your leave, Perdita, and see that everything is done for her that can be. She had no near kinfolk that I know about. Unless you object, Mark, I suppose the best thing would be to bury her quietly on the hill in the family burying ground. She was a connection of the family."

"Petronius has, I believe, attended to everything," the doctor said. "A valuable man."

"Ah, yes. She has been more or less his charge—"

Mark's voice cut suddenly across the conversation. "Cousin Abigail, what did you know of Miss Anna?"

"Not very much," Cousin Abigail answered calmly. "I only came here to stay after the two little girls were so tragically orphaned by the shipwreck of the yacht with nearly all aboard. My impression would be that Miss Anna had been here before I took charge of the children. I was never told anything directly. But I think that such of the servants as knew anything about it, believed or somehow knew that she was a poor girl young Eugenius had got into trouble. At least so old Keziah said. Such things were considered more tragic and irremediable twenty years ago. The alternative to her seclusion—for I do not think anyone but Petronius and old Cousin Eugenius ever saw her—would have been the streets. I remember thinking that Cousin Eugenius, who was a hard man, showed kindness in protecting a fallen girl from that inevitable end. Of course a young woman, as I was then, did not discuss such things with gentlemen."

The two gentlemen present listened without contradiction. Mark said after a moment of silence, "Thank you. I am sorry to seem to go on cross-questioning you, cousin. Dr. De Witt tells me that young Eugenius was interested in the legend of the Oneida woman: the story of the girl who was married to an earlier Eugenius by the Indian rite, and sent from the Red Castle with her child."

"I know the story," she said. There was a faint flush as she answered, and I remembered that she was one of those who was supposed to have suffered from Onnorate the Leaf's curse. "You would ask me if he was interested in it sufficiently to see if he could track down the facts of the legend? Or did you tell Mark that, Dr. De Witt? Yes, he did try, I remember. When I first visited the Red Castle as a young girl, he had just returned from what he called a wild goose chase to the Oneida reservation to see what he could find out. He said that he had supposed, as they were said to keep tribal records, he might come back and prove the whole tale was untrue."

"And he brought back no information one way or another?"

"He was disappointed, I suppose. He was very short about it all; he said it was made of whole cloth, and that nobody had a right to defame the family with such a tale. I remember it, because he was usually gay and good tempered . . . But he was always off somewhere; he went on another trip almost immediately. I scarcely knew him; but he was one of those people one remembers—a vivid personality."

"But Onnorate's leaves still fall when doom is to come," Isobel said. She had not spoken since we left the table. We

247

stared at her, where she sat with her embroidery beside the astral lamp. "And as a dead woman cannot be welcomed back to the Castle in faith and honor, I suppose they always will."

I felt that I could stand no more. The maniac who had killed my father and tried to kill my mother lay dead upstairs. Her daughter, who had tried to strike me down, who, it was almost sure, had twice trapped me to punish Mark and Drusilla, was piously safe among her Anglican sisterhood. And the Red Castle women, along with Mark himself, sat civilly discussing it all as if it was some pleasant *on dit*. I rose and clutched the back of my chair. I heard a scream, and thought it was my own. But it was Isobel. She too had come to the end of her self-control.

"You sit here, all you smug tame people, as if it had happened a thousand years ago, instead of bringing curse after curse on us Red Castle women—Aunt Abigail, Eugenia, Perdita, me, all of us! I cannot stand it—I will not stand it!"

Before anyone could check her she had run screaming from the room: we heard her highheeled slippers racing up the stone stairs. I took a step forward, and found Mark's arm holding me like iron. Miss Abigail had risen too. Her manners never forgotten, she said, "I must apologize for Isobel, she is easily unstrung." She spoke to all three of us courteously and was gone in Isobel's wake, calm as always. I wondered, as she went out of the room, if more lay under that ladylike calm than I had ever thought . . .

The same thought might have come to Dr. De Witt. "With your permission, my young friends, I will follow them," he said, and was gone.

Mark crossed to the room and rang for Petronius, then returned to me, still holding me fast, as if something might befall me. The man, unmoved and immaculate as always, came, bowed and awaited Mark's word.

"You are burying Miss Anna—Miss Juliana—tonight," he said. "Is all in readiness?"

"Yes, Major," the man said quietly. "Keziah and I have attended to everything. The coffin which held the waxen image my mistress worked so long on suffices. I know the vacant place on the hill burying ground. It will be as always. The carryall is ready in the coachhouse. I took the liberty of sending the carriage for Miss Eugenia and the resident priest at the sisterhood, and they await me at the gates."

"As a son of the house," Mark said, looking straight at the man, "you took no liberties."

"I thank you, sir," Petronius said. I honored him, standing there erect and unafraid. His steps sounded up the stone stair. For once they were not silent: they rang.

"Come, my dear," Mark said, and we followed.

It was all light and warmth in our rooms: the grate fire crackled, freshly built. The room we were in, deep-carpeted, brocade-hung, bright with astral lamps, shed happiness and safety. Mark set me down on the *chaise longue* across the bedfoot and sat beside me. We waited silently. Presently we heard the feet mounting the stair and passing our door; Junius' quick young tread, Apollo's heavier plod, Abiah's even, sturdy stepping, Petronius' light feet. I knew them all by now.

"Come to bed, child," Mark said. "It's foolish to wait up for them."

I was only too glad to obey. We were lying at peace, but not asleep, when the steps returned down again, heavier this time, slower. They were carrying away that Juliana Vincent who had thought she was Juliana Somerwell: who had borne young Eugenius a daughter, and then somehow learned she was no wife. She must weigh little by the sound of the foot-steps, I thought . . . and crept into the warm strong arms that closed round me.

"It's all over, darling," Mark said gently, "she's gone for good. Go to sleep now."

But I could not quite yet. I slipped from the bed to the window overlooking the path I knew they must take. I watched till the bobbing lanterns were hidden in the carriage house. They would drive the carryall up the slanting road to the old burying ground near the Post Road, a half mile away. I wondered if Petronius, who knew so many of the Red Castle's secrets, knew which was the unknown grave that held Eugenius, and if he would let Juliana sleep close by him, to be there when they woke on Judgment Day. My mother Honor would not care. It was Jacob Van Dorn she had said she would meet in Heaven . . . I came back and lay down, suddenly quiet. I kissed my husband good night and said my prayer again and went to sleep. . . .

I was very deep asleep, so much had happened. If the light had not flashed across my eyes I would scarcely have waked. I woke, and screamed. For Mark, who had sprung soldier-fashion from the bed at the first noise of the opened latch, stood holding a woman against him, a woman whose hand, gripped helplessly in his, held a knife . . . Eugenia . . . but how had Eugenia found her way through the locked door? I lighted the astral quickly from the nightlight and saw.

It was not Eugenia: the figure was smaller, less slender. The curls that flooded from the lace cap were fair: the blue garment . . .

It was Isobel.

Holding the hand with its knife fast, Mark moved her round to face me. "You tried to kill my wife," his voice said —a voice I scarcely knew, so hard it was.

She did not try to get away from him. She only turned her head so that the scarred cheek was hidden on his breast. She lifted the golden head. Her blue eyes were hurt and wet. She had looked at me, heartbroken, like that, so many times!

"But Mark—but Mark," she said like a child. "I haven't killed her, you stopped me. I picked up Juliana's knife and it gave me an idea. It wasn't any worse than trying to kill Eugenia with Papa's razor when we were little, and she pushed me against the grate. And nobody punished me . . . Oh, Mark darling, don't you see? I couldn't bear seeing you catch Dita in your arms today and push me away . . . I wasn't sure what to do, and then when I saw you asleep with her head against your shoulder . . . Don't you see I couldn't bear it?"

There went through my mind quickly old Eliza's words: "The little girls were double cousins, two brothers marrying two sisters. Why, they were as good as sisters themselves, the doctor said."

Sibylla's daughter, that drowned young Sibylla everyone had forgotten, who, sane herself, could pass on the insane heredity of the Vincents. The madness had always been as deep in my poor Isobel as in Eugenia—deeper perhaps, for being hidden. I heard Mark's voice again, very quiet: "Go on, Isobel." I knew that gentleness. I knew what was under it, but Isobel did not. "How did you get in through the locked door?"

"Why, I've lived here since I was born," she said in a surprised voice. "There was a key to another door that I knew fitted this." She was nestling against him. However he felt, he held her fast. "Tell me, Isobel, something else. Was the story you told Perdita, that Eugenia said the Olivers' housekeeper knew who her mother was, true?"

She gave a happy little laugh. "Oh, Mark, you are clever. No, of course not! But you were angry at Eugenia, and not at me. I thought if Stephen Huntington's man got Perdita out of the way, you would have me. I was her closest friend: we would be sorry together and that would make you care for me more—"

His voice was still soft. "But how did you know about Stephen Huntington?"

I heard the little satisfied laugh again. "But he was Etienne Ducross! And you never knew, neither did Arthur Lawrence! He made friends with Arthur on purpose to reach Perdita. Arthur brought him to Laura's ball, and he saw me look at Perdita and hate her, he said so. It was a clever plan, he said nobody would suspect if they thought we were lovers. But those stupid Olivers came home unexpectedly and spoiled it, so we had to try again. So I pretended I was wild to have Esmerelda tell my fortune." She glanced at me, triumphant. "Remember, Perdita? If you hadn't picked up that wretched street Arab, who knew more about wicked things than was decent for a little boy his age . . ."

"That isn't all," Mark said, still very gently. His face, above her curls, was a hard mask, but she could not see it. "Did you know who Miss Anna was?"

"Old Keziah knew. She always knew everything. She slipped about the house and listened. I was her nursling and she told me. She told me about Onnorate the Leaf, and her curse: that women brought to the Red Castle were always shamed as she had been shamed: I thought of course Perdita would be, too. But she ought to have told me that Onnorate protected Perdita, it wasn't fair. The bough with the brown leaves dropped down between her and Aunt Juliana, just when she wanted to kill Perdita. I thought the curse would come sooner or later, but it kept delaying. What could I do? I did make Aunt Abigail sick with strawberries to give me an excuse to follow her. Etienne sent her the red castle, of course."

"But the curse is done," Mark said. "Do you know what Perdita's real name is? It is Onnorate, and she has been brought to the Red Castle in all faith and honor."

Isobel's scream rang out. "No, no! Mark I love so, it can't

be true. My God, do not tell me that it was Aunt Abigail and I who lifted the curse from the Red Castle women. And all the while we thought her a low foundling she was Onnorate the Leaf!" Isobel's little body went limp against Mark's breast. I thought her feigning; but it was an actual swoon. I did not realize that I was coming toward her till his hand warded me off.

"Stay away from her, my darling fool! Go find me something strong to tie her hands and feet with. Where is the sash you had on tonight?"

I went to the drawer where it lay. It was heavy satin. Mark tied her hands before he released her, then her ankles from a length he cut from it. "One doesn't trifle with homicidal maniacs," he said at my shocked look. "I've too nearly lost you before this to take chances. Show me where her bedroom is."

I hoped we had gone softly enough to disturb no one, but as we opened Isobel's door Cousin Abigail opened the one next to it, where she slept.

"I missed Isobel—I thought I heard her scream. Oh, what is it?"

"Isobel seems to have inherited her share of the Vincent homicidal mania," Mark said. "I am going to lock her in until we can reach the doctor tomorrow. Perdita, isn't there another room, farther off, where Cousin Abigail can sleep in safety?"

"The guest room that was Eugenius and Juliana's is made up on this floor," Miss Abigail answered for herself . . . "Oh, Mark, it isn't like the time she attacked Eugenia when she was a baby?"

"Very much like, or so she said," he answered grimly. "Did it not warn you?"

"She was only four," poor Cousin Abigail said. "We thought it was only a baby's fury, and that the burn when

Eugenia pushed her away was punishment enough . . . Oh, my poor little girl!"

She bent over Isobel, prone on her bed, still in a dead faint. She looked like a pretty punished child, her curls out over the pillow, and the bright ribbons on wrists and ankles.

"You mustn't stay here, Cousin," Mark said. "You are not well enough, for one thing—and it is not safe."

She made no demur. Her face was drawn, but she collected her possessions for the morning quietly with my help, and we escorted her to young Eugenius' room. Juliana's wax flowers, incredibly real, stood before his likeness; the exquisite statuettes of Spring and Summer on the mantel, still. I knew now that Juliana had made it a shrine. I saw Miss Abigail safe in bed and kissed her goodnight and went. Just as I was leaving she spoke.

"She gave me something without my knowledge," she said, "once before, to make me ill—or so the doctor said—I would not believe it. If she did it this time, it would have given her an excuse for following me here. But she could not have sent me the chess castle—"

"Don't think about it," I said. "It doesn't matter now." Ducross—Huntington—had probably sent it. If Keziah knew everything about the Castle legends, so did Isobel. But there was nothing to be done about it tonight. I kissed my old friend goodnight again, and went where Mark waited for me beside the door. The portrait of young Eugenius faced me from over the mantel as I passed: the smiling warm dark eyes, the charm that persisted even in his likeness, followed me till I left the room. Young Eugenius, who was my father as well as Eugenia's.

"Are you leaving Isobel alone?" I asked Mark. He shook his head. "When Petronius returned, I sent him for Keziah," he said. "She is locked in there. She insists she is safe—and I

254

let it go; she is to blame for a good deal of this. I can only hope she does not have duplicate keys like her mistress!"

Petronius, behind us, spoke. "Major, with your permission, I will watch outside till morning."

"Very well. Get yourself a comfortable chair." Mark spoke as matter-of-factly as if he was ordering one of his soldiers. Petronius said, "Thank you sir. Yes sir."

"But can you trust him?" I asked, as we gained our own room.

"Certainly: Isobel needs to be guarded. And from now on, my darling, I think you will find that you will be included in his devotion."

I had forgotten . . . Yes—I was one of the Somerwells, a Red Castle woman. Petronius Somerwell, kinsman by the left hand, would consider me his charge now.

"You are to go to sleep," Mark said, in the voice which gave orders. I smiled up at him—how could I, I thought, after all this. He was there; he guarded me. My eyelids drooped. My last thought was relief that Keziah was with Isobel. Isobel was always so worn out after one of her wild spells. Incredibly—or was it that I always obeyed Mark?— I did go to sleep, heavily and quietly.

He was gone when I woke. It was late morning, from the sun that glimpsed through the Venetian blinds on the river side of the room. In a corner, knitting placidly, was Janet. When I opened my eyes she spoke as placidly. "Would Madame like breakfast brought up? The Major thought so."

"Where is he?"

"In Miss Isobel's room with the doctor," she said. "She was taken ill in the night."

"Yes, bring the tray; and ask the Major to come in when he is at leisure." When she had gone I slipped down by the bed and said a little prayer thanking Our Lord for keeping us

255

safe; and added a prayer for Isobel. We had been sisters for so many years . . .

Janet's routine, the silk bed jacket, the scented water for my face and hands, the blind drawn up enough to let sun come in, the slow Scottish-turned usual words, helped to make the terrors of the last day and night seem unreal. Was I unfeeling, I wondered, that I could rest and eat and like the morning sun? I wondered how Cousin Abigail was after all this. She was not young, and she had been ill.

Mark came in presently. In answer to my questions he said that Abigail was dressed and sitting with Isobel. The doctor had come and gone. Isobel herself seemed to have forgotten everything about last night. "She talks and acts like a child," he said with faint distaste. "When I left she was asking when she could be rowed over to play with Perdita, she had a new doll to show her, with a real hoop that Petronius had made out of wire and ribbon, and a lavender taffeta dress like Miss Abigail's. I am not as sure as De Witt and my cousin seem to be that it is genuine."

My eyes filled. "She did come over with the doll in lavender taffeta," I said. "We were only eight that year . . ." I found I was sobbing uncontrollably into my pillow. The tears seemed to release me. The arms that always meant safety closed round me. I dried my eyes and sat up. "What else does the doctor say?" I asked.

"His friend Reading has come and gone," Mark said. "I liked him. They seem to agree that her mind will remain like this. They think she will not regain her strength, but fade out slowly, increasingly childish. Reading says he has seen other such cases."

I said timidly, "Please, Mark, will you allow me to see her?"

He stood back from me. "My God, what sort of spell has that madwoman woven around you?"

"Only—we loved each other, a good many years," I said. I lay back, quiet. Close on that came a knock, Janet's knock. She said: "The doctor says, if Madame could come . . . It is quite safe. She is very weak. We think it would quiet her. She keeps begging for her."

I looked up at Mark, silently pleading. Dr. De Witt stood in the doorway now. He said, "Isobel could not harm a kitten in her present state. But there is a chance of her working herself up into some sort of dangerous mood if she doesn't see Mrs. Harradine, Major. I know it is a strange thing to ask under the circumstances. But it might be the difference between life and death, or hopeless madness and a hope of sanity."

"You ask that in spite of the fact that my wife came close to death at her hands last night?"

"Yes," the old doctor said. "That was insanity. She is not insane now."

"The worse for her!" Mark said. "I shall see that she stands trial when she recovers, as you seem to think she may. Very well."

Mark, still silent, helped me into my wrapper, and, still holding me fast, led me into Isobel's room. Lying against her pillows, she tried to hold her hands out to me, but they dropped again.

"Dita," she said eagerly in her weak voice, "I had to see you. I can't remember our doll's name, you know. The one I had for my birthday that I said we'd share. I have to remember it. You always remember things for me . . ." her breath gave out.

I moved away from Mark and stood by the bedside. "Her name was Flora," I said.

Isobel drew a long satisfied breath. "Of course. I knew you'd remember . . . Who is that tall man with you?"

"He has come to take care of me now that Uncle Jacob can't any more," I said.

"Can't he? Why not? . . . Oh, you look taller, too . . . Have I been sick a long time?"

"Yes, Isobel," the doctor said, moving between us. "A very long time. And you must rest now Dita has told you the doll's name . . ."

He gestured to us to go. As we went we heard old Keziah sobbing aloud.

CHAPTER NINETEEN

All houses wherein men have lived and died
Are haunted houses. Through the open doors
The harmless phantoms on their errands glide,
With feet that make no sound upon the floors.

H. W. LONGFELLOW

Cousin Abigail returned to her Peekskill house as soon as Isobel was able to travel with her. Petronius, at his own request, went with them.

"It is as well," Mark said. "I will feel safer about Cousin Abigail."

"I will see that she is safe," Petronius answered gravely; and cared for the removal with his usual silent capability. Shadow of Juliana, shadow of Eugenia that he had been, the place was more freed of them now that it was freed of him. The light through the stained glass was brighter: the servants spoke in less hushed voices.

Mark reported Stephen Huntington's supposed whereabouts to the New York police, who had the affair in hand. He also put it into the hands of Allan Pinkerton. But the bird had flown. Contact with the county-seat nearest the Huntington plantation was equally useless. As Edgar had feared, there was a certain amount of feeling at that time against Northern police and Northern officers. Mr. Stephen Huntington, it seemed, who had been caring for his cousin's property so assiduously in her prolonged absence, had at her request sold slaves, plantation and house property. He had also then, it was understood, joined her in Europe. Which was around the time that young Mr. Etienne Ducross had appeared in Tarrytown, and then New York City.

We never knew whether he had forged a power of attorney, told the authorities the facts of Drusilla's birth under pledge of secrecy, or even—though this seemed less likely—given proof of her death. When Mark notified the Eatons, as he had thought, they preferred to let sleeping dogs lie, rather than take a chance on having her mother's race known.

When Mark and I had, with Dr. De Witt's assistance, talked everything out with Lawyer Granger, we traveled up to Canandaigua, where my parents had been married. Like so many things, now we had the clue, as Mark had said, it was simple. The marriage was on record in the county clerk's office. Without being asked, he said, "I suppose you are going to Mr. Leighton's house?"

Mr. Leighton, it appeared, was my mother's brother; her parents were dead, and so was his wife. He had no children. We could see that the family was much respected, from the registrar's attitude.

It was a beautiful old house, lying in wide grounds. And my uncle—it seemed strange, but that was what he was, of course—was a handsome kindly elderly gentleman, who, after the first surprise was over, was pleased and welcoming. I was so like the Leightons, he said, that no other introduction was necessary. There was a portrait of his sister at seventeen in the long still sunny drawing room where he received us. We stood together and looked at it a long time: the gold-glinting brown hair done in the quaint piling of the twenties, the eyes and color like my own, the smile of innocent expectancy, the little ruche close to the lifted chin. My uncle, Ellington Leighton, had gone out for the moment to give orders to his housekeeper, for he had insisted on our being his guests. Mark's hand closed over mine. We kissed each other, and looked at her a little longer. Then my uncle came back in.

"Everyone loved her," he said. "Then young Somerwell came, the namesake of our ancestor. It was like a whirlwind carrying her away."

He showed us, then, the painting opposite, their mother. It was the face in the locket, from which young Eugenius' portrait had been torn. His own wife, slender, fair and aristocratic, with his own portrait done perhaps fifteen years back, hung in the living room beyond.

"Honor and Alice spoiled me for other women, I suppose," he said, smiling a little.

Over the dinner table he filled in the lost pieces of my mother's story.

Young Eugenius, as Cousin Abigail had remembered, had actually gone upstate to find out how much of the story of the Oneida girl of the Iroquois was true. There were tribal records, and there was an old Indian who was the historian. Eugenius the second *had* married her by the Indian rite. She was a chief's daughter as she had said. They had lived with the tribe over a year, and then gone away together: she had returned alone with her son. She had not lived long after that. The child, who was fair-skinned and handsome, attracted the attention of a trader's wife whose own child had died. She had begged him of the tribe and been given him. The trader, Ezra Leighton, ended as a rich man; they had settled in Canandaigua of the Finger Lakes. The boy grew up and married, but he did not forget his Indian heritage.

He visited the Oneida people from time to time and knew his story: he named his first daughter for Onnorate the Leaf, as did the eldest son of each generation after him.

As far as my uncle Ellington knew, there had never been any mention of what befell the first Onnorate at Grandison— or indeed, of her return at the time of Eugenius' marriage to Isobel Van Vooren. When my father, young Eugenius, following the clues given him at the reservation, came to Canandaigua, and looked up the Leightons, the family of course learned a little more, though he seems not to have said anything of Onnorate's return. He and my mother fell immediately and violently in love.

"But why was there any objection to their marriage?" I asked.

"Because, although he was unmistakably wellborn and well bred, he refused to give my parents any information about his background or family. He was so charming, so delightful in every way, that they had been won over up to that point. My sister loved him so much that as she said she would have married him no matter what his background. His charm," my uncle said, as Dr. De Witt had, "was like a spell." He pulled his long white mustache. "Ah, well—but he couldn't move my father. So Honor and he went away secretly. She wrote back a week later that she was married and happy, but that the reason why her husband could not tell them who he was was sound: he was entirely dependent on his own father for money and the parent wanted him to marry someone else and would have stopped his income if he learned he had not obeyed. There were relatives of his in Canandaigua who would have found out and passed on the information. Her husband told her that it would soon be all right, and his father and everyone satisfied. Her own people, she said, would be pleased. Her husband said so."

I remembered what the doctor had said—that Juliana had

been supposed to be dying or at least her life was precarious. Once out of the way, Eugenius could admit his marriage to my mother . . .

Mark set his lips; but he only said, "Was that the last they heard?"

"No," my uncle said. We had been talking over the walnuts and wine; we went back to the drawing room. "There was a last letter. It came over four years after they had gone, when all our searches and inquiries had been abandoned . . . Fools that we were not to look at home for the register of their marriage! It did not occur to us that there had been time or audacity. Everything was wonderful, she wrote, everything was straightened out, and soon, if our parents were willing, she would return and explain everything. And that was all . . . We had not known her husband's real name; he had called himself Edward Summers. The marriage, you say, was recorded in his actual name; but my parents supposed it had taken place after they left the city from what the note said, and searched everywhere but here. The letter was postmarked New York City. She spoke in the letter of her little daughter and how much she had wanted to tell us about her and everything else. And that was the last we heard."

Mark said, "What was the date of that letter?"

It was close, it seemed, to the time when she and I were found on the road to the ferry.

We would never know what actually happened. What seemed probable was that Eugenius had told the truth to Juliana, perhaps to the father. Certainly something had shocked Juliana out of her precariously balanced sanity: she had killed Eugenius and summoned Honor Leighton by the token of the red chessman. How she returned home, how her father-in-law dealt with it all, we would never know, excepting that Nicholas and Sibylla's death by drowning gave him the opportunity to hide what had actually happened. He must have given Juliana, when she came out of her spell of mania, her choice of trial, an asylum, or her seclusion in the upper rooms.

It all seemed strange and wild, sitting there in that peaceful, softly lighted drawing room. My uncle Ellington drew a long breath.

"At least we know—nearly—now," he said. "From what you say my sister Onnorate was happy through it all: even after she lost her memory."

"She was happy," Mark said. "Perdita was almost too little to remember: her mother died when she was six. Honor was loved and taken care of. She lived with the people of the ferryhouse: Van Dorn, who was a very fine man, brought my wife up as his own child: he loved Honor Leighton. Indeed, most people who knew her did."

I thought of Uncle Jacob, and the song that meant Honor Leighton to him:

> . . . *a maiden loved and cherished*
> *By high and low,*
> > *But with Autumn's leaf she perished*
> *Long time ago.*

We stayed with my uncle Ellington two days; he would not take no for an answer: there was a real tie of kinship that I felt. He would come to stay with us, he promised; which, indeed, he did later. He had friends, indeed, in Grandison. It seemed that he was more of a personage than we had realized.

Back at the Red Castle, Mark summoned the old doctor and lawyer for a last talk, a last tying of threads together. Lawyer Granger sighed.

"Your grandfather's one idea," he said, "seems to have been to spare the Somerwell name."

He spoke to both of us: for the first time I realized that old Eugenius was my grandfather too. Mark had married his cousin after all.

"There are only the two girls left who bear it," he said, "three if you count my wife."

"Old Mr. Somerwell took for granted you would assume it when you married Eugenia," Granger said. "I thought he had said so to you."

"He said so, but I refused," he said carelessly. He turned and smiled at me. "Well, my child, do you feel I should, now that I am married to my cousin Onnorate Somerwell?"

I shook my head. I could not feel that it was my name. "Oh, no, no," I said. "Too many dark memories cling about that name."

"So I think," my husband said.

Lawyer Granger sighed again. "What with poor little Isobel mentally shaken, and Eugenia's resolves what they are—"

"What are they?" I asked.

"I have remonstrated with her for refusing an eligible offer," he said. "She says that she will not pass on her mother's heritage."

I did not think she would hold to that; she was young and handsome. But to anticipate, she did. The repression, the hard control, did not soften, as her doctor had hoped it would. But it held her, as far as could be seen, from any darkening of her mind. Dominant, severe, apparently incapable of feeling, she presently became a well known figure in the charitable organizations of New York City. Our paths, later, therefore sometimes crossed. She was my half sister, but Mark advised me not to make any effort to draw nearer her. It would only lead, he said, to a recollection on her part of her actual status, and more bitterness toward me.

As for mine—it became known that my mother had been

Onnorate Leighton, of a distinguished upstate family. My mother, the story went, had been married to a connection of the Somerwells. After her husband's death she had been on the way to visit his relatives when her accident occurred. My uncle Ellington's visits to us and ours to him verified the truth; and it spared my father and Juliana, not to say Eugenia.

Isobel, I heard from Cousin Abigail, was unchanged, except for becoming weaker and more childlike month by month, a gentle child who recalled none of the storms and legends that had driven her so long.

"She keeps asking where her Perdita is, and why she cannot be rowed over for lessons with Miss Letty and Perdita at the ferryhouse," the poor lady wrote. When I showed the letter to Mark his brow darkened.

"You have done and suffered enough for her," he said. "You are not to go near her, imbecile or normal, darling, unless she is at death's door."

So I obeyed.

We lived happily together at the old Grammercy Park mansion; we would have been happy together anywhere. Our little Marcus, and little Onnorate we called Norah, played with Janet's guardianship in the green park beneath our windows. In the summers we went where other people did; Saratoga, Newport, abroad, once to Canada to visit Cyril Eaton and his wife Drusilla. They were still grateful beyond words to Mark. We did not tell them how dear Drusilla's rescue had cost us—what use? They had one dazzlingly fair little daughter, like Drusilla's mother, she said, and named Eveline for her.

Neither we nor they for some years after that knew anything more of Drusilla's cousin and enemy, Stephen Huntington, who had called himself—it seemed it was his grandfather's name—Etienne Ducross. It was after the end of the

Rebellion, indeed, that a fellow officer of Mark's told of something which might have been his end.

After one of the last great battles, a Southern officer was found shot through the back. One of his friends, a Confederate Captain, captured, related in horror that the dead man's valet, who had been admired for his devotion in staying close to his master in the battle, had shot him, and escaped in the melee. A handsome nearly white nigra, the young Confederate said. The names were different; there had been a mass burial by a detail. The description of the dead man might have been that of Ducross ten years older—or not. But I always wondered if Cassius Huntington had not taken the short way to his freedom. . . .

It was seven years after Cousin Abigail took Isobel with her to her Peekskill home that Petronius rode down with the message. Isobel was going. Nothing special; the springs of life were failing, that was all. She asked for me. Would I come? She was dying.

I mounted and rode back with Petronius.

She looked, as they had said, like a child. Her gold curls were pulled forward to the scar in the old pitiful way. The great blue eyes came wide as I entered the room.

"She is very weak; you need not be afraid," Cousin Abigail murmured. I had not thought of being afraid.

"I had to ask you about the curse," Isobel whispered. "You know, you live in the Red Castle. Will it ever be lifted?"

Cousin Abigail spoke before I could. "Dear child, the curse was lifted years ago. Onnorate came back to the Castle, an honored, happy wife. Nobody need fear her again."

Whether because Cousin Abigail unwittingly looked at me as she spoke, or that Isobel's mind cleared with dying, she opened the blue eyes and said, "Perdita! Were you Onnorate all the time, and you never told me? But you loved me."

I said as well as I could, "Yes, darling, I am Onnorate. I shall always love you."

"Oh, then it's all right about the curse," she said with the ghost of her little laugh, and was gone.

Petronius escorted me back after the funeral. But it was scarcely two months before Miss Abigail wrote again. As if, now there was nobody his own to take care of, there was nothing to keep him, he had died, quietly and suddenly. Could he, she asked, being a servant of the Somerwells, be buried in the servants' section of the family burying ground?

She came with the cortege. She stayed with us, and our children loved her. When I spoke to Mark he approved. He had always been fond of her. She has never gone away.

Mark had resigned his commission at the end of his year's furlough, with a colonelcy. But in 1861 he was recalled to the Army, with a brigadier generalship. We had of course spent our summers at the Red Castle, and visited it otherwise from time to time. It was a great estate, with its responsibilities. Of necessity I took charge of it when he was gone. I did not dread it: my children loved it. Janet, I knew, had told them romantic tales of its romance and beauty. The servants and tenants, as well as our neighbors, were warmly interested and pleased that General Harradine's wife and children had come home to the old estate.

There had been leaves, of course; there had been times when he was in Washington and I joined him. But when the Rebellion was over he came home to me, unwounded, thank Heaven, bronzed and strong and stately. It seemed too wonderful to be true: we were together again for good. Here were our home, our children, our love and peace and prosperity, like that of our country.

Laura and Edgar, with their sons, came to stay with us a couple of weeks after Mark's return. We had been with them for a long horseback ride along the other side of the river, which had meant, of course, a visit to Eliza and the Blackwaters on the way over. Now we were meeting our children —Oh they were shooting up so, and Laura's eldest wore cadet gray—in the grape arbor. It was a heavenly autumn afternoon. Marcus and Norah heaped piles of the Concords on a table, and Junius had brought out a trayful of cakes and tea and chocolate for us, with wine for the gentlemen.

"Oh, the estate is so beautiful, the old castle and its gardens and great trees," Laura said.

I said, "Yes, I love it and so do the children. I hope Mark loves it as much as we do."

"I think I have never felt what was after all mostly superstition about its gloominess, love," he said, smiling a little. "It seems everything peaceful and beautiful to me; after all, my mother's people have lived here for generations. It's as much my ancestral home as my father's house in the city." He laughed a little. "Either you, my Honor, or these children of ours who have taken such complete possession, seem to have effectually exorcised all ghosts and such things."

Laura laughed too, swinging a great bunch of grapes in her fingers.

   "From turret to foundation stone
   The castle is the young's alone," she misquoted.

"Perdita, I think my demons and yours have hunted over every room and every inch of it for years. And as far as one can see and hear your ghosts are gone as completely as the Iroquois girl's curse. It's what your poor Isobel, you told me, believed when she was dying; 'Onnorate the Leaf was brought back to the Castle in peace and honor.'"

"Who was she?" my Norah asked, pressing close to her father's knee where he sat beside me. "Does she mean me, Mama? That is my real name."

"Don't forget it is your mother's real name too," Laura said. "She was brought here to the Castle and lives here, an honored wife. That was all the poor Iroquois girl wanted."

Heedless of our cousins Mark put an arm around me. As yet I could scarcely bear him out of my sight, though I tried to hide it, and I think he felt the same way. "She *is* my faith and honor," he said.

"No more ghosts, then," Laura said lightly.

"None," he said.

A great red and gold leaf fell gently on my hair like a caress. I lifted it and put it carefully in my reticule. I did not answer.

The week before, we had given a housewarming. The Castle, lighted and warm, was filled. Guests from New York City, from up and down the river, all the friends and kinfolk who had made Mark welcome must be welcomed to him again. It had been all warmth and gayety, a dance, a reception, the friends and neighbors who loved us and we loved. There had been officers from Mark's staff in Washington; ladies and gentlemen from the city, returned young officers: all the rejoicing of a homecoming that was not only ours but America's.

"There is a happy feeling in the Castle all over, isn't there, Mama?" my Norah had said when it was over, and the servants, who had been proud and pleased as if it was their own, had set the place in order again.

We were standing on the portico. Mark was taking our son with him on a round of the place with our overseer. "It will all be yours some day," he said, as they waited for the grooms to bring the horses. "You must learn to know it, lad."

Marcus, tall and straight like his father, smiled, "I love it, and I know it now," he said. Norah and I watched them go.

"I think it will always be happy here," I answered what Norah had said a little before.

"I hope so—even the poor lady with the colored servant, the one who brought the presents, was smiling a little."

I looked at her; she was smiling too, my pretty Norah with her gold-brown ringlets and sash-ribbons blowing in the light wind. "I don't place her, dear," I said. "Tell me about her."

"It was after almost everyone else had gone," she said. "I was up on the third floor. You know we'd all been playing hide-and-seek up there, and I'd dropped my locket somewhere. I was hunting in the room with the portrait they call young Eugenius—you know, the handsome one that looks almost alive, as if he loved you. He's very like Marcus. What relation is he?"

"He—he was your grandmother Eleanor Harradine's brother," I said.

"I thought he must be some kin. Well, I looked up and the lady was coming in at the door. She must have had slippers on. I hadn't heard her. She was tall and thin, and she had on very old-fashioned clothes. Her hair was done in queer high loops. I think she must have been handsome when she was young. Her colored man followed her with a basket on his arm, and oh, Mama, she took a couple of the loveliest colored wax statuettes from the basket—Mama, what is the matter?"

"Nothing," I said through a choked throat. I put my hand on the pillar we stood by, and pulled her close. "Go on."

"She put them on the mantelpiece—shouldn't she?—and went and stood and looked and looked at young Eugenius . . . Oh, Mama, it was pitiful, he was so young and gay and charming, and she was so old, and she must have been his age once, and in love with him."

I looked at her. Her cheeks and eyes were bright, and the lips quivering with pity yet smiling . . . She had not been afraid, my little daughter; she must not be.

"Then?"

"Oh, she didn't do anything wrong. She only got some vases from the closet, and found a couple of clusters of flowers in the basket her man held. She put them under young Eugenius' picture and looked a long time more. I was so sorry for her. *She* was so sorry."

"Well?"

"Mama—you're holding me so tight—" I loosened my hold. "That was all, really," she said. "She saw me staring—I was rude really—and she smiled at me, and turned to go out. The colored man bowed as if I was a grown person. He had a high white stock, old-fashioned. I like him. He looked at me as if he had always known me. You know—that sort of taking-care and kindness, the way you and Papa look at us sometimes. Do you know who they are?"

Did I know who they were? Petronius, looking at the child who would have been his grandniece if such as he had kin. The look of taking-care—yes, of love—I had seen on his dark, fine cut face for Isobel, Eugenia, for—me. Petronius, out there on the servants' side of the burial hill, with the stone saying Faithful Service over him, with his white stock wrapped under his Somerwell chin, under his shut lips and eyes . . . Petronius, still guarding Juliana, who lay near him.

I must not scream, I would not scream. And then, as I stood trying to smile at my daughter Onnorate with stiff lips, and saw her beginning to stare at me, down from the windless air drifted the great leaf. As one had twice, three times, lovingly, gently, it stroked my cheek. As when I first came to the Castle. When I came with my bridegroom. When

I leaned, happy, against my returned husband. And as each time before, there was reassurance and happiness and love.

"I think I know who they were, dear," I said. "They smiled at you, you say? They were—distant connections. Like the other guests, they came to wish us well in our happiness."

J23